SEASONS
UNDER THE
Sun

DEBBIE K MEDLIN

WESTBOW
PRESS®
A DIVISION OF THOMAS NELSON
& ZONDERVAN

WestBow Press books may be ordered through booksellers or by contacting:

WestBow Press
A Division of Thomas Nelson & Zondervan
1663 Liberty Drive
Bloomington, IN 47403
www.westbowpress.com
844-714-3454

ISBN: 979-8-3850-1470-5 (sc)
ISBN: 979-8-3850-1471-2 (e)

Library of Congress Control Number: 2023923765

Print information available on the last page.

WestBow Press rev. date: 02/06/2024

Each of us tread upon the same path of synonyms and antonyms:
Birth ~ Death ** Joyfulness ~ Sadness ** Dependence ~ Independence
Success ~ Failure ** Bravery ~ Cowardice
Benevolence ~ Greediness ** Compassion ~ Apathy
Love ~ Hate ** Hopefulness ~ Hopelessness
Some paths may be longer, steeper and more difficult than others,
yet we strive to march onward mindful of our
steps with one goal in mind.
To trust and follow God's straight and narrow path.
Our Gracious Merciful Guide leads us to
the end of our earthly journey
and with open arms lovingly welcomes us to yet another journey—
Our eternal home where only Joy and Happiness abide.

For everything there is a season,
and a time for every matter under heaven;
A time to be born, and a time to die;
A time to plant, and a time to pluck up what is planted;
A time to kill, and a time to heal;
A time to break down, and a time to build up;
A time to weep, and a time to laugh;
A time to mourn, and a time to dance.

Ecclesiastes 3:1-4
English Standard Version of the Bible

CONTENTS

INTRODUCTION

Seasons Under the Sun begins where *Heart of Texas* ends and follows the Franklin Bailey family twelve additional years—1934 through 1946. Although the narrator of *Heart of Texas* was the Bailey's limestone house, each chapter in *Seasons Under the Sun* holds an account of each character—a blending of short stories. *Seasons Under the Sun* expands from within the walls of the house in Central Texas and travels with the reader to other cities in Texas, California, Arizona, and spans across the Pacific and Atlantic Oceans.

The Baileys, both corporately and individually, discover joy, adventure, disappointment, anguish, happiness, dreams fulfilled, and dreams unrealized.

A recap of the family members and their ages as of 1934 is listed below for those who are acquainted with the Bailey family and as an introduction for those who are meeting the family for the first time:

Franklin Stuart Bailey – A graduate of College of Pharmacy in Galveston, Texas; Marries Margaret May Bond and together rear eight children; Opens Bailey's Drugstore in Oak Hill; Entrepreneur investing in Oak Hill's city development; Dispensed medicine during the Spanish Flu pandemic and during the installation of the Missouri, Kansas, Texas Railway. Head of Household; Age 47

Margaret (Maggie) Bond Bailey – Marries Franklin Bailey, her brother's best friend; Mother of six boys, two girls; Gains the right to vote; Homeschools her children during the Spanish Flu pandemic; Cares for her brother Ernie and his six-week-old son after being abandoned by his wife; Offers encouragement to her pregnant unwed teenaged niece; Introduced to indoor plumbing and electricity; Teaches piano in her home; Church volunteer and gardener; Age 45

John Cameron Bailey – Eldest son; Graduates from Dallas Business College and marries Emily Moore; Resigns banking position at onset of the stock market crash; Son Edward is born in 1931; Moves to Sacramento, California, where Emily interns at Sacramento Memorial; Wholesale grocery manager; Age 25

Emily Diane Moore Bailey – Daughter-in-law; Moves to Oak Hill with her family; Infatuated with the two eldest Bailey boys; Considering Art's career path lacking monetary value, marries John; Their son's unplanned birth does little to alter her desire to become a doctor; Intern Sacramento Memorial; Age 23

Jonathan Edward (Eddie) Bailey – Son of John and Emily; Age 3

Arthur (Art) Tilman Bailey – Second eldest son; His love for horses seconded only by his love for Emily Moore; After hearing Emily is engaged to his brother, bolts immediately to the King Ranch in Kingsville, Texas; Horse wrangler; Age 23

Rosa Valentina De León – Daughter of Juan De León, King Ranch foreman, and Camilla Garcia De León; Independent and an accomplished equestrian; Pampered by her father and overly protected by her four brothers; Age 23

Samuel James Bailey – Third eldest son; After high school works for his Uncle Ernie's construction company; Marries Trina Jones; Takes classes at the University of Texas to become an electrical engineer; Age 21

Trina Louise Jones Bailey – Daughter-in-law; Hired as secretary to a Municipal Judge after high school; Marries Sam and reside over the drugstore; Age 21

William Franklin Bailey – Fourth eldest son; A sophomore at Austin High; Plays baseball for the Austin Maroons; Loves dogs and baseball; Age 16

Clayton Stuart Bailey – Fifth eldest son; 7th grader at Fulmore Junior High; Along with younger brother, is mischievous, high-spirited and loves to tease; Age 13

Patrick (Paddy) Thomas Bailey – Sixth eldest and youngest son; 6th grader at Oak Hill Elementary; Looks up to his older brothers; Age 12

Lucinda (Lucy) Mae Bailey – Loraine Rae Bailey – Twin daughters in 2nd grade at Oak Hill Elementary; Only girls in a household of boys; Spoiled and coddled by all family members; Age 7

Beatrice (Bessie) Long Bailey – Mother to son Franklin and daughter Lorna Joelle; After husband dies, moves with Lorna to Oklahoma; Comes to Oak Hill to escape Oklahoma's deadly dust storms; Moves to Galveston and then to Sacramento to care for Eddie, her great-grandson; Answers to Granma or Gran; Age 64

Ernest (Ernie) Randall Bond – Maggie's older brother; Franklin's best childhood friend; Abandoned by his first wife, hires Elizabeth Foster to be his son's wet nurse; Marries Elizabeth and welcome a son, Carter Eugene; Opens Bond Construction Company in Oak Hill; Age 47

Elizabeth Foster Bond – First husband dies during the Great War; Has three children—Anne, Dottie, and Harold; Employed as Owen's wet nurse and marries Ernie, who is five years her junior; Age 52

Anne Foster Collier – Marries Grayson Collier and serve as missionaries; Have one son, Grant Allister Collier; Ages: Anne 30; Grayson 32; Grant 8

Dorothy (Dottie) Foster – Single and a registered nurse in Colorado; Age 26

Harold Howard Foster - Single; Montana Forest Ranger; Age 21

Luis (Santos) and Delores (Tia) Santiago – Leave Kingsville, Texas, after their only son Tomás dies in a rodeo accident; Hired by the Baileys; Santos cares for the grounds, garden, and horses; Tia helps with the children and household chores; Beloved by the Bailey family; Santos age 59; Tia 57

SAM AND TRINA
1934

Trina hurried down the backstairs and pushed through the French doors leading from the back vestibule into the drugstore. Hastily pulling a white apron over her floral dress, she flipped the switches for the overhead light in the main room and the light in the compound room. The hardwood planks squeaked as she rushed across the floor. Entering the front vestibule, Trina pulled up the shade and turned the sign hanging from the top of the door from "Closed" to "Open." She quickly unlocked the door. The grandfather clock which sat in the corner by the two glass-enclosed display cases chimed seven gongs.

The store seemed devoid of color with its sterile white walls, cabinets, and counters. The red checked tablecloths topping the three tables by the soda fountain along with the merchandise in the display cases produced the only color. Trina grabbed the feather duster hanging behind the first display case and gave each glass candy jar a good going over—peppermint, licorice sticks, gumballs, lemon drops, Boston Baked Beans, Cinnamon Imperials, candy buttons and chocolate nuggets. She looked up as Franklin, her father-in-law, entered through the back door.

"Morning, Trina. Thanks for opening for me." He kissed her cheek. "I have six orders to fill before eight. Do you have time to manage the front before going to work? Maggie will be here soon. This is your last day, isn't it?"

"Yes, of course, and today is my last day. Judge Newman is taking us all for lunch. Supposed to be a surprise, but you know how that goes."

Franklin chuckled as he pushed through the swinging gate that divided the long counter in half and headed to his workroom. The "compound" room as he referred to his workroom was brightly lit with white oak cabinets on two walls. One wall cabinet held drawers, five rows high and five rows deep, neatly labeled with names of dry powders and herbs. Pharmaceutical Journals and medical articles catalogued by year were stacked neatly on the shelves underneath. Stationed at the other cabinet's center, a white stone mortar and pestle were housed to grind composites for prescription tablets. Corked glass bottles of all colors and sizes with the content labels well secured under a thin slice of glass lined the shelves above. Although he could buy ready-to-sell remedies from wholesalers, he enjoyed measuring the compounds and rolling and cutting the tablets himself.

Because of her father-in-law's example, she knew Sam would be a wonderful father. She stroked her rounded stomach lovingly. During these past few weeks, thinking of being a mother triggered Trina's giddiness into overflowing joyfulness. She was to be the mother of Sam's baby. What could be more perfect?

The bell dinged over the door. Maggie entered followed by Lucy, Loraine, Paddy, and Clayton. The morning's peaceful serenity destroyed in seconds.

"But I don't want my hair braided!" Loraine protested as she stomped across the floor and plopped into the nearest white cane-back chair. She laid her head on the table and covered her wavy, frazzled blonde hair with her hands.

Maggie placed a green cloth tote on the table while Loraine continued her childish theatrics. Ignoring her daughter, Maggie pulled a brush and two red ribbons from the tote's side pocket.

"Morning, Trina," she said, as if this daily routine for the seven-year-old required any explanation. She gently coaxed her daughter to a sitting position. Maggie grasped her child's unruly hair in one hand and pulled the brush gently through the mane. Loraine squirmed. "If you continue to squirm, you'll have crooked braids. But that's up to you."

Lucy skipped across the wood floor to where Trina continued dusting the candy jars with the yellow feather duster. Lucy stretched her arms as best as she could around Trina's waist and hugged her gently. She placed her head sideways against Trina's middle and listened.

"Do you think your baby can hear me in there?"

Trina smiled as she put the feather duster down. "Well, I don't know about that. But I do know before too long you can talk to him as much as you'd like."

"Him? A boy? You're going to have a boy?"

"Oh, I really don't know. Easier to refer to the baby as a boy, I suppose."

The bell over the front door chimed again. An older gentleman in his sixties entered. His hair and eyebrows were white and unkempt—a sure candidate for Maggie's brushing table. He wore frayed denim overalls, a blue denim shirt, scuffed brown boots, and spectacles balanced on the end of his nose. He carried small bundles of newspapers and magazines in his large-knuckled arthritic hands.

"Good morning, Bailey family," he greeted.

"Mr. Hatcher, good morning," Maggie answered. "Hope today finds you and Mrs. Hatcher well."

"Fit as a fiddle." He eyed the two boys impatiently waiting for him to unload the daily order of ten newspapers. "The comic books are in the truck." As he winked, one eyebrow wiggled. "You're welcome to four. Only four, mind ya."

Clayton and Paddy rushed from the store to the black truck parked at the front curb. They peered over the side panels and saw the stack of *Famous Funnies* tied with twine in groupings of four. Dell reprinted their newspaper comic strips in a magazine format. The boys didn't care if they'd already seen them or how often they'd read them. They couldn't read enough of "Hairbreadth Harry" or "Joe Palooka" or "Mutt & Jeff" or "Flash Gordon." The twins preferred "Blondie."

"Would you care for a cup of coffee, Mr. Hatcher? It's fresh." Trina clasped Lucy's hand and led her away from the display case.

"Nah, thank ya, just the same. I'll just collect my fee and be gone."

"Of course." Trina slipped behind the counter and opened the cash register. "Here you are. One dollar and twenty cents—two cents apiece for the newspapers, ten cents apiece for the comics and twelve cents apiece for the *Better Homes and Gardens*." Trina placed the coins in Mr. Hatcher's outstretched palm.

In their haste coming in, the boys almost plowed over Mr. Hatcher as he was leaving. They voiced their apologies and hurried inside. The bell above the door dinged announcing their arrival and echoed with Mr. Hatcher's departure. The boys plopped down at the nearest round table and Lucy eagerly joined them.

"Loraine, thank you for being still. Your braids look nice," Maggie said.

Loraine rolled her eyes and joined her siblings at the table. The boys were sitting side by side reading and snickering, enjoying the first page of comics. Clayton and Paddy took turns reading the characters' written parts.

When they turned the page to "Blondie," Paddy pointed to the page. "Ya know, Mr. Hatcher looks a lot like Mr. Dithers, Dagwood's boss. Look!"

"Only needs a suit and tie!" Clayton exclaimed. Looking up at Trina, he wriggled his eyebrows up and down which caused his sisters to giggle.

Trina smiled, suppressing her own laughter, and wondered if this is what it will be like rearing children. A pleasant thought indeed.

"We don't have time to read the comics. It's time for school. But we always have time to be kind," Maggie said as she scooped up her tote and herded her brood toward the door. "Have an enjoyable day at work, Trina. Will you and Sam be joining us for dinner tonight?"

"Thank you, Mama Bailey. I don't think we'll make dinner. It's Tuesday. Sam has a class tonight at the university." Trina followed her family to the door.

Maggie kissed her daughter-in-law's cheek. "Maybe Sunday then?"

Trina nodded as Maggie followed her children outside to their car. Franklin appeared from the back and looked around.

"Has Maggie taken the kids to school?"

"Yes, they just left. Mr. Hatcher was here, and I paid him for the order. He had comics and magazines this time, too. I recorded it in the ledger."

"Excellent! I can oversee the front now if you need to get to work."

Trina nodded and retrieved her clutch and sweater under the counter.

"You're not walking, are you?"

"It's not far and it's a beautiful day. Sam is picking me up after work."

Trina waved and walked out to greet the crisp March morning. She pulled on her sweater and strolled toward the courthouse only six blocks away. The sun was making its debut over Main Street's rooftops. The wind was stirring about trying to decide whether to be mellow or menacing.

As Trina neared the simple red brick two-story office building, she was grateful the building was not as intimidating as the Travis County Courthouse. Last year, she accompanied John Davenport, Oak Hill's attorney, to serve as a witness for a deposition arranged at one of the offices in the courthouse. She recalled standing on the top step to the courthouse gazing up at the lintel carved above the bronze doorway—a detailed depiction of a bearded man, undoubtedly a judge, holding a staff in one hand while seated before six men in shackles. The men were barely clothed in strips of linen, waiting their turn for punishment or pardon. Behind the judge ten or more people were carved in a dance-like celebratory manner. Were all the prisoners set free? Was justice served? Realizing she was spending too much time daydreaming, she hurried inside.

At half past four, Sam pulled his royal blue Chevrolet pickup to a stop in front of the Municipal Building. The truck with its black fenders and silver spoked wheels appeared too fancy for traveling the countryside hauling tools and lumber. Sam got out of the cab and checked the back tire which seemed low when he left Bastrop. The tire looked fine now. He'd add air in the morning. He leaned against the truck's side and waited for Trina.

When he saw his wife exit the building, he purposely waited to watch her approach. She was beautiful; motherhood suited her. Her face held a certain maternal glow. She was carrying a bouquet of mixed flowers and a box of candy. Trina saw him and hastened her step. As she neared the truck, he opened the passenger door for her. He could smell her lilac perfume as she embraced him.

"So is Judge Newman wooing my girl?"

"What?"

"The flowers and candy." He nodded toward the flowers and box she held.

"No, of course not!" she laughed. "A gift from the office. You smell of wood chips and sweat! You need to clean up before class."

"And there I thought you liked that smell on me," he teased.

Sam pulled his truck into the private fenced-in area behind the drugstore and parked. They got out and went upstairs to their apartment. Trina pulled off her sweater and straddled it across the back of the dark blue sofa. She proceeded to the kitchenette to warm the stew. While she waited, Trina sat down at the table and propped her swollen feet up on a dinette chair.

"You look nice," Trina smiled as Sam entered.

"Sit still. I'll get dinner."

Sam returned with two bowls of stew and placed them on the yellow tablecloth. Trina pulled her feet from his chair so he could sit down. He ate quickly.

"I may be a late coming home tonight," he said between bites. "Want to talk to my professor about my last test score. I need a better class grade."

Finishing his stew, Sam placed their empty bowls in the sink. He kissed her goodbye, grabbed his books and hurried out the door. Trina decided the dishes could wait; her legs were hurting, and she wanted to soak in the tub.

In the bathroom, she sat on the edge of the club-foot tub, turned on the faucet and waited for the water to warm. She poured a tiny bit of bath oil into the water, turned off the faucet, and stepped in. Stretching back, Trina rested her head against the back of the tub and relaxed. She rubbed her hands lovingly over the mound in her belly. A little life nesting inside, growing, developing a personality, becoming a little person. She lifted her hand. The oily water slowly trickled down like a rain drop pooling from a leaf. Suddenly, she felt a little kick under her hands. Tears flooded her eyes as she cradled her hands over her baby.

Trina was lying in bed, fully awake, when Sam came home.

"You're still awake," Sam whispered while undressing.

Trina pulled up the blanket. He crawled underneath next to her and placed his hand on her tummy. Suddenly, they both felt a flutter.

"That's my boy!" Sam announced excitedly.

Trina rolled to one side as Sam curled beside her. The room was filled with their rhythmic breathing—in and out, in and out. They quickly fell asleep.

Trina awoke Saturday morning to an empty house. Sam left before sunrise for Bastrop. The project there was almost finished. Trina pulled back her covers, sat up and stretched her arms. As she slipped on her housecoat, she smelled coffee and smiled. Sam made a pot of coffee before he left. She would have one cup—doctor's orders. She quickly toasted two pieces of bread.

As Trina stood to carry the dishes to the sink, she felt a small stabbing twinge. She grabbed her side and waited. The pain subsided as quickly as it came. Relieved, Trina hurried to dress and went downstairs to help Franklin with the monthly inventory. Maggie was bringing the children to help as well. Although Trina was unsure how helpful the twins would be.

"Good morning, Trina," Maggie greeted as she steered the twins to a table and quickly topped it with drawing pencils, crayons, and buff-colored paper.

Trina, dressed in her favorite pastel yellow loose-fitting shift, crossed the floor, and kissed her mother-in-law's cheek.

"Good morning, girls. What are you drawing today?"

Lucy scribbled quickly then held up a picture of a large yellow circle perched on stilt legs. "It's you!"

Trina laughed. "Lovely! I never looked better."

"Trina, good morning," Franklin entered from the compound room, carrying two clipboards under his arm.

"Morning, where are the boys? Is William coming?" Trina asked.

"The boys carried out the trash. William had a meeting at the high school. Something about summer baseball camp. Oh, here they are," Franklin replied as the boys hustled through the back door.

"Okay, Paddy, here's your list. Clayton, here's yours." Franklin held out two pens and the two clipboards with inventory sheets attached. "When you're finished, help yourself to a root beer or a coke at the fountain!"

"Hurry!" the twins cried in unison. Franklin chuckled.

"Would you help me, Trina?" Paddy asked.

Trina draped her arm around his shoulders. "You bet. You count; I'll record."

Paddy slid the back glass panels open on the first case and placed the individual boxes of items on the top of the case. The first display held men's articles—key fobs, straight-edge razors, tubes of Palmolive shaving cream, boar hair bristle shaving brushes, Bonafide Beards mustache wax, and musk scented cologne. Once counted and recorded, they moved to the second case.

This display held women's accessories—rouge, lipstick, lace embroidered handkerchiefs, jeweled covered pill boxes, rose scented bath oils or bath salts, and colorful spritzer cologne bottles with matching tassels attached. For the children—hair bows and clips in bright colors and assorted sizes for girls and for boys an assortment of ankle or knee length socks and black or brown suspenders.

"I have a game Thursday night. Are you comin'?" Clayton asked Trina.

"I'll certainly try."

"Yeah, Clayton plays right field and has been practicing batting left-handed...wants to be Fulmore's Babe Ruth," Paddy snickered. "Think you'll beat Babe's sixty homerun record, too?"

Standing on the stepladder while counting unopened boxes of merchandise, Clayton reached over and popped his brother on the head with his clipboard. Not hard, but enough to get his attention. Paddy pantomimed a serious affront. Trina laughed as the bell over the front door rang.

Mrs. Eunice Rogers, clearly a woman on a mission, entered and walked briskly to the main counter where Maggie stood. Mrs. Rogers, a tall, slender woman in her sixties, was the 'gab-about-town.' If you wanted to know what was going on or even didn't care to know, it was of little concern to Mrs. Rogers. She would tell you anyway. Felt it her sole duty to keep Oak Hill's town folks well informed about local and national news...but mainly local news.

"Morning, Maggie. I'm here for Erwin's medicine. He's waiting in the truck." Mrs. Rogers dropped her large purse with a thud on the counter and crossed her arms across her chest.

"Of course, Eunice, it's ready." Maggie pulled out the prescription basket and thumbed through the envelopes until she found the one labeled 'Erwin Rogers.'

Trina recorded Paddy's last item and felt that same stabbing pain she'd felt earlier. Sharper this time. She used the display to lean against. Clayton noticed her discomfort and stepped off the ladder.

"You, alright, Trina?"

Trina nodded but suddenly felt hot and faint. "If you guys don't mind, I think I'll go upstairs and lie down a bit."

"Thanks for your help, Trina," Paddy said. "Yeah, thanks," Clayton echoed.

Trina smiled at them both and walked toward the stairs. Halfway up the stairway another pain hit, wrapping her midriff in a vise. She stopped and rested her hand on the wall until the pain receded. Slowly she went up to her apartment.

Downstairs, Maggie said, "That will be thirty-five cents, Eunice."

"Thirty-five cents! Prices these days! Just for rheumatiz medicine." Eunice fumbled around her purse. "Gets higher and higher. At least Roosevelt's AAA—Agriculture Adjustment Act—pays us farmers to plant a third fewer acres than we normally do and produce a third fewer animals. A good plan, really. Helps us make a decent wage after the drought from last year."

Mrs. Rogers pulled a coin purse from her larger purse and wriggled her finger around looking for coins. "Did you hear about Clyde Barrow and Bonnie Parker helping five prisoners escape from Eastham State Prison in January? Eastham is up north of Huntsville. Used a machine gun they say. Those two have been stealing cars and robbing stores all over north Texas and even parts of Louisiana. What's this world coming to?" Mrs. Rogers scooted the counted coins across to Maggie.

As Maggie dropped the coins in the till, a thud followed by a crash was heard above them. Clayton and Paddy exchanged glances. The boys dashed from the room and ran up the stairs, taking two at a time.

Clayton, followed closely by Paddy, charged through the apartment door. Trina was lying on the floor. Liquid with a tinge of blood puddled between her thighs discoloring her yellow dress. The hurricane lamp which usually sat on the end table by the sofa now lay in shards of broken pieces beside her.

"Trina!" Clayton belted, sliding beside her on the floor. He reached for her hand and grasped it tightly.

"Sam! Sam! It's too soon!" She was screaming hysterically.

Clayton pushed damp hair from her face. "It'll be okay, Trina. Shush, now."

As Paddy turned to go downstairs for help, Maggie rushed into the room.

"Paddy, tell Papa we need Doc and to send word to Sam! Hurry, now!"

"Will she be okay, Mama?" Paddy asked, backing slowly out of the room.

"Paddy, hurry, son!" Maggie commanded, kneeling beside Trina.

Paddy bolted down the stairs and entered the drugstore as Franklin exited the compound room.

"What is it, boy? What's happened?" Mrs. Rogers demanded.

"Papa! Papa!" Paddy huffed, ignoring the woman.

Franklin could see panic welling in Paddy's eyes and placed his hands upon his son's shoulders to calm him.

"It's Trina! Something's terrible wrong! Mama said to get Doc and get word to Sam!" Paddy blurted.

Without hesitation or asking further questions, Franklin ran past Mrs. Rogers who still stood by the counter with her oversized purse slung over her right shoulder. Loraine began to cry. Paddy squeezed into the chair beside her. Lucy crawled onto his lap and tucked her head under his chin.

Maggie came back downstairs as Mr. Rogers, a short, stout man dressed in faded overalls, hurried through the door. The bell over the door clanged overhead.

"What in the world is going on? I just saw Franklin shoot out the door like a nest of hornets had been dropped on his head!"

"It's their girl," Mrs. Rogers whispered. "Doc's been called."

Maggie smiled weakly as she neared her three children huddled together in one chair. She pulled up a chair and took her twelve-year-old son's hand. "Paddy, I'm taking you and your sisters home. Trina will be taken to the hospital. I'll call Jewel Jeter to come stay with you until Tia and Santos come home."

"Forgive me, Mrs. Bailey." Mr. Rogers stepped forward. "Eunice and I can get your young'uns home. No need for you to leave your girl."

Maggie stood to face the couple. "Thank you, that would be so helpful."

Maggie helped Paddy gather the girls' things and kissed her children. Paddy took his sisters' hands and followed the Rogers outside. A 1930 Ford Model-A pickup sat parked at the curb. Paddy led his sisters to the back of the truck and lifted them up over the tailgate into the back. Once safely loaded, Mr. Rogers backed the truck out and drove slowly toward the Bailey's house nine miles away.

William rolled the family's 1932 Packard to a stop in front of the drugstore. As William grabbed his varsity letterman jacket from the passenger seat, he saw his dad and Doc Lawrence running into the store. William exited the car quickly and chased after the men as they ran through the drugstore to the back stairway.

Doc patted Maggie's shoulder as he entered the apartment. He knelt beside Clayton who still tightly held Trina's hand. Trina winced when Doc touched her abdomen. Doc stepped over her and knelt once more.

"Maggie, call Nelson's Funeral Home and tell Jack we need him now. We need to get Trina to Brackenridge. Franklin, think you and William can carry her downstairs on the stretcher?"

Franklin unfolded the stretcher he'd carried from Doc's office. He and Clayton aligned it alongside the length of Trina's body. Maggie rushed from the room. Doc pulled Trina's shoulders gently toward him.

"Trina, dear," Doc softly said, "we're going to move you. Gently, now. Clayton, roll her legs toward me. That's it. Slowly. Push the stretcher underneath. That's it. Now, let's roll her back."

Trina began to whimper. Clayton squeezed her hand.

Maggie entered the room. "Jack is here."

Maggie covered Trina with a white sheet she had stripped from the bed and bent to kiss Trina's cheek. Franklin and William carefully maneuvered Trina through the door and down the stairs. Jack stood at the back of the hearse; its two wide doors fully extended. Jack helped Franklin and William lift Trina up and scoot her onto the raised platform used for transporting patients or caskets. Doc climbed into the back of the hearse, sat beside Trina, and strapped her in.

Jack quickly closed the back doors and climbed into the driver's seat. He started the engine and pulled out into the street. Dazed, Maggie and Franklin and Clayton watched until the hearse pulled away.

"Aren't we going to follow?" William asked, concern edging his voice.

"Yes, yes! Maggie, ride with the boys. I'll come in my truck," Franklin said.

"Franklin, check to see if Bridgett found Sam. Call Trina's brother. Nathan and Charlotte need to know. Jewel is staying with the children."

"Okay. We need God's protective hand now. I'll meet you at the hospital."

Maggie kissed him and followed her sons back through the drugstore.

An hour later Maggie, William, and Clayton arrived at the hospital. After assuring the receptionist Clayton was over twelve, the three were directed to the waiting room on the second floor. The room was large with spacious windows stretched across one wall. Maggie led her sons to an unoccupied sofa that faced a bank of chairs. The three sat on the sofa. The waiting began.

"Here, Mama." William, noticing his mother shivering, held up his wool Austin High letter jacket and helped Maggie place her arms within the sleeves. Once settled, he placed his arm around her.

Clayton leaned against his mother and placed his head above the maroon jacket's large letter "A" machine-stitched in white on the jacket's left side. The fabric was itchy, but Clayton was too worried about Trina to care.

Twenty minutes passed. Franklin entered the waiting room carrying a brown paper sack. "Matilda brought sandwiches and cookies as I was leaving the store. Boys, are you hungry?"

He placed the sack on the small rectangular table between them. No one seemed to be hungry. Mrs. Lawrence's generous offering remained untouched.

Focusing on Maggie, Franklin said, "I called the house. Tia and Santos are home. Told them I'd call with updates. Jewel and Fred wanted to come to the hospital, but I suggested they wait. Bridgett was able to contact Mr. Gower, their client. He'll get word to Sam. I also called Nathan and Charlotte as you suggested. Nathan couldn't leave the feed store until closing but will come as soon as he can."

Franklin, extremely restless, crossed and uncrossed his legs twice. He leaned forward and patted Maggie's knee. Words were unnecessary after living with someone over twenty-five years; thoughts understood without voicing them.

Clayton slowly lowered his head onto Maggie's lap. As she rubbed his shoulders, Elizabeth, Ernie's wife, arrived. William stood, offering his aunt the seat next to his mother. Clayton sat up. Elizabeth hugged Maggie tightly.

"Is Sam not here?" Elizabeth glanced about the room.

"No….no, he's not," Franklin answered.

"Ernie called me. As soon as Mr. Gower notified Sam at the site, he left. That was over an hour and half ago…closer to two now."

"Something's wrong, Franklin," Maggie's voice quivered. "Shouldn't take that long to get here from Bastrop."

William placed his hand on his father's forearm. "I'll go find him."

"We both will! Clayton, stay with your mother."

As Franklin and William neared the waiting room's exit, Ernie and Sam rushed through. Fear and anxiety edged Sam's eyes.

"We were so worried. What happened to you?" Maggie asked.

Ernie answered. "Sam left immediately after Mr. Gower told him about Trina. Halfway to Austin, his back tire blew out. His spare was also flat. I left the site after I spoke to Elizabeth. Found Sam parked on the side of the road and drove him straight here."

No sooner had Ernie explained the situation, Doc entered through the door marked "No Entrance-Medical Staff Only." The room fell silent. Everyone bunched together, waiting. Franklin watched the man who'd been his friend over twenty-one years and who'd delivered five of his eight children at home...William being the first. Doc looked tired; stress and tension etched his face.

Franklin moved closer to where Sam and Maggie were standing.

Doc approached Sam. "Sit down, son."

Sam held his shoulders back. "I'm fine, Doc. How's Trina and the baby?"

Doc glanced at Franklin and then said, "Sam, Trina will be fine. Needs rest and time to heal. She's a healthy young woman." His voice quavered as he touched Sam's arm. "We lost the baby, son. I'm so sorry. His lungs were premature; couldn't breathe on his own. We did everything we could to save him."

With Doc's last words, Sam's knees buckled. Ernie side-stepped in front of Maggie and grabbed Sam's arm; Franklin caught the other. They eased Sam into the closest chair before he collapsed to the floor. Sam propped his elbows on his knees and cradled his head. Suddenly the room erupted in sobs and stifled cries as the family responded to the news.

Clayton crumbled onto the sofa. All his pent-up emotions of the afternoon escaped through unrestrained whimpers. Elizabeth sat next to him and consolingly patted his shoulders. Ernie grabbed Maggie. Together they cried. Franklin rubbed Sam's back. William turned away; his tears flowed freely down his cheeks.

Doc took a knee in front of Sam. "Son, Trina is sleeping now and will probably sleep through the night. It's best you all go home and rest. Visiting hours are in the morning from nine to noon."

Sam looked squarely into Doc's eyes. "Does Trina know?"

Doc shook his head no.

"Then I'm not going anywhere! I'm not leaving her!"

Doc could see determination and fire in the young man's eyes. He would not have wanted to leave either if the situation were reversed and had concerned Matilda and their first child. Doc placed his hand on the arm of the chair, using it for leverage, and pushed himself up. Standing, he patted Sam's shoulder.

"Okay, son. Franklin, take your family home. I'll make sure Sam gets a cot in Trina's room. The nurses will fuss at me, but I don't care. Come along, Sam."

Standing slowly and still dazed, Sam allowed Doc to lead him from the room.

"Good night, son. We love you," Maggie called out tearfully as Sam and Doc exited through the "No Entrance" door.

Sam sat in the dark by Trina's bed. He held her hand and watched her chest rise and fall with each breath. He was still uncertain what exactly had happened that afternoon that led them here to this room, to this moment. Doc's announcement seemed too surreal. A dreadful nightmare.

He squeezed Trina's hand trying to wake her. Trina's night nurse, Mrs. Ambrose, had assured him she would sleep through the night. Sam laid his head on the side of the bed and placed Trina's hand on the side of his face. Her hand was warm on his skin. He closed his eyes as tears trickled down the side of his nose.

Mrs. Ambrose pushed open the door and moved toward the bed. She pulled up a flashlight and shielded the bright light with one hand as she flashed it over Trina's face and checked the IV in her arm.

"Just checking on her," she said. "We don't usually allow overnight guests, but I can secure a cot from the nurses' lounge if you'd like to sleep."

Sam whispered, "No, thank you. I want to be right here when she wakes."

Mrs. Ambrose smiled. "More than likely, it will be breakfast time before that happens. Have you eaten? I can get you something."

Sam shook his head. She patted his shoulder and slipped out quietly.

Sam didn't know how long he'd slept. It was still dark. Trina rested peacefully. He slipped out into the hall in search of the men's facilities.

He saw Mrs. Ambrose exiting another patient's room and asked for directions.

Exiting the second floor, he took the stairs down one flight. After leaving the men's room, he walked aimlessly up and down the hall. When he noticed a sign pointing to a chapel three doors down, he followed the sign and entered.

The chapel was small and dark with the only light filtered through a stained-glass window at the back of the room. Sam sat down in the middle of the third row of pews. The room was quieter and more reverent than any church service he'd ever attended. Void of people and their consistent chatter and unintentional distractions. Only peaceful silence.

Staring at the stained-glass, Sam just sat there; his mind a jumbled wreck. Bright colors of yellow and green and blue and brown glass depicted Jesus carrying a white lamb over his shoulder. Hanging underneath, a framed wooden sign read, "The Good Shepherd."

"The Good Shepherd!" Sam exclaimed aloud. "What's so good about what happened today?" He questioned the glass, "How could you bring this life into our lives and fill us with excitement and happiness and then take him away before we could hold him? How is that good? How could you let Trina suffer so? She would have been a wonderful mother. Oh, God, are you there? Are you listening? Are you truly a good Father? How am I going to tell Trina we lost our son?"

Sam's voice cracked as a wail of sobs ricocheted off the four walls, splintering the small peaceful space. He cushioned his head on his arms and rested them on the top of the pew in front of him. Amid uncontrollable crying, he continued voicing his unanswered questions to the empty room. After draining all the tears he thought he owned, Sam sat up. Sitting still, he stared at the stained-glass image. He wiped his wet face with the back of his hand.

Suddenly a Bible verse he'd learned as a child filled his mind. He couldn't remember it word for word, but it had something to do with never being afraid or discouraged. God is always there. Sam closed his eyes; emotional exhaustion overpowered his body as he sat back against the hard-backed pew.

Startled by muffled sounds filling the hallway hours later, Sam opened his eyes. Lying on his back; one leg outstretched on the hardwood pew; one foot on the floor. Alarmed, he stood and exited the chapel. Three nurses, deep in conversation and dressed in brilliant white head to toe, approached.

"Excuse me," he asked. "What time is it?"

One of the nurses answered without stopping, "It's almost nine, sir."

Sam hurried to the stairwell and bounded up the steps to the second floor. He passed the nurses' desk. Mrs. Ambrose was no longer there. A heavyset woman with dark hair swept under her white nurses cap sat in Mrs. Ambrose place. She adjusted the brown round rimmed glasses over her ears and smiled.

As Sam neared Trina's room, he heard a scream. Behind him he heard the nurse rise from her chair. Sam pushed open the door in time to hear Charlotte say, "Oh, Trina, I'm so sorry. I thought you knew."

Sam's eyes darted swiftly between Charlotte and Trina. Trina's brow furrowed at Charlotte's words of sympathy. Reality registered across her face when she saw Sam. Shock followed by anguish and unacceptance completely distorted her face. Sam's heart split into pieces.

"Sa-am," she whispered, tears falling freely down her cheeks.

Sam hurried to her side with tears in his eyes. "I didn't want you to find out this way," he whispered, holding her hand. "I wanted to tell you."

"No! Sam, no! Our baby! It was a little boy!" she wailed, pushing his hands away, thrashing her head side to side on the pillow. He reached out to softly hold her shoulders, but she slapped his hands as her hysteria grew.

"Charlotte, on your way out, send in the nurse!"

"I'm here, Mr. Bailey. I'll call Doc Lawrence for something to calm her. Ma'am," she turned toward Charlotte. "May I escort you out?"

"I'm so sorry, Sam. I thought she knew. Nathan told me last night…" Charlotte's voiced trailed off as the nurse gently guided her from the room.

Five days later Sam entered the hospital lobby carrying a bouquet of fresh flowers in one hand and a grin on his face. Earlier that morning,

Tia and Maggie picked a fresh bouquet of flowers for him to take to the hospital. He had prayed on the drive to town that Trina would be as excited about coming home as he and his entire family. Doc had cautioned him that some women who've lost a child often take longer to recover than others. Doc also assured him this was normal. Trina needed time, patience, love, and reassurance.

In his eagerness to see Trina, Sam had not noticed her father standing in the lobby until the man abruptly stepped in front of him.

"Mr. Jones! How nice to see you. Trina will be thrilled! And Mrs. Jones?"

"Yes, yes. She's with Trina." Mr. Jones took Sam's arm and tugged slightly. "Sam, we need to talk. Would you join me over there?"

"But, Trina, I must…"

"Her mother is with her. I need to talk to you. It's an urgent matter. Please."

Mr. Jones moved toward a grouping of chairs; Sam respectfully followed.

When Sam was seated across from his father-in-law, Mr. Jones began, "First of all, let me say how truly sorry we are for your loss. You know that Trina is all that matters now. She needs time to heal emotionally and physically. Her mother and I agree she cannot do that here with your being gone most of the time. She needs to be properly cared for; she needs her mother now."

"Mr. Jones, I respect your concern for your daughter, and I know how much you love her. But she is my wife. I will take care of her!"

"Well, you certainly haven't done such a grand job so far!" a woman voiced gruffly behind him. "If you hadn't left her alone, this might not have happened!"

Sam stood and turned. Mrs. Jones, anger in her eyes, stood with her arm interlinked within Trina's.

"Trina!" Sam held out his hand, reaching for his wife. Trina stared ahead in a dazed-like stupor. Mrs. Jones stepped forward, creating a barrier.

Hands poised on her hips, she asked, "Has Mr. Jones told you our plans?"

"No, was just beginning, Doris," Mr. Jones addressed Sam. "We are taking Trina to Hereford until she's ready to come back. Thought about her staying with Nathan. But with his four little ones running about, she couldn't easily rest there. Trina has agreed, haven't you, pet?"

"Trina? What are you doing?" Sam moved around Mrs. Jones. "Trina?"

Trina stiffened. "I'm going home, Sam. Please, don't stop me."

Mrs. Jones turned her daughter toward the front door. "Amos?"

"The car is parked out front, dear." Amos Jones clapped Sam's back and picked up Trina's small suitcase. "We'll take care of her, son. Don't worry. You agree we must do what's best for Trina. And this is best."

For a moment, Sam stood, as if sucker-punched in the gut, confused and shocked; unsure of what had just happened. Mentally slapping himself back to reality, he hurried through the hospital entrance and down the steps. "Trina! Please, wait! Don't do this! I don't want you to go! Trina! Please, don't go!"

Without looking back, Trina lowered her head as her father opened the car door. She slid into the back seat and placed her head against her mother's shoulder. Mrs. Jones tapped on the back of the front seat alerting her husband they were ready to go. The car eased away from the hospital grounds.

Sam sat on the bottom step and watched the car inch out of sight. Now what? How much more misery could one man undertake? The bouquet of flowers slipped from his fingers and tumbled onto the ground. Distraught and completely not knowing what to do, he rose and slowly walked to his truck. He sat in the cab and cried. His only solace now, it seemed, was to also go home.

****

"It's been over two weeks now," Tia said, helping Maggie clear the Saturday breakfast dishes from the kitchen table. "How is Sam, really?"

Maggie shook her head. "I honestly don't know, Delores. Ernie gave him as much paid time off as he needs. Sam's so miserable. I'm worried about him."

"Any word from Trina?"

Maggie shook her head again. "No, not a word. Sam's written every day, but she's not responded."

Loraine and Lucy, snickering noisily, skipped from the mudroom through the kitchen. Their laughter plus the slamming screen door preceded their arrival. Lucy held Miss Daisy, her light gray cat, in her arms. Arlo, the family's black Labrador pup, scampered behind them.

"What are you girls up to?" Maggie asked.

"Nuttin,' Mamma," they replied in unison.

As the foursome neared the study, Arlo lead the way and bounded inside. Sitting on the sofa, Sam stared at the wall; his thoughts clearly elsewhere. Arlo jumped into his lap. Tip, William's dog now old and grayed, lay on the rug watching the pup and the twins curiously. Choosing not to investigate, Tip remained alert and watchful but stayed curled in his comfortably warm spot.

"Hello, there, Arlo!" Sam said, playfully stroking the dog's neck. When Arlo began licking Sam's neck and chin, he was gently pushed to the floor.

Loraine plopped down beside her brother and laid her head against his arm. Lucy crowded against Sam's knees intently watching his every move. Miss Daisy, tired of being held, squirmed about until she successfully climbed up Lucy's dress sleeve. Perching on her master's shoulder, Miss Daisy, too, stared—piercing him with her golden-green eyes. Sam smiled at his sister and her cat, a comical duo. He placed his arm around Loraine as she snuggled closer.

Franklin entered the study with the intention of asking the girls to leave Sam alone, but stepped back when he heard Lucy's voice. He leaned against the door jamb and merely listened.

"Remember when Peaches died? We were all so sad. Loraine and I cried for days. Remember? You told us not to be sad 'cause Peaches was in doggie heaven."

Sam nodded.

Lucy crept closer. "You've been sad for a long time. Don't be sad. Do you think your baby boy is in baby heaven with Jesus? I do."

Sam blinked at his seven-year-old sister...such innocence; everything so literal, so easily understood. He picked her up, kitten and all, and placed her in his lap. Miss Daisy jumped to the back of the sofa and licked her white paws. Too much human contact for the cat it seemed. Sam held his twin sisters tightly.

After two weeks passed, Sam moved back to his apartment and began working forty to sixty hours a week for his uncle. Despair, depression… too many sleepless nights and loss of an appetite…countered his interest in anything. He dropped his night classes at the University. Work became his new outlet; his focus. He continued to write to Trina although he'd received a discouraging letter from her father that letters were unnecessary and a waste of Sam's time and postage.

Bond Construction won a bid for a two-story brick office building in Caldwell, a small community of less than two thousand people, eighty miles east of Austin. The job would require at least four to five months to complete. Sam took it…anything away from Oak Hill and so many memories enclosing in on him.

Spring morphed silently into summer. The first week of July heralded blistering hot days and warm nights. With the building completed in Caldwell and the client pleased, Sam packed up and headed home. Chalk up another successful project and a healthy paycheck.

The windows on Sam's truck were rolled down to welcome air, any air. He leaned his elbow on the door ledge. The hot sun baked his skin, but Sam was oblivious. He dreaded going home to face its emptiness. He refused to go back to his parents. He was twenty-one; a grown man, after all. By mid-afternoon as he neared Oak Hill, his thoughts suddenly centered on a big juicy steak at Cal's Diner, a long, hot bath, and a good night's sleep in his own bed.

Deciding to clean up first, he pulled his truck into the fenced-in private enclosure behind the drugstore and parked. He climbed out and lifted up his suitcase and coat from the truck bed.

"Sam?"

Startled, Sam looked up. There she stood….Trina. After all this time. Trina.

Sam dropped his suitcase and jacket back into the truck bed. He stood immovable as if his boots had been nailed to the ground. Trina took two steps toward him. He could smell her lilac perfume as she drew closer. She looked beautiful. Her blonde hair had grown longer and fell below her shoulders.

"Sam?"

When he remained still with no attempt to move toward her, tears filled her eyes. In a soft voice, she explained, "Sam, I'm so sorry. I'm sorry for so many things. For not writing—for leaving you alone—for losing…" Her voice cracked. "After losing our baby, I felt like a failure. I was wrong to have left you. I'm so ashamed of my behavior."

Trina paused allowing Sam time to speak. When he remained silent, she continued. "Sam, you were hurting! I wasn't here for you. My grandmother helped me see I was wrong. She said you should never hurt the ones you love. I'm here now. Please, forgive me. Sam, say something. Have I lost you, too?"

Sam felt as if he were walking on wooden stilts as he breached the gap between them. He hesitantly reached out and gently rubbed her arms. "Are you real? Or are you just the same dream I've had every night these past four months?"

She placed her arms around his neck and kissed him softly. He grabbed her tightly, lowered his head and blubbered into her neck. They stood holding each other as their tears and sorrow melded together.

"Can you forgive me? Can we start over?" Trina whispered.

He kissed her again.

She touched his face. "I've missed you so."

Sam fumbled in his jeans pocket for the house keys and led her toward the building. Leaning against the unlocked door, he took Trina's hand.

"Sweetheart, I've dreamt of this moment for so long! We're finally home!"

ART AND ROSA
1934

Art lay on his back in his bunk; his left arm curled above his head. It was Monday....sunrise. A pinpoint of light and far less air stirred through the open windows of the bunkhouse. He shared the small living space with three other cowboys, horse wranglers like himself. Art called these living quarters on the Laureles division of the King Ranch...home.

His thoughts bounced about never settling too long on any single thought. This weekend was the cutting horse competition in Kingsville. Most cutting horse wranglers living on the King Ranch would compete. The four-year-old stallion he'd trained the past two years was ready. The young quarter horse, a strawberry roan, had a red coat intermingled with white hair—giving it an almost sun-bleached look. His name, Fuego, meant fire. Fuego's mane, tail and head, as well as his legs from the knees down, were solid reddish-brown. His brown eyes were large and curious; his body muscular; his nature feisty.

But mostly, he thought of Rosa. They were dreaming about and planning their wedding and future together. He had not been able to afford the ring they liked in the jewelry store window in Kingsville. So for now, they would wait. Like Art, Rosa didn't mind waiting, but not too long.

Art was uncertain if Rosa's father, the foreman of this horse training section of the ranch, had truly given his blessing for their marriage. Art always felt comfortable around Rosa's parents and her four brothers and their families. He enjoyed being a part of the family events and especially partaking meals with them. The De Leóns were a large family like his own.

Rosa, his dark-haired, amber-eyed beauty, was the center of his every thought. One day soon—or he hoped would be soon—she would become his wife; his life companion. Emily Moore, his high school sweetheart, had been his first love. But Rosa had shown him what true love meant. Hers was not a fleeting nor fickle flimsy. Of that he was certain.

When he heard Rojo, the old red rooster, crowing and demanding the sun to rise, Art swung his legs off the bed and dressed. He grabbed his hat that hung on a peg by the door and walked out onto the porch.

It was still dark with just a hint of light forming on the eastern horizon. Rojo, perched on the porch railing, cocked his head around and pierced his beady eyes in Art's direction. Completely annoyed by the interruption of signaling the day, the rooster spread his red wings and flopped to the ground. Rojo strutted away unaware his constant crowing was only a disturbance and had no control over the sun.

Art walked toward the cookhouse which was centered between two oak trees in the wranglers' living compound. Prickly pear cacti, scattered over the grounds, exposed their yellow-orange blooms. Positioned around the cookhouse, the six bunkhouses stood. Each bunkhouse housed four to six wranglers. All the buildings were made of earthy-colored adobe brick and topped with a red clay tile roofing. The adobe was cool in the summer and enclosed heat during the winter.

The Laureles, originally a Spanish land grant named after the groves of laurel trees growing there, is the largest of the four King Ranch divisions. Its two-hundred-fifty thousand acres span twenty-two miles south of Corpus Christi and is bordered on the east by the Baffin Bay, an inlet to the Gulf of Mexico.

Art entered the cookhouse and hung his hat on the first peg of thirty that lined the wall. Four oak wood tables, spaced three feet apart, extended down the length of the room. On the back wall five blue speckled granite coffee pots warmed on a cast iron wood stove. Like the café in town, a four-sided cut-out in the wall divided the dining area from the kitchen, making food distribution easier to manage.

Marta Garza, busy rolling out tortillas, eyed Art through the cut-out window.

"Buenos días, Arturo. You're up early."

"Buenos días, Marta."

Marta and her husband, Oscar, had worked for the De Leóns for over twenty years. Marta cooked three meals a day for the De León family and two for the wranglers. Oscar was an expert at everything--carpentry, gardening, tack and saddle making, cattle driving, horse wrangling and excelled exceedingly in running errands for Marta. The couple, Art mused, reminded him of the *Mutt and Jeff* cartoon comic strip in the newspaper. Oscar stretched six-foot-two while Marta was barely five-feet tall and only then if she stood on a box.

It was five o'clock. Choosing the table at the back, Art pulled out the bench and sat down. Other wranglers began to file in and nodded in Art's direction. His three bunkmates joined him. Jake and Lance Young, twenty-something-year-old brothers from Falfurrias, had joined the crew last summer. Still novices as far as the seasoned wranglers were concerned. Eduard Pérez, a forty-year-old veteran cowboy, felt obligated to teach all the greenhorns. Although he loved to tease, his advice about horses and cattle was well respected and followed without argument.

"What got you up so early?" Jake asked Art.

"That noisy old rooster, I bet!" Eduard answered. "Don't know why Marta doesn't serve him for Sunday dinner!"

"Surprised you even heard the rooster," Jake teased. "More likely it was your snoring that woke Art!" Lance laughed in agreement with his brother.

"I keep telling you boys I don't snore! I just dream deeply!" Eduard grinned and took a big gulp of coffee.

With as much vigor as she could muster, Marta clanged a cast iron striker against a triangular chuck wagon dinner bell as she announced, "Come and get it!"

The twenty-four cowboys formed a single line near the serving window and waited their turn to receive their breakfast fare—fried bacon, sausage patties, scrambled eggs, fried potatoes, pinto beans, jalapeno peppers, green tomatillo salsa, and tortillas. The wranglers scarfed down their food. Their long twelve-hour day began in twenty minutes.

As Art and a couple other wranglers headed for the horse barn, Art saw a black car speeding down the road toward them. Dust was billowing out behind the 1928 Chevrolet two-door sedan. The car skidded to a stop in front of the barn and Roman, Rosa's youngest brother, jumped out. Rosa rose from the driver's seat and waited for Art by the car.

"Sorry I'm late!" Roman called as he ran past Art.

"No problem for me. I'm not the one you report to!" Art laughed.

"Think my brother will give me some slack? How long does the newlywed exemption last anyway?" Roman yelled over his shoulder.

"Wish I knew!"

As Rosa neared, Art pulled her close for a morning kiss. Shrill whistles and catcalls escalated from the barn. Art kissed her again. She smiled but her face reddened as the whistles intensified.

"Art," she said, "I came not only to bring my lazy love-sick brother but also to tell you I'm taking Mamá to Kingsville to shop for curtains. She wants to redo Abuela's room before Saturday. My grandmother is coming to live with us. Her cousin with whom she had been living in Mexico City remarried seven months ago. Abuela felt like an intruder. Good thing our house is big and roomy. One day we too may live in the big hacienda along with my brothers and their families." Rosa smiled coquettishly.

"Maybe," Art grinned. "Have a good day with your mother. I can have Bonita saddled and ready for our sunset ride. Meet me at the barn?"

"Art," Rosa apologized. "I'm sorry. I won't have time. Have so much to do. Come to dinner Saturday night and meet Abuela. I know she will love you."

"I have the cutting horse competition all day Saturday. But I'll try."

"Oh, I completely forgot! Don't know where my head is. I know you and Fuego will do well! If we get everything done, I want to come watch."

"I'd like that."

"Art!" A male's gruff voice sounded behind him.

Art turned to see Rosa's eldest brother, Rafael, standing in the doorway of the barn. "Rosa, leave him alone. He has work to do. Pedro has Fuego saddled."

Art and Rafael watched Rosa back the car around and head back toward the family's house. Turning, Art followed Rafael into the barn. Art, Roman and Rafael were the only three horse trainers besides Rosa's father. Mr. De León had trained all four of his sons when they were quite young. Reynaldo and Ricardo, however, preferred to be out on the range. Rafael, appointed head trainer five years ago, taught Art the skill of training cutting horses.

Saturday had finally arrived. Art woke early. Cowboys who were competing in the local rodeo—team roping, steer wrestling, cutting horse competition, or bronc riding—had already chowed down and were making their way to the barn. The rodeo competition held every year at the end of May was a demonstration of the daily working skills of each cowboy and his horse. The top scores in each category won cash prizes. Claiming bragging rights was always motivation to enter. Saddles and tack were gathered and placed in the back of pickup truck beds. The horses had been fed, brushed, and readied to trailer. It was an hour's drive to Kingsville. The cutting horse competition began promptly at ten o'clock.

Art didn't realize how frazzled he was until their convoy of pickups pulled into the unloading area at the rodeo grounds. Pickups, trailers, and cars were already parked in designated parking areas. Cowboys from the other King Ranch divisions—Encino, Norias, and Santa Gertrudis—had arrived. Red and yellow tents were set in two long rows walking distance from the arena, the largest corral. Small red, green, and yellow triangular-shaped flags were strung together and tied above the spectators' bleachers and across the judges' raised platform inside the arena. Crowds of people mingled around the tents. Across the grass-stripped field, the wind carried aromas of chili, cotton candy, churros--sweet Mexican fritters--and barbeque all intermingled with the smell of cattle, horses, and hay.

Art registered for the cutting horse competition and was given number seventeen. Still a long wait before he and Fuego would compete. More time for the anxiety churning in his stomach to increase.

It was time. The cutting horse competition had begun. Art sat astride Fuego and observed the competitors from outside of the fence. Contestant seventeen was called to the main arena. Art reined Fuego's head to the right and steered the horse toward the entrance of the arena and stopped. He waited for the head judge, who was sitting on the raised platform, to raise a flag to start the clock. Seeing the fifteen heifers in the far corner of the arena, Fuego's front legs danced in anticipation.

The judge raised a green flag. Art nudged Fuego forward. There were four other riders in the arena. Two were judges who counted off points if the rider directed his horse in any way after a heifer was selected. The other two men controlled the herd in the corner. As Art and Fuego advanced, Art pointed to a small brown heifer standing in the herd's center. He reined Fuego forward. The heifer started to move with the herd as they all circled away from the horse. Fuego followed closely, forcing the animal to leave the herd. The heifer trotted toward the center of the arena trying to escape from the horse. Art relaxed the reins. For two-and-one-half minutes, he was now only a spectator sitting in the saddle rather than in the bleachers. It was now up to Fuego. His call; his show.

The heifer circled and faced the herd. Fuego stopped three feet away. He lowered his head and watched the smaller animal. When the heifer moved to the right, Fuego shadowed her direction. The heifer tried again to run past him back to the herd, but Fuego cut her off. His quick maneuvers stirred up the loose dirt on the arena's floor. The heifer turned again to the left. Fuego mirrored her movements. His quick turns and stops finally caused the heifer to stand still. The young heifer stared at this tall red animal blocking her path. Time was up. Art reined Fuego out of the arena. The heifer ran back to the herd. Art's score would be announced after all the cutting-horse contestants had competed.

The annual event in Kingsville ended. All the challenging work of training had paid off. Art came in second with Rafael placing first.

Now he was eager to get back to Laureles, bathe, and put on his blue suit. Rosa was waiting for him.

Art smoothed down the front of his Sunday suit jacket as he approached the De León's hacienda. The horseshoe-shaped house was a remarkable sight. Its adobe walls were painted bright yellow which contrasted well with the red clay tile roof. The rounded tiles gave the roof a scalloped-looking edge. Tall palm trees and squat cacti skirted the perimeter of the yard. Cedar benches sat against the inside walls on either side of the arched entryway.

Large multi-colored ceramic pots held either dark rose bougainvillea vines or purple vincas or orange lantana plants. An oval ceramic sundial hung on the wall adjacent to the massive oak door leading to the main house. The dial captured the sun's face in tiny red, blue, green, yellow and orange mosaic tiles.

The patio's royal blue three-tiered fountain boasted center stage. Water trickled slowly from tier to tier and collected into a circular basin that spanned four feet across. Wide enough for sitting, the basin's ledge as well as its sides were decorated with dark blue and bright yellow tiles that formed geometric floral shapes. The patio welcomed guests and residents alike.

Art stepped toward the door and posed his hand to knock. The door sprang open, and Rosa appeared. She looked stunning. Her dark wavy hair fell loosely over her shoulders. She wore a traditional Mexican dress—peasant-style white blouse tucked into an emerald green skirt. The tiered skirt, embellished with red and yellow and blue yarn, fell inches above her sandaled feet. The ends of a red and yellow striped sash, tied around her waist, touched the hemline of her skirt.

"Art!" Rosa kissed him. "Congratulations! Rafael told me you won second place. I'm so proud of you! Oh, and thank you for wearing the charro tie."

Art grinned as she ruffled the ends of his red satin balloon tie. "For you, anything. The tie doesn't look too out of place with my Sunday suit?"

"Not at all. You're my handsome cowboy, mi guapa vaquero."

He leaned in for another kiss but was interrupted by Reynaldo.

"Hey, Rosa, come on! Abuela asked for you."

Rosa grabbed Art's hand and led him to the main sitting area. All the De Leóns, except for the nine grandchildren, were gathered, waiting for dinner to be announced. The men—Mr. De León, Rafael, Reynaldo, Ricardo and Roman—were standing. They wore either black or dark blue charro suits—charro, a Spanish nickname for cowboy or equestrian. The fancy suit jacket was short and close fitting, touching the waistline. White embroidered designs stretched across the back, around the collar and around the sleeve cuffs. The scrolled designs down the length of the pant legs matched the ones on the jacket. Mr. De León's and Rafael's jackets were each fastened at the top by two silver conchos. Their knotted ties created a billowing of satin at their necklines.

The women, an artist's pallet of bright colors, were seated. Each wore a skirt similar to Rosa's but in assorted colors. Mrs. De León, wearing all white, was seated on a black leather sofa next to an older woman—Abuela, Art assumed. The old woman's dark eyes examined Art curiously. Abuela was dressed in black, and a black lacy shawl embraced her stooped shoulders.

A knock pounded against the front door. Mr. De León excused himself. The room became soundless as Rosa led Art to her grandmother.

"Abuela, I want you to meet Art," Rosa said cheerfully. "He is my fiancée."

Art reached out for Abuela's hand, but she kept it secured in her lap. Her dark eyes never wavered from his.

"It's an honor to meet you. Es un honor conocerte," Art smiled, slowly retracting his hand.

The woman sat there like a cold slab of stone pretending not to understand what was said nor acknowledging the man who stood before her. Mrs. De León patted her mother-in-law's wrinkled hands and smiled apologetically at Art.

"Ahem, excuse me," Mr. De León entered the room. "Look who has come! He claims Senora Sofía De León invited him. Mamá?"

"Gabriel!" Abuela exclaimed, rising from her seat and stepping past

Art to meet the visitor. Her shawl slipped from her shoulders onto the floor.

Art noticed how quickly the atmosphere soured. Rosa stepped closer and grabbed his arm. Rosa's brothers seemed agitated and exchanged side glances with each other and with their wives.

"Come! Come!" Abuela, speaking excitedly in Spanish, held up her arms motioning the young man to hug her. "So good to see you, Gabriel! You're still so handsome! Rosa is here." Abuela chuckled and pointed to where Rosa was standing.

Art was confused and could see Rosa was upset and embarrassed.

"No greeting for an old friend?" Gabriel asked.

"Hug the man!" Abuela commanded, smiling broadly.

Rosa reluctantly dropped Art's arm and stepped uneasily toward Gabriel. The mystery man reached out for Rosa's hand. He pulled her into a hug. Art clenched his teeth and stepped up beside her.

"There will be time later for us to catch up." Gabriel squeezed Rosa's hand.

Mrs. De León, trying to break the tension and relieve her daughter's uneasiness, stood. "Marta has prepared a lovely dinner. Please, let's go in."

The couples filed out of the room. Gabriel retrieved Abuela's shawl from the floor and spread it around her shoulders. Abuela took Gabriel's arm subtly requesting an escort. Art pulled Rosa back when she started to exit with the others.

"What's going on? Who is that guy?"

"Rosa?" Abuela called from the doorway. "Come, my dear."

Rosa whispered, "Please, not now. He's a nobody. Come, Abuela is calling."

Suddenly Art's first impression of Rosa's grandmother was most unfavorable, and he felt childishly jealous. But for Rosa he would give the elderly woman another chance. Consideration for that shifty scoundrel who acted as if he had claims on Rosa was clearly out of the question.

Abuela took over the seating arrangements as if the house were hers rather than her son's. "Rafael, you and Catalina, sit there. Ricardo and Elena on the other side there; Reynaldo and Maria at the end by your father. Roman and Carmen by your mother. Rosa, come sit here. Gabriel, sit here on my right next to Rosa."

"You," she practically snarled, pointing at Art. "Sit across from Rosa there next to Ricardo."

Dinner was soon underway. Conversation eased the tension caused by Gabriel's arrival. The rodeo was the main topic followed by ranch business, Abuela's cousin's recent marriage, stories about the De León's heritage and of course, the grandchildren. Art, not knowing the extended family nor past family stories, felt left out and soon lost interest in trying to follow the discussion.

When he'd finished eating, he placed his napkin in his lap. He kept his eyes trained on Gabriel. He bristled every time the man leaned toward Rosa and spoke in hushed tones. Art's attention suddenly turned to Maria as she scooted her chair slightly from the table. Maria patted Reynaldo's arm and smiled. Reynaldo looked down and lifted a beautiful child onto his lap.

"Sorry, Abuela," Reynaldo apologized, wrapping his arm around his daughter. "Both Luna and Luis were asleep before we came down. She must have awakened and became frightened when she couldn't find us. She won't be a bother."

Luna, the little three-year-old, leaned her head against her father's chest and stared at Art who was sitting diagonally across the table. Her hair was dark and fell in ringlets to the middle of her back. Her eyes were pitch-black and her lashes dark and long. Art smiled at her, but she continued to stare. Curious, he thought. Being the second eldest of eight, he usually fared well with children. He smiled once more. No reaction. But at least she did not turn her head away.

Art remembered a game he once played with his twin sisters when they were Luna's age. He reached for the napkin in his lap and wrapped it around his right hand. Pulling up one corner between two fingers to form ears, he slowly lifted the napkin from his lap. He wiggled the napkin from side to side like a rabbit or a long-eared puppy trying to see over the table edge. Luna grinned at him.

"So, married a year and no baby?" Abuelo bluntly asked Roman.

Carmen's face turned a brilliant shade of red as Roman answered, "We're not ready, Abuela. We've not been married a full year."

"Ready? Who plans these things? Reynaldo, it's time for another. Luis is almost weaned, is he not, Maria?"

"Abuela, I'm not a cow listed on the ranch's stock breeding calendar!" Maria snapped, looking helplessly at her husband.

Gabriel coughed into his napkin attempting to disguise his laugh.

"Sorry," Maria whispered to Reynaldo. Detecting distress in his wife's eyes, he placed his hand over hers. Luna fidgeted in his lap.

"Mamá," Mr. De León said, "The dinner table is not the place for these matters. I am immensely proud of my family and my nine grandchildren."

"Children are God's blessings." Abuela added with a twinkle in her eyes.

"Why don't you ask Art and Rosa?" Roman suggested, hoping to divert any attention that might come back his and Carmen's way.

"Why? Why should I ask them?"

"We are getting married, Abuela," Rosa answered. "I told you. Art and I."

"No! No, you are not! Are you Catholic?" Abuela addressed Art directly for the first time that evening.

"No, ma'am. I'm protestant."

A quirky grin spread across Gabriel's face. He was relishing this interview.

Abuela pounded her hands against the table; anger washed over her face. "No! Rosa, I forbid it! He may speak our language and dress as we do but he will never be part of this family! Juan! I forbid it!"

Trying to buffer the situation, Rosa's father, said, "Yes, Mamá, you're right, of course. Come, let's enjoy our dinner and speak of this another time."

"Papá!" Rosa stood to face her father. "What are you saying? You know Art! If you didn't agree to our marriage, why have you not said anything until now?"

"Enough, Rosa!" Mr. De León exclaimed angrily. Rosa's disrespectful outburst in front of his mother was embarrassing. His mother might conclude he had no control over his children, especially his only daughter. Rosa threw her napkin onto her plate and stormed from the room.

Art stood. All eyes fell upon him. "Thank you for the meal, Mrs. De León. It's been a long day. I bid you all a goodnight." Art nodded toward Mr. De León.

"Yes! Time to leave! You should never be a guest in this house! You are a simple hired hand!" Abuela was furious as she stood. "And stay away Rosa!"

"Oh, Señora De León, sit down. Don't upset yourself." Gabriel held the back of Abuela's chair as she slowly sat down. Gabriel pulled his chair closer and lovingly put his arm around her. He smirked as Art quickly exited the room.

Carmen slipped out onto the patio and saw Art standing by the fountain. She rushed up to him. "Oh, Art! I am so sorry how Abuela treated you!"

Art nodded awkwardly. "It's okay, Carmen. Help me find Rosa."

Carmen ran up the stairs. Three minutes later, Rosa descended. Art stayed by the fountain. As she approached, he reached out for her hand.

"Not here! Come with me!"

Rosa led him into the yard toward a group of palm trees standing statuesquely under the midnight-blue sky. They stepped behind a twenty-foot-tall palm—its trunk narrow, its bark course and its long pointed green fronds spread like a canopy over their heads.

Art pulled her to him. "Rosa, what just happened? Are you okay?"

"Oh, Art," she began to cry. "I'm so sorry! Abuela was so hateful. I've never seen her act that way. She's trying to stop us from getting married!"

"That won't happen! I promise." He kissed her and held her tightly.

Carmen remained at the house and stood under the archway. Chirping crickets and rustling palm fronds were the only sounds stirring the night. She strained her eyes toward the yard, but the night was too dark to see clearly.

"Carmen!"

Startled, Carmen turned quickly.

Mrs. De León, with resolve in her eyes, asked, "Are they out there?"

"Who?"

"Don't play games with me, child. Is Rosa with Art?"

Carmen looked down at her sandaled feet. "Yes, ma'am."

"Go to bed, Carmen!" Mrs. De León briskly brushed past.

Mrs. De León followed the graveled path to its end and easily spotted Rosa and Art. "Rosa, come inside. Art, please return to your quarters. I'm sorry about tonight. You are a good man, but Rosa must come in with me now." Mrs. De León held out her hand, but Rosa was hesitant to take it. "Rosa!"

"Go," Art whispered and squeezed her hand.

With tears in her eyes, Rosa took her mother's hand and was led back toward the house. Rosa looked back over her shoulder. Art remained by the tree.

Carmen, resentful of being treated like a child, leaned against the adobe wall deciding what to do when she saw her father-in-law escorting Abuela to her room. Gabriel was trailing behind them. Once Abuela was in her room and her bedroom door closed, Mr. De León turned to face Gabriel.

"You have some nerve coming here tonight! We were only cordial because my mother invited you. Does she know how you treated her granddaughter?"

"I'm sorry, Señor. I don't understand. I thought all had been forgiven. It was just a little misunderstanding. I still solemnly vow to marry your daughter and can now offer her a bright future."

"I don't think my daughter will agree. It's best you leave, Gabriel. If my mother had not been here tonight, I would not have allowed you inside my house!"

Carmen slipped further into the shadows as Gabriel huffed past. A few minutes later Mrs. De León and Rosa enter the patio.

"Good night, Rosa," Mrs. De León kissed her daughter's cheek. "Go to bed, sweetheart. All will be better in the morning."

Rosa remained by the fountain and watched her mother enter the main house. She was hurt and confused. Her mother trusted she would obey and go to bed. Rosa was not usually defiant, but Art deserved an explanation. She turned to go back out to find him when she heard something rustling in the corner by the front gate.

A dark form appeared and slowly advanced toward the fountain. The patio was dark except for the moonlight invading the cloudless sky. But even though the light was dim, Gabriel's cologne, musky and strong, identified him. She turned hastily to escape up the stairs. He hurried toward her and grasped her arm.

"You have been avoiding me all night. Oh, mi amore." He took her hands and kissed her knuckles.

She pulled her hands away. "Gabriel! Why did you dare come tonight? I thought I had made myself clear! I never wanted to see you again!"

"Oh, but you don't mean it." He smiled that charming smile she once loved and tipped her chin up with his fingertips. "I've missed you, Rosa. Your gorgeous amber eyes. Look at me. You can't say you haven't missed me. I've not stopped loving you. You once loved my kisses. Kiss me like you used to."

Gabriel leaned forward. Rosa turned her head to avoid his kiss and hit his chest with her hands. He scoffed at her futile efforts to avoid his advances.

"Rosa, don't fight me." Persistently, he tried kissing her mouth.

"Stop! Gabriel! You're hurting me!" She continued to struggle against him, but his grasp was too strong. His strength and her fear immobilized her.

"Take your filthy hands off her!"

"Art!" Rosa squealed, trying to pull away.

Art bounded toward Gabriel and shoved him. Bumped to one side, Rosa backed up near the fountain. Surprised by the sudden attack, Gabriel turned to meet his adversary. Art doubled his fist and pummeled Gabriel's left jaw. Gabriel's head snapped backwards. With anger in his eyes and fire in his gut, Gabriel swung hard. Art ducked. Gabriel skirted around and swung again catching Art's upper jaw. With clinched fists, Art targeted Gabriel's nose and hit it dead center. Gabriel, blood streaming down his face, returned the punch squarely connecting Art's left eye and upper brow. Art stepped back and raised both fists readying to box. With a deep guttural sound, Gabriel plowed into Art's midsection jarring him off balance. Gabriel cinched Art's waist tightly and continued to push. Like two felled trees, the men dropped upon the tile flooring. Art hit first and hard; Gabriel did not release his clinch. They scuffled and rolled toward the fountain like two tumbleweeds blown about by the South Texas wind.

"What's going on?" Roman shouted as he and Ricardo pulled the men apart.

Carmen rushed to Rosa's side. "Are you all right? Did he hurt you?"

Rosa shook her head and blinked tears from her eyes. She rubbed the sides of her aching arms. "Thank you, Carmen, for bringing my brothers."

Pulling Gabriel up by his collar, Roman pushed him toward the gate. "You're scum! Thought you'd learned your lesson! If we weren't standing in my father's courtyard, I'd let Art finish what he'd started! Stay away from my sister!"

Roman continued to shout as Gabriel started his car and sped away.

"Let's get you to Oscar's," Ricardo suggested, helping Art to stand.

"Nah, it's too late. I'll be fine." Art dabbed the blood at the corner of his mouth with his finger.

"No, Art, please," Rosa pleaded. "Let them take you to Oscar's. Who do you think doctored my brothers when they came home after a brawl?"

"Ah, come on now, hermanita. Be nice. We were much younger!" Ricardo laughed. "And unmarried!" Roman added. "Thanks, Art, for rescuing our baby sister. Thought we were through with that guy!"

"Okay, Roman, you can take me to Oscar's but first I want to talk to Rosa. Meet you outside by your truck?"

"Good night, then," Ricardo nodded and climbed the stairs to his and Elena's room. Roman took Carmen's hand. They walked out to wait in their truck.

Art looked into Rosa's eyes. "Now tell me about Gabriel. Who is he?"

Rosa looked down at her hands, took a deep breath and began, "Gabriel Sanchez and I dated all through high school. Our parents are…were friends. When I was accepted to St. Mary's University in San Antonio, he was afraid I wouldn't come back. He proposed the night after graduation, and I foolishly accepted. When I came home the summer after my sophomore year, I heard from several friends that Gabriel had been seen with other women. I didn't believe Gabriel would do such a thing. I trusted him. One weekend Carmen went with her family to her aunt's birthday party in Corpus. Gabriel was there with Carmen's cousin. He hadn't met Carmen and didn't know she and Roman were dating. When Carmen and Roman and I confronted him, he, as usual, denied it and called Carmen a liar. That only incensed Roman. When I gave his ring back, Gabriel became angry and raised his fist to hit me. Roman shoved him. A fight broke out right here on this very spot. My father heard the raucous, broke it up and sent Gabriel away."

"So, why does your grandmother love him so much then?"

"Oh, I just told Abuela I'd called off the engagement but didn't explain why. She's tried to get us back together ever since. I should have told her. This would have never happened if I'd been honest with her and with you."

"Who could know what would have happened? It's not your fault. Abuela has other issues with me. It's late. Roman and Carmen are waiting for me. If my lips weren't busted, I'd give you a big kiss right now."

Rosa kissed his cheek. "We'll work this out. I want Abuela to love you as much as I do."

"Well, maybe not that much!" he teased. "I'll call you tomorrow."

A light shone brightly through the front window at Oscar's and Marta's small adobe house. Roman drove Art's truck and parked near the front porch. Carmen followed, driving Roman's truck. As Art opened the passenger door, Oscar opened the door to his house and stepped out onto the porch.

"I heard you coming. What's going on?"

"A tussle with Gabriel," Roman answered. "Oscar, will you patch him up? May have a couple cracked ribs. Took a nasty fall."

"Yes, of course. Come this way." Oscar motioned toward the kitchen.

Roman removed his arm from under Art's shoulder as he and Oscar eased Art into a kitchen chair. Marta appeared wrapping a housecoat about her. She asked no questions. Art's condition said it all.

"Art, sorry you had a rough time tonight," Roman chuckled. "But this time Gabriel got the message! You'll get the best of good care here. Talk to you tomorrow. Need to get my bride home. Goodnight, all." Roman nodded and left the house.

Oscar opened a cabinet above the sink and removed gauze, tape, scissors and iodine. Marta sat beside Art at the table and patted his uninjured hand.

"Arturo, answer one question."

Art looked into her deep brown inquisitive eyes.

"Did you win?"

Trying to smile, Art flinched. "Don't make me laugh, Marta."

Marta and Oscar attended Art's cuts and wrapped his ribs with gauze. They worked methodically as a team. Clearly not their first rescue.

"Marta," Art began, "Why is Señora De León, Abuela, so set against my marrying Rosa? Abuela asked if I were Catholic. Is my being protestant a problem?"

Marta glanced at Oscar. "Oh, mi hijo, yes. Someone should have explained this to you. In the Catholic Church, God blesses marriages. Marriage is sacred."

"Same as my church."

"But marriages between a Catholic and a non-Catholic cannot receive a blessing and would be invalid in the eyes of the Church. Marriage is one of our sacraments. Baptism is the first. Rosa must be married in the Catholic Church where she was confirmed and where she receives Holy Communion."

"I don't understand. I am a believer and have been baptized. We believe in and worship the same God, do we not?"

Marta smiled weakly, "Yes, I suppose. But we Catholics are very faithful to our traditions. There is no other way."

Art squirmed as Oscar dabbed more iodine to the cuts over his eyebrow. "There must be something! I cannot imagine my life without her!"

"If you're not willing to convert to Catholicism, there's no other way."

"Wait, Marta," Oscar interjected, "what about a permission letter sent from Father Montoya to the Bishop Diocese in Corpus? It's been done before."

"I didn't think of that. Talk with Rosa and then visit with Father Montoya. He will know what to do."

"First, I must speak with Señor De León. Thank you both. Now will you direct me to your sofa? I feel like I've been bucked off a mustang."

Monday morning Art dressed in his best long-sleeved white shirt and non-working denim jeans. With difficulty, he pulled on his black boots. He still smarted all over. His face was scratched, had a split lip, a black eye, and three cracked ribs. The bump on the back of his head prompted his decision to leave his hat where it now hung on the wall. He'd gained permission from Rafael to take the day off. Sunday afternoon he'd called Rosa from the cookhouse to explain his plan to see her father. He'd also prayed fervently that Abuela would change her opinion of him.

When Art entered the courtyard, birds flittered about the patio from one roof top to another. The water in the tiered fountain trickled into the tiled basin. The flower heads bowed gracefully as he passed by. The courtyard was peaceful during the daytime, Art thought. He knocked on the front door and waited. Mrs. De León opened the door.

"Good morning, Señora De León."

"Art," she replied. Her eyes quickly examined his injuries. "Rosa is not here."

"Yes, ma'am, I know. I've come to see Señor De León. May I come in?"

Rosa's mother scrutinized his wounds a second time then stepped to one side allowing his entrance. She turned without saying anything further. Art followed her even though he knew the way to Mr. De León's study. She rapped on the door three times and waited until her husband invited her inside.

She opened the door and announced, "Art is here to see you."

Mr. De León looked up from a pile of papers strewn across the top of his desk. With a quizzical brow, he said, "Well, come in, young man. Come in! Art, would you care for coffee?"

"Don't go to any trouble on my account, sir."

"No trouble. Camilla brought in a tray just a few minutes ago. Marta makes the best coffee, agree? Cream?"

"Very well then," Art agreed. "No cream, thank you."

Mr. De León closed his journal and pushed it to one side. Motioning toward the sofa, Mr. De León said, "The coffee is on the table there."

Art followed Rosa's father to the sofa and sat down. Mr. De León poured coffee into two large white ceramic mugs. "Never understood why the ladies prefer those tiny finger-sized cups. I need a manly cup; one I can grip! Here you are."

Art took the mug from Rosa's father and watched the man pour a copious stream of cream into his mug. Mr. De León stirred the contents and eased back.

"Sir?" Art began. "I've come…."

"No, no, there's always time for other matters. Come, enjoy your coffee. Drink up." Mr. De León's eyes twinkled as he crossed his legs.

Mr. De León placed his mug on the silver tray. To one side of the tray sat a medium-sized wooden box with red and blue ceramic tiles decorated across its top. Mr. De León opened the cedar-lined box and removed a cigar. He tilted the box toward Art in an invitation to join him. Art declined the offer. Mr. De León bit off a small piece from the tip of the cigar. Striking a match, he twirled the cigar encased with dried tobacco above the flame and began to puff. Inhaling deeply, he turned his head and exhaled the smoke away from his guest.

"So, what is it you've come to see me about? A raise? You certainly deserve one after doing so well at the cutting horse competition."

"Thank you, sir. I appreciate that, but that's not why I'm here." Art gulped; his mouth dry; his hands sweaty.

Mr. De León took another big puff from his cigar and viewed Art through squinted eyes. He spat a small piece of dried tobacco from his lip and smiled. "No, I didn't think so. I owe you much more than pay raises for coming to my daughter's rescue Saturday night. Don't look alarmed; Rosa told me all about it. Gabriel had been forewarned to stay away from her, but the man is stubborn. Did Oscar and Marta get you patched up okay?"

"Yes, sir, they did. I have something important to discuss with you. I'm sure you are aware of how much I love your daughter. Sir, we want your approval and blessings for our future together. We want to be married at St. Gertrude's. But our differences of faith pose a problem. We need your help."

Mr. De León stood and returned to his desk. He sat down in his overstuffed leather chair and took a couple more puffs from his cigar. Art, unsure of what to do, returned to the chair opposite Mr. De León's.

"Before we talk about differences of faith and getting married in my church, I have other questions for you, son, which will determine whether I approve of your marriage to my daughter. They may seem trivial to you but are of extreme importance to me. Rosa is my only daughter and as such, is my pride and joy. Her security and happiness will always be my utmost priority as her father. Whomever she marries must provide for her in a manner that cause little concern to me and her mother about her welfare and well-being. You are a horse wrangler and own no property nor have any other means of wealth. Is this true?"

"Yes, sir, that is true. I have those same concerns. I have seen an abandoned adobe house down by the creek. Do you know the owner? I have saved some money and would like to buy it for our first home. Rosa plans to teach full-time in Kingsville this fall. With our combined incomes, we can afford to start small."

Mr. De León flipped a burning ash into the ashtray on his desk. He took another big puff from his cigar as he considered Art's declaration for his daughter. Art remained composed but his insides were as skittish as a colt bearing the weight of a saddle for the first time.

Suddenly, two female voices raised in a quarrel sounded in the hallway. As Art and Mr. De León turned their heads toward the disturbance, the door abruptly swung open. Rosa, closely followed by her mother, barged into the room.

"What is the meaning of this, Camilla?" Mr. De León demanded.

"I tried to keep her away, but you know how strong-willed our daughter is!"

Art stood to his feet as Rosa sidled next to him. Her brows furrowed; determination painted her face. "Art told me he was coming to speak to you this morning, Papá. I, too, have something to say! I know you think of me as a child, your baby girl. But I am twenty-three years old and can make my own decisions! Art came today to receive your blessing for our marriage. If you refuse to bless our union, we will leave the ranch and be married elsewhere! I love him and am determined to marry him with or without your blessing!" Never having spoken to her father in this tone, Rosa's face reddened.

Art clasped her hand as Mr. De León cleared his throat and said, "You're being a bit hasty, mi hija. I have not yet given my answer. Camilla, Art was explaining how he was going to provide for our daughter. They want to buy that little adobe house by the creek. What do you think? Would that be a suitable place for a young couple to start out?"

Mrs. De León raised her eyebrows in confusion. But as she searched her husband's eyes, she smiled. "That little house by the creek was where your father and I lived after we married. We welcomed two of our five children there. That little adobe has sentimental value and is not for sell."

Rosa glanced at Art and easily observed his disappointment. Mrs. De León continued, "If that is where you'd like to live after you marry, you may do so without buying it. Consider it a wedding present if my husband agrees."

"Yes, yes, of course," Mr. De León grinned, "but we have bigger hurdles, I understand. I will make an appointment with Father Montoya. He will tell us what to do. Rosa, you must do exactly what Father says, understand?"

Rosa clinched Art's hand. "Does this mean you've blessed our union?"

"If you two can be married at St. Gertrude's in our Mexican tradition, promise to raise your children in the Catholic Church and do all Father Montoya instructs, then your mother and I whole-heartedly agree."

Rosa moved swiftly around the desk, plopped onto her father's lap as she loved to do as a child and hugged his neck tightly.

Mrs. De León laughed. "That's enough. Get up from there! You're too old for such behavior!" Rosa stood and embraced her mother.

Mr. De León shook Art's hand. "Welcome to our family, my son."

THE WEDDING
1935

The summer afternoon was mild in temperature but high in excitement for this long awaited event had finally arrived. A slight breeze lifted the sweet fragrance from the lilac wisteria vines that wound over the arch at the end of the walkway. Yellow and red rose bushes in radiant full bloom filled the flower beds. White dyanthis lined their borders. Behind St. Gertrude Church six white tents erected for the reception held round tables and folding chairs. One tent was dedicated to food—tacos, tamales, enchiladas, chile rellenos, barbecoa, carnitas, and salsas. Another to desserts—the four-tiered wedding cake accompanied by tres leches cake, flan, Mexican wedding cookies, and pan dulce. After the ceremony, the wedding guests mingled outside by the gardens waiting for the wedding party to exit the church.

Finally, the church doors opened and the wedding party was led outside by two couples—Tia and Santos Santiago and Marta and Oscar Garza. Rosa and Art had chosen these couples to be their padrinos and madrinas—a special honor selected by the bride and groom to serve as sponsors or mentors. Marta and Oscar provided the white lace kneeling pillows and the wedding lasso for the ceremony; Tia and Santos offered the Bible and the wedding coins.

The Bailey and Bond families stood together under the shade of a tent and watched the wedding procession come down the steps. Maggie took Franklin's arm and squeezed it. "They are all so beautiful," she whispered.

Rosa's brothers served as Art's groomsmen. Each wore a dark blue charro suit accented with a light blue satin charro tie and cumberbund. The scrolled designs on their jackets and pant legs were stitched in gold thread. In their right hands, the groomsmen held white sombreros embroidered in gold.

Rosa's sisters-in-law were her attendants. The ladies wore a folklórico style dress but each a different color—peach, yellow, light blue, red, and green. The over-the-shoulder frilly collared tops were tucked into a long free-flowing three-tiered skirt decorated in rows of multi-colored ribbons and lace. The women wore their hair pulled up in a bun with a large yellow peony secured on one side.

The groomsmen escorted their wives down the church steps and formed two lines on the walkway. One beside Tia and Santos; the other beside Marta and Oscar. When the bride and groom appeared on the threshold, Father Montoya announced, "It's my pleasure to present to you Mr. and Mrs. Arthur Bailey!"

As the guests cheered and applauded, Art, dressed in a white charro suit trimmed with gold embroiderey, kissed his bride's hand. Rosa looked more lovely than he'd ever seen her. Her long dark hair was curled in ringlets over her shoulders and cascaded down the middle of her back. Her long tulle lace veil stretched four-feet behind her and a diamond tiara topped her head. Wide pleats of white satin criss-crossed over the front and back of the dress forming the bodice. The short capped sleeves and the underskirt were also white satin. The overskirt of silk chantilly lace gathered about her waist. The skirt's edge was scalloped with tatted floral designs evenly spaced overall. The hem swished above her three-inch white heels decorated with white beads.

Art looked out over the crowd for his family, but his search would have to wait. His father-in-law—Art was pleased he could now call Mr. De León by that name—was ushering the bride and groom as well as his parents into the courtyard to form a reception line.

Mr. De León was first in line followed by Camilla, Rosa and Art, then Franklin and Maggie; parental bookends. Art shook hand after hand and received hugs from people he didn't know—businessmen and ranchers or friends and family of the De Leóns—and from those he knew over the course of living near Kingsville for five years. The line was long but soon began to dwindle as the refreshment tent became much more enticing.

"Follow me," Maggie said after Art asked about the Baileys.

When Art and Rosa walked into the tent, his family once again cheered and applauded. One by one the family came to wish them well. Another reception line was formed. This time Art knew them all; knew them well.

Art's eyes welled with tears as the first to greet him grabbed him around the neck. "John! I didn't know you were coming!"

"Sorry, I was a bit late. Luckily, the train station is within walking distance. I slipped in the back, but was there through most of the ceremony. Congratulations!"

"Did Emily, Eddie and Granma come?" Art asked.

"No, Em couldn't get away. Rosa, you are indeed a beautiful bride! Now I can officially welcome you to our family!" John clutched Rosa's arms gently and kissed her cheek.

"Hold up there, bub!" Art protested as Rosa laughed.

"Oh, Art, look whose coming!"

Lucy and Loraine skipped toward them, smiles on their faces, twinkles in their eyes. Lucy rushed to Rosa, looked up and smiled. "You look like a princess."

"And you two look lovely."

As if on cue, the twins swished their skirts about to show off their matching taffetta sundresses, Loraine's yellow; Lucy's blue. Loraine's grin was as bright as the color of her dress; all sunshine and glee.

"There you two are. Rosa, it's time to start the dancing," Mrs. De León said as she and Carmen stepped up behind the bride. "Here, let's remove your veil. Will be easier for you to move around."

Rosa remained still as her mother removed the tiara and unfastened the veil. Carmen scooped the lace up from the grass as it slid from Rosa's head and carefully looped the lacy fabric around her arms. Mrs. De León replaced the diamond tiara upon Rosa's head and smiled lovingly at her daughter.

Art held Rosa's hand, fingers intertwined, as they walked toward the courtyard. Many of the guests had already formed a circle around the tiled courtyard but cleared a path for them to enter.

"Oh, Art! The marachi band is here!" Rosa exclaimed excitedly.

The band of eight players stood in two rows on the church steps. Each man wore a light blue charro suit. White buckles spaced vertically were sewn an inch apart down the length of the outside of each pant leg. Their jackets were adorned with white scrolling across the yokes and were fastened with silver concho buckles; blue scrolls accented their white charro ties; their boots light blue; their sombreros white with blue accents.

Oscar neared the couple. "It's time for your first dance together as a married couple." He nodded to the band and each player readied their instruments.

As the slow-tempoed music filled the air, Art took Rosa into his arms. Looking at her took his breath away. Rosa's amber eyes glistened with tears as her husband danced her slowly across the clay tiles. They swayed to the sounds of the trumpets, violins and guitars as if they were the only two in the courtyard and the music was played only for them.

One of the trumpet players lowered his horn and began to sing. Art was so focused on the moment the lyrics became jumbled….something about the moon and all its beauty, searching for a beautiful woman and leaving flowers at her feet as a vow of love.

When the song ended, Art kissed his bride and the guests applauded.

"If you want to dance with either the bride or groom, you must pay a dollar! Tia is collecting money for Rosa; Marta for Art. Come," the lead vocalist announced. "Don't be shy!"

Clayton, who stood at his father's side within a circle of onlookers, pulled at his father's sleeve. "What does that mean?"

"Just what he said. A Mexican tradition…a fun way of gifting the bride and groom with cash. Need a dollar?" Franklin reached into his wallet and withdrew a dollar bill. He handed the money to Clayton and watched his fourteen-year-old son dash toward Tia.

"Raffi! Catalina!" The crowd began to chant and clap. "Raffi! Catalina!"

Art turned to Rosa. "What's going on?"

"Oh, you will see! Come!" Rosa led Art to the group of spectators who had encircled her eldest brother, Rafael and his wife, Catalina.

The couple stood facing each other in the center of the circle. Rafael with his white sombrero secured upon his head stood erect with both hands poised behind his back. Catalina pulled the ends of her long green skirt up into the air like a bird in flight. Exposing her black heels, she pointed her right toe. With the first note of the folklórico, Catalina stomped her left foot and fanned the ends of the skirt forming a wave of yellow and blue ruffled ribbons. Rafael danced slowly around her stomping and tapping his boots in small deliberate steps without changing the positions of his hands. At times he would lean close causing Catalina to smile. As he danced away, she shook her skirt in more waves and swung her hips as if enticing him back. The trumpets and guitars increased the tempo. The two dancers responded by repeating their steps more energetically. The crowd clapped with the rhythm. When the last note sounded, Rafael dipped his wife over his arm. The crowd yelled and cheered. He pulled her up, readjusted the string of his sombrero under his chin until the hat fell against his back. Catalina winked at him, stepped back two steps, and with a curled finger motioned him nearer. With the other hand, she swished her skirt from side to side as the crowd's enjoyment intensified. Rafael pulled her close and kissed her. The crowd responded with heightened excitement.

"That was fun!" Aunt Elizabeth found an empty chair inside the refreshment tent and sat down "My feet hurt just watching all the dancing."

Maggie laughed, "Yes, this is quite some party! Delores, come join us."

Tia placed her small plate of assorted desserts on the table and sat down.

"Tia? May I ask you something?" Aunt Elizabeth asked.

"Of course," Tia answered then took a bite of a sweet pan dulce.

"What was inside the gold box Art gave to Rosa during the ceremony?"

"That oranate box was filled with thirteen gold coins. Las arras or wedding coins. The number thirteen represents Jesus and his twelve apostles. The coins themselves symbolize Art's commitment to provide for Rosa and to proclaim his wealth now hers; their treasure one to share."

"Oh, that's so lovely. I loved all the symbolism in the service. Especially the rope ceremony—so beautiful."

"Marta and I made the lasso. In Spanish, it's called el lazo. We used small white flowers and tied them onto a white braided rope. And as you saw as Father Montoya blessed their union, the rope was draped first around Rosa's shoulders and formed a figure eight around Art's. The lasso symbolizes two being bound together as one in God's eyes and of their unity and binding support to each other."

"Art is so happy," Maggie added. "Oh, what's all the noise?"

The three ladies followed the noise to investigate.

Santos and Oscar led Rosa to a chair in the center of the dance floor. Rosa's and Art's brothers, all ten, carried the groom high over their heads and circled Rosa's chair twice. The guests howled and yelled excitedly. Art waved his arms in an attempt to surrender. Santos nodded and the brothers slowly lowered Art to the floor and placed him in an upright position.

Mr. De León stood behind Rosa with his hands on her shoulders. "Art," he began, "See all the single men standing behind you? They are waiting, impatiently I might add, to catch the garter Rosa's wearing. There's only one lucky winner!"

"Sir, that would be me!" Art declared as the guests laughed and applauded.

The guests moved in closer to watch. One of the guitarists strummed his guitar strings like a drum roll. Art knelt in front of his bride and removed her beaded shoes. He lifted her dress to her knees. He smiled up at her as he searched her left leg for the garter. She blushed as the crowd whistled.

"Got it!" Art pulled the blue garter trimmed in white lace over her knee, down her calf, over her toes and held it high in the air.

As Art stood, Rosa's four brothers plus John and Sam rushed in and grabbed him up off the floor. They poistioned him over their heads as the marachi band began to play. The crowd responded noisily.

"Throw it!" Rafael shouted as Art was carried closer to the single men. "Wait!" Art yelled as he was bounced about. "I can't see them!"

"That's the fun!" Ricardo exclaimed. "Throw it!"

Just as Art carefully postitioned the garter over his outstretched thumb and forefinger readying to fling it, the brothers turned quickly. After two turns, Art flung the garter in the air not knowing if it would land anywhere near his target. He heard screams and shouts and scrambling before his captors set him down. Ricardo and Reynaldo grabbed his shoulders and spun him more three times. When they let go, Art staggered dizzily and bumped into Rosa. She laughed and kissed him.

"Who got the garter?" Art asked.

"I did!"

Art turned to see William, a grin swept ear to ear, holding the esteemed blue garter. "Nah!" Art exclaimed. "You're too young to get married!"

"Who said anything about getting married? I'm putting this on my rearview mirror!" Art grabbed his seventeen-year-old brother and hugged him.

Unnoticed, the sun slowly inched across the cloudless sky and tucked herself into bed. The high-spirited wedding festivities continued. Torch lights emitted light for the dancers in the courtyard as well for the guests dining or visiting inside the tents. Children chased each other around the yard. Untouched, gifts wrapped in white paper sat on a long table inside the refreshment tent. A few guests lolled about but no one was ready to call it an evening.

When the band took a break, Art and Rosa sat down and shared their second piece of wedding cake. With her napkin, Rosa wiped a bit of icing from the corner of Art's mouth. He fingered icing from his cake and dabbed it on her nose.

"Ahh, you!" she laughed.

Mr. De León entered the tent and clapped Art's back. "Why don't you two slip away? We'll see you in the morning at breakfast."

Art glanced at his bride. Rosa stood on tiptoes and kissed her father's cheek. "Thank you, Papá. I will always remember this day and how much I love you."

"Go! Go!" Mr. De León responded, wiping a tear from his cheek.

The next morning, Art pulled his black truck onto the dirt road leading to the De León's hacienda and drove the short distance to the house. Cars and trucks were already parked in front. Art parked and hurriedly got out. He ran around to open Rosa's door. Hand-in-hand, they walked past a row of cars.

"Look!" Art pointed to a blue garter hanging from the rearview mirror of a 1932 Ford station wagon. Rosa laughed as she linked her arm through his.

As they walked under the archway, their families greeted them with applause. Eight tables arranged in a rectangular shape centered the patio. The tables were laden with pitchers of Sangria for the adults, orange juice for the children, and several bowls of mixed fruit—melons, pineapple, strawberries and bananas. Art held Rosa's hand as they made their way inside to say hello.

"Rosa, there's Trina. I didn't get to speak with her yesterday."

When Sam saw the bride and groom approaching, he stood. "Trina, it's the couple of the hour!"

Sam hugged them both. "Good morning!"

"Good morning," Rosa answered.

Trina remained seated. Art kissed the top of her head and patted her shoulders. Trina turned slightly in her chair.

"Well, who do we have here?" Art asked moving to Trina's side.

Trina fully turned toward Art. "This is Simon Nathaniel."

Trina beamed at the bundle of blue in her arms. She pulled the lightweight blanket down from the baby's face. The baby yawned and scrunched his face, frowning in the sunlight.

"Oh, Trina, he is beautiful! May we hold him?" Rosa asked.

Sam placed his hand on Trina's shoulder. She looked up at him and slipped her hand over his. Art held out his arms. Rosa gingerly held the baby's tiny body in her hands and transferred Simon over.

Art gently held his nephew, mesmerized by this small miracle. He pulled the corner of the blanket back to examine fingers and toes. A pair of blue crocheted booties hid the baby's toes from view. When Simon lifted his small fist to his mouth and eagerly suckled his fingers, Art smiled.

"There you are! Welcome! Welcome!" Mr. De León declared, shaking hands with Art and kissing his daughter's cheeks; first left, then right. Art and Rosa were directed to sit in the place of honor at the head of the table.

Mr. De León returned to the opposite end of the table and announced in English, "Thank you again, everyone, for coming to share this day with Art and Rosa. My wife and I are honored to have you here in our home. Franklin?"

Franklin patted Maggie's arm and then stood beside Mr. De León.

"Please, raise your glasses." Mr. De León lifted his glass of Sangria. "To Art and my Rosa, may your lives be long and prosperous."

"And may God, as your center, guide you through difficulties, bless you daily with happiness and bind your lives in love," Franklin added.

"And may your home be filled with health and joy and laughter and many bambinos!" Rosa's father chuckled.

In a collective salute to the bride and groom, glasses were raised as the toast was voiced. At its conclusion, everyone in unison shouted, "To Art and Rosa!"

"Salud!" the De Leóns cheered.

Rosa looked at Art, "What? Why are you smiling?"

Art kissed her cheek and whispered, "I'm one happy man."

JOHN AND EMILY
1938

J ohn pushed the bedroom door open. His seven-year-old son, Eddie, clad in white pajamas with printed patterns of red bats and blue baseballs, squatted in front of the bookshelf by his bed. The four shelves held books of all sizes, small painted wooden soldiers, a green striped yo-yo, a baseball glove, one mason jar filled with rocks, another with shells—his treausres. Selecting a book, the boy pulled it off the shelf.

"Find a book?" John asked as he sat on the edge of the small bed.

Eddie, holding tightly to his book, hopped up on the bed, bounced twice then plopped back against the pillow leaning against the bed's headboard. John pulled up one corner of the blue tufted chenille bedspread and rolled down the top sheet. The child stretched out his legs and lay still as the covers were pulled back up and tucked under his arms.

"What are we reading tonight?"

Eddie held up the book...a lime green hardback with corners somewhat worn; spine flexible but intact, pages dog-eared from numerous readings. Under his pillow he pulled out a brown and white knitted sock monkey. The stuffed toy bore a big red smile, black button eyes, and red heeled socks. Eddie placed the knitted sock monkey against his pillow.

"Okay, Rocko is ready. Wait!" Eddie's expression noted a sense of panic as he looked across his room. A golden cocker spaniel, stretched across her dogbed with her head resting on her front paws, simply watched the nightly routine. Eddie patted the bed covers, "Come on, girl. Come on, Sandy!"

Sandy scrambled across the wood floor and bounded on top of the bed. Eddie positioned her beside him. Sandy on one side, Rocko the other.

"Ready," Eddie said leaning back against his pillow.

John grinned as he opened the book to the first chapter. *"Peter Pan,"* by J.M. Barrie, of course. Let's see…okay here we go. 'All children, except one, grow up. They soon know that they will grow up, and the way Wendy knew was this. One day when she was two years old she was playing in the garden, and she plucked another flower and ran with it to…"

"No, stop! Gran read that yesterday," Eddie protested and sat up.

John chuckled. "Okay then tell me what happens. I've forgotten."

"Really?" Eddie pulled his knees up knocking Rocko over. "You don't remember the Darlings? Mr. and Mrs. Darling have three children; Wendy, John, like you, and Michael. The Darlings wanted to be like their neighbors and have a nanny. But the Darlings didn't have much money so they hired a big, big dog…a Newfoundland. See, here's her picture!" Eddie pointed at the illustration. Slapping his knees, Eddie laughed. "This one time at bathtime, Nana…that's the dog's name… carried Michael on her back to the tub! Funny, huh?"

After Eddie's giggles subsided, John asked, "Want to tell me what happened at Joey's today?"

"Did Gran tell you?"

"Yes, but I want you to tell me."

"What did she say?"

"What did you tell her?"

Eddie reached down, pulled Rocko up under his chin and crossed his arms over the smiling monkey. John waited.

"Well, Joey and I were play-boxing, ya know? He wanted to be Joe Lewis 'cause their names are the same. He wanted me to be Max Baer. But I didn't want to be the loser! I wanted to be Joe Lewis, the Brown Bomber! I wanted to be the world-heavy-weight champion! So I hit him.

Not hard! He's such a baby. Started crying. Didn't even bloody his nose. Betcha Joe Lewis never cried during a match."

John suppressed a smile as his skinny, long-legged seven-year-old adamantly proclaimed to be the world-heavy-weight champion of Sacramento's 35th Street.

"You didn't intend to hurt him, did you? Did you apologize?"

"Well sort of. His mom made me. I told her we were just playing. But she made me say sorry anyway. Then she walked me straight home to tell Gran."

"Think maybe tomorrow you should apologize and really mean it this time?"

"But tomorrow's Saturday. We're going to the park to fly kites!"

"Maybe Joey could come with us."

"Yeah," Eddie leaned back against his pillow. "Maybe he could. Daddy?"

"Hmm?"

"Will Mommy be home to kiss me goodnight?"

John brushed back a strand of Eddie's dark blonde hair that had fallen across his hazel eyes. "Mommy has patients in the hospital she must see. You know she always kisses you when she comes home."

"But I'm always asleep. Is she coming with us tomorrow?"

"I hope so. Tomorrow is a big day. Need to get some sleep."

Eddie nodded his head as he wrapped an arm around Rocko. Sandy burrowed in the crook of his legs. John kissed his son's cheek.

"Let's say our prayers," John took his son's hands. Eddie squinted his eyes.

Together they recited, "Father, we thank you for the night and for the pleasant morning light. For rest and food and loving care and all that makes the day so fair. Help us to do the things we should. To be to others kind and good. In all we do in work and play, to grow more loving every day." Without prompting Eddie continued, "God bless Mommy, Daddy, and Gran. Oh, and Sandy and Joey. Amen."

"Good night. Sleep tight, son," John whispered.

John remained seated on the side of the bed until Eddie finally closed his eyes without peeking to see if he were still there. As he stood,

Sandy wagged her stumpy tail but didn't budge from her warm spot. John patted the dog's head, crossed the braided floor rug and quietly closed the bedroom door.

Down the hall, John found Bessie, his sixty-eight-year-old grandmother, sitting in her favorite gold overstuffed chair with her feet propped upon the matching ottoman. The chair was pulled up near their Zenith floor-model radio—a handsome piece of oakwood furniture. Had a black-faced tear-drop dial in its center; three round control knobs jutted out at its base for tuning and volume. John sat in his brown leather chair and crossed one knee over the other.

An announcement sounded over the radio. "Good evening. National Broadcasting Company invites you to sit back, relax and enjoy these swinging sounds from Glenn Miller and His Orchestra."

The band—saxophones, clarinets, trombones, a bass violin, a guitar, trumpets, and drums—began to play while a male quartet harmonized. Bessie turned down the volume and smiled.

"Get our boy to bed?"

John nodded. "He sure loves Peter Pan, doesn't he?"

Bessie laughed. "Indeed, he does. Oh, here's the newspaper." She extended the printed pages to her grandson.

"Anything good?"

"Same ole stuff, really. Congress passed a Wages and Hours Act. Minimum hourly wage is now 25 cents and the maximum work week is 44 hours."

"Hmm, that's interesting. Guess I'll be checking personnel records."

"Oh, in the world news Hitler accompanied his German troops into Austria yesterday. Austria's Chancellor was forced to resign the day before and asked the Austrian forces not to resist. Enthusiastic crowds welcomed Hitler into Vienna. Can you imagine? He's up to no good, I'd say."

"Yes, quite the bully." John shook open the paper. "What's this about the foundation the President began?"

"Oh, the non-profit program to help children with polio? Such a wonderful thing. All because President Roosevelt has polio. I forget the name...national something or other."

John grinned. "How can I rely on you to summarize the news for me if you can't remember it word for word?"

Bessie laughed as John read, "Says here it's called the National Foundation for Infantile Paralysis."

"That's it! Started in January. Donations are being collected and are doing quite well. Glenn Miller is over. Time to call it a day. Going kiting tomorrow?"

"Yes, Eddie may invite Joey. Sorry to have interrupted your radio program." John folded the newspaper and placed it over his knee.

"That would be nice." Bessie stood and patted her grandson's shoulder. "I always enjoy time spent with you, John. See you in the morning."

"Nite, Gran."

John stood and placed the folded newspaper in his chair. He turned off the radio and checked the time on his wristwatch. It was after ten. Another late night for Emily. But then, they all were late nights lately. Eddie was right. She always seemed to be gone. Working at the hospital or attending a medical convention or a conference. He turned off the floorlamp and retired for the evening.

"One or two pancakes?" Bessie asked Eddie early Saturday morning.

Eddie still clad in pajamas knelt in his chair and leaned against the table. "Two, please. Morning, Daddy!" Eddie beamed when John entered the room.

Bessie handed John a cup of coffee. "Thanks, Gran."

"Ready to go kiting?" Eddie asked eagerly.

"Yes, it's a beautiful day for kiting." John ruffled his son's hair and sat down.

Bessie placed Eddie's order in front of him. "John? Two as well?"

"Yes, please. Thank you."

Eddie reached across the table for the brown bottle of Log Cabin syrup. Removing the lid, he tipped the bottle and poured a waterfall of syrup over his pancakes. A moat of maple stickiness surrounded the cakes. John grinned at him.

Bessie returned to the stove and ladled batter from a bowl onto the hot griddle. She glanced up as Emily entered the kitchen.

"Morning, Emily," Bessie greeted. "Pancakes this morning?"

Emily kissed the top of Eddie's head. "Not this morning, Gran. Thank you, but I'm running late as it is. Have so much to do for our upcoming fundraising gala next weekend for the new hospital wing."

"You're not coming with us to the park?" Eddie slumped into his chair.

"I'll try to meet you for lunch. Mommy has a very important meeting this morning. John, if I'm not at the park by noon, I won't be coming." Emily hurried out the door without waiting for responses from her family.

Three weeks later John came home late from work. He entered the kitchen through the back door. Bessie looked up and smiled. Rinsing a plate, she placed it face down on top of three plates that were drying on a red dish towel on the counter.

"Sorry to be so late, Gran. Inventory took longer than usual." John kissed his grandmother's cheek. "I grabbed a bite on the way home."

"Daddy!" Eddie, clad in blue pajamas, squealed as he ran toward John. "Mommy's home! She let me play with my boats in the bathtub!"

John scooped up his son. "Sounds like fun, buddy."

Emily appeared with a bath towel strewn over her shoulder. "I want to talk to all of you before Eddie's bedtime."

Eddie asked excitedly, "What time is it?"

"Seven-thirty...not quite your bedtime," John answered.

"Seven-thirty!" Eddie exclaimed. "It's time for *The Lone Ranger*!"

Emily smiled at John. "Okay, we'll listen to your show first."

Eddie scooted the ottoman closer to the radio and turned the dial to "on." The introduction to the program swelled loudly over the radio speakers. The theme music played as hoofbeats sounded in the background. A male's melodramatic voice announced, "A fiery horse with the speed of light, a cloud of dust and a hearty hi-yo Silver! The Lone Ranger!...With his faithful Indian companion, Tonto, the daring and resourceful masked rider of the plains led the fight for law and order in the early western United States. Return with me now to those thrilling days of yesteryear..."

With his legs straddling the ottoman, Eddie bounced and flailed his arms about as if he were riding a horse. He cried loudly, "Hi-yo Silver! Away!"

Emily whispered, "John, may I speak with you in the bedroom?"

John followed Emily into their bedroom and sat on the bed. He scooted to one side, making room for her.

"John, Doctor Collier has accepted a position at Baylor University teaching introduction to medicine to pre-med students. He's also obtained a lease on a space close to the campus for a clinic and has offered me a position at the clinic making twice what I do now. While I'm studying for the Texas Board, Doctor Collier wants me to organize the clinic and be ready to open by late September."

"That's wonderful, babe! What an opportunity! I'm so very proud of you!"

"Dr. Collier had often talked about the possibility of teaching and continuing his practice but I had no idea that included me. I'm overwhelmed! I've referred my patients to Dr. Smitty. John, you'll have to resign and find another job. We'll have to sell the house and move to Waco. There's so much to do!"

John studied Emily's face. His wife looked frantic, like a young girl on the first day of school not knowing where to find her classroom. He took her hand.

"We'll work out all the details together. We can do this! I can always find another job. I'm not worried about that. Just think how wonderful this is, Em! You'll be working in a clinic! I'm excited for all of us! Now let's go share your good news with Eddie and Gran! We're going home!"

WACO AND NEW BEGINNINGS
1938

Balancing a medium-sized cardboard box on her hip, Emily unlocked the door and pushed against it with the rounded toe of her brown shoe. Crossing the worn linoleum flooring in the small room, she placed the box on the walnut desk. Finally the marketing flyers had arrived. Placing her hands on her hips, she turned to survey the room and smiled. Collier Clinic had taken up residence in what was once someone's home and the house suited the clinic's purpose perfectly.

Opening day had been delayed due to the beginning of the fall semester at the university. The postponement turned out to be beneficial as there was so much yet to do—placing newspaper ads in the *Waco News Tribune*, displaying marketing flyers in hair salon, barber shop and store windows, scheduling staff meetings at the hospital as well as with the department heads at Baylor University and its women's counterpart, Mary Hardin-Baylor College in Belton.

Hearing the front door open, Emily turned. "William, how nice to see you!"

"My class is over and I have an hour or so before I report to work. Want to join me at the café for an early dinner?"

Emily laughed, "But don't you work there?"

"Yeah, but Elite Café is the best place in town to eat plus we're the only diner in town with air conditioning!" William's eyes twinkled. "Besides it's almost five!"

"Is it? Oh my, I didn't realize it was so late. Well, yes then. Let's go eat!"

William opened the passenger door to his two-door willow green 1936 Chevrolet pickup—rounded fenders and large radiator grille, tan upholstered interior, steel spoked wheels; and a hood ornament of wings spanned backwards horizontally. Settled in the passenger seat, Emily placed her purse in her lap. William slid behind the steering wheel and pulled away from the curb. Emily laughed and jiggled the blue lacy garter that dangled over the rearview mirror.

"And what is this, Mr. William Bailey?"

"Oh, it's Rosa's garter. I was the lucky guy who caught it at her wedding. Oh, sorry. Didn't mean to bring up sour grapes."

Emily laughed and patted her brother-in-law's arm. "Art and I are ancient history. I'm happy for them. Truly."

"That's good. We're here." William parked his car in the designated employee's lot and exited. Rounding the vehicle, he opened Emily's door. She got out and the two entered the crowded café.

"Look there's a booth." William took Emily's elbow and led her through the throng of Baylor students who sat on barstools around the green u-shaped counter.

Emily slid across the gold and green striped vinyl seat and rested her hands on the slick tabletop. William took a seat across from her. A bubbly waitress wearing a gold checked dress with short puffed sleeves and a white collar approached and handed William two menus.

"Hello, William," she said, pulling a pad and pencil from her green apron.

"Hey, Darlene. Um, this is my brother's wife Emily."

"Hello," Emily looked up at the girl whose blonde frizzy hair escaped from underneath a white frilly headband.

"What may I get for you?" the girl asked sweetly.

"What would you like, Emily?"

"You know what's good. Order for me."

"Okay. Darlene, we'll both have the chopped beef patty with green beans, mashed potatoes and gravy."

Darlene smiled as she took the menus from William. "And what will you be drinking with your meals?"

"Oh, William," Emily blurted. "I've heard about the Dr Pepper floats here, but have not had one. Could we?"

William looked up as Darlene twisted a loose strand of hair over her ear. "Of course! Two Dr Pepper floats and two waters, please."

"I'll bring those right out." Darlene smiled. Emily wasn't certain but thought the girl actually winked at William.

When their waitress walked away, Emily whispered, "So tell me about Darlene. She's very cute. Blonde hair; blue eyes. She definitely has eyes for you."

"What? Darlene? No way. We just work together."

"William, you're blushing."

"Could we talk about something else? How's Eddie liking school?"

"You're clearly changing the subject!" Emily teased. "Eddie is doing wonderfully. It's only been two weeks and he's making friends. I was able to go with him on the first day to meet his teacher. John usually does that. Eddie loves being with his cousins. I think Gran was homesick and is really glad to be home."

"Yeah, I missed her, too. What's the latest from Sacramento?"

Before Emily could respond, Darlene set down two frosted mugs of Dr Pepper poured over three scoops of vanilla ice cream. Foam fizzled over the top and slithered down the sides of the ice-cold glass mugs. She pulled two paper straws from her apron pocket and placed them on the table.

"Thanks, Darlene." William slid Emily's mug and straw toward her.

When Darlene turned from the booth, Emily was certain their waitress had winked at her handsome but very timid twenty-year-old brother-in-law.

* * * * * * * * * * * * * *

Standing on the corner, Emily pulled her white gloves over her chilled fingers and wrapped her blue linen suit jacket tightly about her. The early morning already carried traces of autumn's nippy air. A black 1936 custom-built Cadillac stopped near the curb and its passenger door swung open.

"Get in."

Emily stooped slightly to see Doctor Collier sitting behind the wheel. She quickly stepped off the curb and got into the car.

"We're unable to meet with Doctor Harrison, the university's president. Instead we are meeting with the Dean of Women. I don't recall her name."

"Doctor Olivia Crandall. I made the appointment, remember?"

"Hmm? Oh, yes, of course."

Emily looked forward to meeting Doctor Crandall. Over their previous telephone conversations, Doctor Crandall's voice professed friendliness and openness. Someone with whom Emily would like to develop a friendship.

Emily's anticipation grew as the car drove underneath the *Mary Hardin Baylor 1845* archway. Doctor Collier followed the curved driveway and passed several red brick three-story buildings each styled with Greek facades and white pillars. Since it was a Monday morning, the campus grounds were busy. Students were hastily walking to class or sitting on benches under well-canopied trees.

Doctor Collier pulled the car to a stop in front of the administration building. Raised brick flower beds holding gold marigolds and purple chrysanthemums lined the walkway. Emily smiled recalling the school's colors being purple and gold.

After asking directions from the receptionist, Emily and Doctor Collier proceded down a hallway and stopped at the third door on the left. Stenciled boldly in bright purple letters, "Dean of Women" centered the oak door's top half of glazed glass. A receptionist sitting behind a walnut desk greeted them as they entered.

"Good morning. Doctor Crandall will be with you momentarily. Please have a seat. May I get you coffee or water?"

Doctor Collier scowled clearly not appreciating having to wait after changing his first set appointment time. He took a seat next to Emily. She slipped off her gloves and placed them in her black handbag.

The intercom on the desk buzzed. The young woman answered the telephone. "Doctor Crandall will see you now. Just through that door."

Doctor Collier sighed and opened the door. As Emily stepped across the threshhold, a thin woman who stood at least six-feet tall rose from behind her desk.

"Emily!" The woman rounded the desk and extended her hand.

"Olivia, it's so wonderful to finally meet you."

"How was your drive? Oh, please have a seat here on the sofa. Those straight-back chairs in front of my desk are reserved for students."

"The drive was fine. A beautiful day."

"Indeed. It's so nice to put a face with a name."

"Yes, I agree. Oh, I'm sorry. Pardon me. Olivia, this is Doctor Craig Collier. Sir, this is Doctor Olivia Crandall."

"Yes, it's a pleasure to meet you." Doctor Crandall extended her hand. Doctor Collier shook it hastily. "Please be seated, Doctor Collier. Emily, did Gwendolyn offer refreshments?"

"She did. Thank you," Emily answered. "Gwendolyn is charming."

Doctor Collier cleared his throat. "Ladies, this is a business meeting. Is it not? You can exchange pleasantries another time. As you may know, Doctor Crandall, I am opening a small practice in Waco. I also teach at Baylor. My time is vitally important as I'm sure yours may be as well."

Olivia Crandall squared her shoulders and eyed this insolent man as he continued, "We have come today to present ideas about providing an infirmary here at Mary Hardin-Baylor for your students. I understand you don't have a health clinic to speak of as yet. Health is as important as education in the life of students. This is what we propose..."

"Excuse my interruption, Doctor Collier. But Emily...Doctor Moore...and I have spoken at length over the past several days. We are ready to initiate our plan. There's a vacant room in our Presser Hall that will be suitable for a clinic. Emily will come two days each week... Tuesday and Thursday afternoons...to see patients. All minor needs I pray and pro bono per your gracious generosity. Gwendolyn will manage the appointments so as not to disrupt Emily's duties in Waco. I think that covers it. Did you have anything to add?"

Doctor Collier glanced between the Dean of Women and his colleague suddenly feeling outnumbered and outfinessed.

"Granted your plan sounds well thought out, but I will wait until Doctor Harrison has given his permission to proceed. Tweaks may be in order."

Doctor Crandall stood, stretching to her full intimidating height. "Doctor Collier, I assure you Doctor Harrison will be advised. I certainly do not need nor require his permission to do what's best for my students. Since the morning is slipping away and I do have other appointments, I must insist this meeting be considered concluded if you have nothing further…"

Doctor Collier rose slowly to his feet. Emily smiled at Olivia.

"Emily, I'll see you next Tuesday! Welcome aboard."

That evening Emily entered her hotel room at the Alamo Plaza…. another long day. She placed her purse on the bedside table and kicked off her shoes. Leaning her head against the bed's headboard, she recalled how perfectly the week had gone. The telephone on the sidetable suddenly rang, interrupting her thoughts.

Emily jerked the receiver off the hook. "Hello?"

"Hello there, beautiful!"

"John! I was hoping you'd call early."

"I've got good news."

"I do, too. You go first." With her legs criss-crossed, Emily eagerly listened.

"Well, I have good news and bad news…bad news is the house has not sold; good news is I've hired a real estate company to manage the sale without my having to be here. I can join you soon!"

"Oh, John! I've missed you so much. You're actually coming here?"

"Yeah, don't get too excited. Still have to arrange a place for the movers to deliver our belongings. Is this the weekend William takes you to Oak Hill?"

"No, next weekend. Such a great kid giving up his time to take me to see Eddie. Eddie will be excited to know you're coming soon!"

"Em, don't tell him. I want to surprise him. Now, what was your news?"

Emily spent the next few minutes telling John about the week—her appointment with Olivia Crandall to start a clinic in Belton and her excitement to begin; how much she enjoyed William's company and finally how much she missed her husband. She spoke at a blabbering-non-stop pace not wanting to omit a thing.

She reluctantly ended her conversation. "Is time up? I love you, John,"

"I love you, too, Em, and yeah, it is."

"See you then."

"See ya then."

The following Thursday Emily hurried across the clinic's linoleum floor. As she turned the doorknob, the telephone on the desk began to ring. Deciding whether it could be important enough to answer, Emily glanced back over her shoulder. If she were to make the connection from the city bus to the Greyhound Station, she should leave within the next ten minutes to arrive in Belton on time. The phone continued to ring, mocking her dilemma. Emily sighed and hurried back across the floor. She picked up the receiver from its black base.

"Good morning, Collier Clinic."

"Emily? Oh, good! You're still there!"

"Yes, I was just headed out to catch the bus. May I help you with something?"

"Did you finish grading my second period vocab papers?"

"Yes, I put them in your satchel."

"Well, that's just it. I forgot my satchel this morning. Was in a hurry to meet Professor Billings and Professor Smith for breakfast. Completely slipped my mind. Be a dear and bring it to me. It's on my desk in my office."

"But I'll miss my connection to Belton."

"Won't take but a minute. The city bus comes right by the campus. Easy on; easy off." When Emily was hesitant to answer, Doctor Collier added, "I really need those papers this morning."

"Okay. I'll be there as soon as I can."

The brown leather satchel was easily located in the center of the Doctor Collier's desk. Emily opened it to make sure the folder of graded papers was where she'd placed it. Seems of late she had also been tasked with grading papers. Whenever he had an activity to attend he deemed more important, she also recorded the grades in the grade book. He had taken up golfing with his colleagues and Mrs. Collier had become more demanding of his time. Emily certainly wouldn't begrudge any time Ruth spent with her husband.

Exiting the city bus, Emily hurried across the well-manicured quadrangle toward Carroll Science Building. Taking the twelve steps up to the main door of the gray stone building, she stopped and took a breath. A courteous young man held the door open for her as she breezed by. Doctor Collier's office was on the third floor. Three more flights to climb. Out of breath but finally standing in front of his office door, she knocked softly.

"Enter." Emily heard Doctor Collier say.

She opened the door to a small reception area. Doctor Collier greeted her warmly and offered a cup of coffee. "No, thank you. I really should be going. Your papers are in a yellow folder in the side pocket there."

"I insist. Come join me in my office." He took his satchel from her.

"But, I need to hurry or I'll miss the Greyhound bus."

"Emily, come be seated." Doctor Collier's voice was stern and demanding.

Emily followed her employer into his office and was seated on a dark green upholstered chair positioned in front of a massive oak desk...one Mrs. Collier had purchased, no doubt. He took a seat in a black leather chair behind the desk.

After taking a sip of coffee he asked, "Sure I can't get you a cup of coffee?"

"I'm sure. Thank you. Why did you want to see me?"

"Well, since you've always preferred coming straight to the point, here it is. I have spoken to Doctor Harrison at Belton and have withdrawn my monies to sponsor the clinic there. And I..."

Emily stood to her feet. "What? I've only been there one week! What happened? Did you do this because Doctor Crandall and I arranged it without you?"

Doctor Collier slightly frowned and continued, "Sit down, Emily. No, I seriously trust you don't find me that shallow. I have decided to add a couple more classes this semester. I didn't realize how much I love teaching. I want to devote more time and energy instructing upcoming medical students."

"You are an excellent instructor. I have learned so much from you. And the clinic? Are you turning that over to me?"

"No," he exhaled. "I have sublet the building to a gentleman who wants to rennovate it and sell it. It's prime real estate so close to campus. The clinic was just my hobby you might say."

"A hobby?" Emily screeched. "But you asked me to move my family from California and be your number two at the clinic!"

Doctor Collier rose from his chair, walked around his desk and sat on its edge. He slid closer to Emily and placed his hand on her shoulder. She was glaring up at him as he said, "But you have helped me tremendously, Emily. How could I have foreseen the necessity for switching gears? I have a proposal for you. Be my teaching assistant. You have such outstanding organizational skills and your clinical experience is truly valuable. I'll continue to pay your current salary. I'll even place a downpayment on a house for your family. What do you say? You may still be my number two but only here at the university instead."

Emily could hardly believe what he was saying! "I am a doctor first and foremost," she said, pushing his hand away. "I am in the process of moving my family here. John has resigned his position! We have sacrificed so much! How can you just haphazardly change your mind midstream?"

"Well, my dear, it is my venture after all; my investments. What have you contributed?" Doctor Collier's tone changed vehemently. Arrogantly he stared at her, daring her to answer.

Emily sat tongue-tied for a moment searching for the right words. "I have been the mechanical gear behind this entire project from the very beginning. You may have the capital, but I've organzied everything for the clinic here and in Belton. I graded your papers and made sure your appointments were kept. I..."

"Emily, Emily, you've been most helpful. There's no denying that. Your administration skills plus your pretty face will be an asset wherever you go."

"I am not a secretary! I am a doctor! That you well know!"

"Yes, yes, a fairly young doctor with very little experience. There are only a few female doctors on staff at Baylor Medical. But I can introduce you to a couple of physicians I've met on the golf course and see what they can do for you."

"That won't be necessary."

"I assume from your surly attitude you no longer wish to be my colleague?"

Emily grabbed her medical bag and stood. "Your assumption is correct, sir!"

Doctor Collier rose from the side of the desk. Cocking his head, he said, "I must admit my disappointment in you, Emily. Granted you carried much of my load in Sacramento as well and for that I'm thankful. We were a good team. Ruth even said so. There's nothing I can do or say to persuade you to stay?"

Fighting back tears, Emily replied, "No, if I'm not working alongside you as a doctor and only as a doctor, then my answer remains the same."

Doctor Collier took her hands and squeezed them. "I will write a glowing letter of recommendation for you. Come by next week and pick it up."

Emily pulled her hands from his grasp and turned toward the door. As she opened it, she heard Doctor Collier say, "I'll call Alamo Plaza then and prepay your room through Sunday. Good luck, Emily, and the best to your family."

Sunday afternoon William leaned against the side of his truck and waited outside Emily's motel room. He looked around the courtyard. Two rows of eight flat-topped cabins exact replicas of the other stood facing a small spanse of grass. Constructed of white stone each had a window on either side of the front door with the number of the cabin distinctly posted in black numbering on the door frame. Supposedly, the Alamo Plaza's entrance was a replica of the Alamo in San Antonio.

With a box secured under her arm, Emily stepped off the porch and handed the box to William. "I almost forgot my hatbox. That's everything."

Finally loaded, William drove his truck under the Alamo Plaza's arches.

"Sorry about Doctor Collier and all that happened. What did John say?"

"I've not been able to reach him. Can we talk about something else?"

William gripped the steering wheel and darted his eyes toward his traveling companion. She had closed her eyes and settled in for the two-hour drive.

"Ya know, Em, when God closes one door, He opens another one."

Emily looked at him and grimaced. "Well, why didn't He reveal His plans before we altered our whole lives and moved from our home in California?"

"Sometimes we have to continue through whatever we find ourselves in to better understand God's intentions. Later we'll see how God was leading us."

"William, one day you will be a wonderful pastor. Right now, I don't need counseling. Okay?"

William nodded. "Care to listen to the radio?"

Emily leaned up and turned on the radio. Ella Fitzgerald's "A-Tisket, A-Tasket," a jazzy number accompanied by the Chick Webb Orchestra, was playing. William turned up the volume and began humming along as he drummed the steering wheel with his left hand. Emily tried not to smile, but couldn't help it.

An hour later, the willow green coupe pulled into the Bailey's driveway and stopped. Emily got out and straightened her dress—a dark blue silk cotton covered in a print of tiny white roses.

"You look nice, Em." William removed two suitcases from the back.

They proceeded up the porch steps. Three bright orange pumpkins with large toothy grins aligned the steps on either side. A black flowerpot of red geraniums sat near the porch swing. Still in bloom, the dark coral honeysuckle with bright yellow sticky tips snaked over the trellis. Emily breathed in their sweet fragrance. As usual the limestone house looked stately and beautiful. So many cherished childhood memories dwelt here. As Emily neared, the door swung open.

"Mommy!" Eddie cried as he rushed toward her.

Emily dropped her hatbox, grabbed Eddie and lifted him in the air. "Look how much you've grown in two weeks!"

"William! Emily! Come in! Come in!" Holding the door open, Maggie cheerfully greeted them.

Maggie patted William's arm as he slid past her. "William, take those up to John's old room."

Emily balanced Eddie on her hip and leaned forward to kiss Maggie's cheek. "Thank you, Maggie. You were so encouraging when I phoned."

"Of course. It will all work out. Tia has made her infamous cinnamon-sugar cookies. Eddie, why don't you bring in your mother's hatbox?"

Eddie subtly pushed against Emily's shoulder in an effort to get down. He picked up the hatbox and followed his mother and grandmother into the foyer.

"Tia showed me how to roll out cookie dough!" Eddie proudly announced.

"She did? Well, then, I must sample those cookies! Where are the twins?"

"With Grandpa," Eddie answered.

"They'll be home soon. They help Franklin at the store on Saturdays," Maggie explained. "Franklin pays them to sweep the floors and dust the display cases. Not much money but to eleven-year-olds, it's a fortune!"

William trotted back down the stairs. Emily looked up as a cocker spaniel bounded down the stairs behind him. With her ears flying, the dog charged past him and ran at full speed toward Emily. Emily dropped to her knees.

"Sandy!" she squealed. The dog's entire body wagged with delight. Emily lifted her chin as the dog bestowed her neck with slurpy kisses. Emily rubbed Sandy's silky ears. "If you're here, then…"

"Look, Mommy, it's Daddy!" Eddie squealed, pointing toward the stairs.

Emily pushed Sandy gently to one side and stood. Smiling broadly, John slowly descended the stairs. Emily rushed up to meet him. At the landing, she stumbled on the top step and crumpled there at his feet. She didn't move only looked up at him. John knelt beside her and pulled her into his arms. She grabbed his neck.

"Hey, beautiful! Are you okay?"

"No," she whispered, clutching him tightly. Her tears escalated to sobs.

"Shhh, baby. It's okay. I'm here. I'm here now."

The couple, held in a tight embrace, remained on the top step of the landing. William smiled and looked down at Eddie. "Hey, there, Eddie. Why don't we go find those cookies you made."

Maggie turned to follow the boys to the kitchen and glanced back over her shoulder. John and Emily were no longer on the stairs.

****

The house, as was customary on Sunday mornings, was as still and silent as an undisturbed field of freshly fallen snow. The tick-tocking of the stately grandfather clock in the parlor or sometimes a random creaking in the walls or hardwood flooring briefly disrupted the serenity. The mid-morning sun penetrated its bright rays through the oval-shaped stained glass window on the east wall. Blurred images of rainbow colors danced upon the stairway. The dining room table, previously set, held eleven place settings of blue-and-white patterned English china. Three places awaited the children at the kitchen table. At one o'clock, the grandfather clock chimed and as if on cue, the front door opened. The Bailey family entered.

Eddie and the twins, Loraine and Lucy, boisterously led the way. Sandy and Arlo, the golden cocker spaniel and the black lab now fast friends, charged out from the study where they'd been napping to greet the family.

"Fine sermon this morning." Franklin removed his suit jacket.

William answered, "Pastor Edwards always shares inspiring messages."

"You'll be preaching behind your own pulpit one day," Maggie boasted.

"One day," William smiled.

"Won't take long to get lunch on the table. Girls, take Eddie to wash his hands," Maggie instructed. "Franklin, would you let Sandy and Arlo out for awhile? Tip might enjoy stretching his legs, too."

William raced his younger brothers up the stairs. Franklin opened the front door. Tip pushed through the front door first. His tail wagged eagerly as his canine companions followed. The dogs raced into the yard to explore and chase squirrels.

"Are you sure he's not too heavy? He's almost four," Trina asked Emily as the two women entered the house.

"What? This itsy-bitsy boy?" Emily carried Simon on her hip. The toddler giggled as his aunt tickled his tummy.

Trina smiled and turned toward John. "Thank you for carrying the baby."

"It's been so long since Eddie was this size. David has Sam's dark hair and eyes, doesn't he?" John studied the four-month old he carried in his hands.

"Nice looking kid, huh?" Sam boasted as Trina took the baby.

The Baileys settled down to eat—the adults plus a highchair for Simon in the dining room; the other three children in the kitchen. After Franklin offered the blessing, lunch began. Conversation and laughter bounced from one side of the table to the other. Midway through lunch, an uproar of giggling and table banging erupted from the kitchen.

"I'll go check on that." John excused himself from the table. A few moments later, he returned and explained. "It seems neither Lucy nor Loraine had heard about Wrong Way Corrigan! Eddie was entertaining them."

Gran suppressed a giggle.

"Who? What about him?" Clayton asked.

"You've not heard of him either? Well this is a true story. In July of this year, Douglas Corrigan filed a solo flight plan to travel from Long

Beach, California, to New York City. He had been denied permission for a transatlantic flight to Ireland. When he reached New York City, instead of flying back to Long Beach, he flew to Ireland. When questioned upon his return, he claimed a navigational error. Fog and heavy cloud cover obscured landmarks and caused him to misread his compass."

"That's quite an error! All the way across the Atlantic!" Paddy exclaimed.

"But the funny thing is Corrigan was an experienced pilot. Would have never made such a mistake," Gran, a current news enthusiast, added.

"Who wouldn't want to go to Ireland?" William interjected.

"So it was on purpose then?" Trina asked.

"He's yet to admit it. Being called Wrong Way Corrigan must not bother him," John said. "Eddie finds the story quite hilarious. I think Gran may, too."

Gran wiped her mouth on her napkin and smiled at her eldest grandson.

"Dessert?" Maggie asked as the doorbell rang. "Expecting anyone?"

"No, I'll go see who it is. Don't eat all the pie," Franklin said and pointed at his sons. "Cut very small slices for them, Maggie!"

"Emily, someone is here to see you." Franklin returned a few minutes later. "She's waiting in the study."

Emily looked confused. "What? For me?"

Emily almost tripped over the rug when she saw Doctor Olivia Crandall.

"I trust I'm not interrupting your family's afternoon."

"Olivia! What a wonderful surprise! How did you find me?"

"This is the address you left with personnel. I had to see you in person."

Still confused, Emily apologized, "I'm so sorry, Olivia, about the clinic."

"What I have to propose is a thousand times better," Olivia said. "Doctor Harrison, the Mary Hardin-Baylor school board and I would like to extend to you the position of campus physician. We'd also like to offer a campus cottage for you and your family. Belton is a thriving community. John should be able to find employment. What do you say?"

"I...I..." Emily stuttured.

"Ah, the financial details...forgive me. We would provide clinic space on campus to organize and practice as you please. Whatever Doctor Collins paid you, we'll match. Please, say you'll agree."

Instead of an agree-to-the-deal handshake, Emily hugged Olivia tightly.

"Come meet my family and join us for dessert. I want to tell them the news!"

WILLIAM
1940

I n the bottom of the eighth inning, Baylor led 4 to 0. Eastern New Mexico, a four-year college from Portales, took the field. Sitting on the home bench across from first base, William draped his jacket over his right shoulder to keep his arm warm. He had pitched the entire game.

Baylor's leadoff batter, shortstop Niles Bertrum, took his stance by homeplate. The pitcher wound up slowly then delivered a fast curve ball. Niles swung but missed. Strike one. Four pitches later the count stood at three balls and two strikes. Niles waved the bat in small circles over his shoulder enticing the pitcher to throw the ball. Eastern's pitcher nodded at the catcher. The ball was thrown fast and outside. Niles swung. A whack could be heard as the bat connected with the ball. The ball whizzed over the second baseman's head, bounced off the ground then rolled toward centerfield. Niles hurled the bat behind him and raced down the white chalk line toward first base. Eastern's centerfielder advanced toward the ball. The first baseman stretched his body and extended his arm to field the ball when it was thrown his way. Eastern's centerfielder scooped up the ball and hurled it to his shortstop. Niles pumped his arms and lifted his knees as he neared the base. Eastern's shortstop aimed the ball like a projectile to the first baseman. The ball landed with a whump in the first baseman's glove milliseconds after Niles ran through the base. The first base umpire declared the runner safe. The fans supporting the Baylor Bears erupted in whoops and rahs and thunderous applause.

Eighth inning ended. Eastern trotted off the field and returned to their bench. Last chance to bat. Could they make seven runs? Doubtful. The Baylor team felt antsy with a win in sight. William faced three batters. Three up; three down. Baylor won 6-0. A non conference game, but a win just the same.

An hour later, William and a couple of his teammates, Bob Clemson and Niles Bertrum, each proudly donning their Baylor baseball sweaters walked into the Elite to meet up with the family. An electrifying burst of shouts and cheers sounded from staff members, Baylor students and Bear supporters. Franklin stood at the back of the dining room waving his hands in the air. William urged his friends to follow.

Franklin grabbed his son in a hardy bear hug. "Great game, son! I'm so proud of you. Great game to you as well." He nodded at Bob and Niles.

"Papa, this is Bob Clemson and Niles Bertrum."

"Yes! Yes! Great batting and fielding today, boys," Franklin said, shaking their hands. "Please come join us. I've reserved this entire back dining room. Mr. Wayne said only the best for his best busboy and dish washer!"

"Really? Mr. Wayne said that?"

Franklin smiled broadly. "Come on. The family is waiting."

Franklin opened the door to the small dining room Elite reserved for special occasions. Another round of applause and cheers greeted the three Baylor players. William looked around the room and was overwhelmed his entire family had come to see the game.

William, with his friends in tow, made the rounds to each table introducing his family to his friends and receiving celebratory hugs or handshakes. As he neared Emily's and John's table, he was surprised by their guests.

"Doctor Crandall! You said you'd come but I had no idea you meant it!"

Olivia Crandall stood and hugged William. "You all played a great game today. I hope you don't mind, William, but I brought my assistant. She brought a friend and her younger sister."

William glanced at the three girls sitting at the table...a blonde, a brunette, and a red head. He felt one of his friends slightly nudge him in the back with an elbow. Bertrum, more than likely...a lady's man or so he proclaimed.

Olivia began the introductions, "This is Gwendolyn Hawkins, a senior at Belton and my office assistant for the past three years. Lynnette Baker and Caroline Hawkins. This is William Bailey and I'm sorry I didn't catch your names."

"Niles Bertrum, shortstop extraordinaire. Pleasure to meet you, ladies," Niles blurted, sporting his charming smile. Gwendolyn and Caroline smiled. Lynnette nodded. Niles continued, "And this is Bob Clemson. Has such an ugly mug, we have to cover it with a catcher's mask."

Bob grimaced, cleared his throat and simply said, "Hello."

Maggie slipped her arm within William's. "Why don't you and your friends join us at our table? Gran is anxious to see you. Doctor Crandall, you did surprise him after all, didn't you?"

Olivia Crandall nodded and took her seat.

"Thank you all for coming," William said to the young ladies sitting with Doctor Crandall. "Thanks again, Doctor Crandall. Your being here means a lot."

****

Two weeks later William worked the two to six afternoon shift, busing tables. He pushed a two-shelved cart across the dining room floor toward a table that required cleaning. Thursday afternoons were not busy and he was easily bored. Sometimes he felt like a vulture hovering over a table until the patrons finished eating. Grateful for the spills and untouched food left behind for it gave him something to do. Glancing at his watch, he was relieved to see his shift was almost over. He wheeled the cart to the kitchen and helped Rick Garner unload it. They worked methodically separating the plates from the glasses and the silverware.

"Hey, William! Your little friends are back," Darlene teased as she entered the kitchen to pick up an order. "Quite habit forming. Second week in a row. Not all habits are good for you, ya know."

William grinned. Balancing a tray of food and beverages in one hand, she pushed backwards through the swinging doors into the dining room. Rick slapped William on the back.

"Better get out there, my friend."

William pushed the empty cart through the swinging doors and easily spotted the girls…Gwendolyn, Lynnette, and Caroline…sitting in a corner horseshoe-shaped booth under a bank of windows. He stopped the cart at their booth.

"What brings you ladies to the Elite?" he asked.

"We're here for a soda…had to order something. We're actually meeting Niles and Bob at Nell's at six. Would you like to come?" Gwendolyn asked.

"I work 'til six. But yeah, I can come over after."

Lynnette smiled. "See ya there, preacher boy."

William's face reddened. He noticed Caroline frown and gently elbow Lynnette's arm. Lynnette whispered something to Caroline which caused her noticeable distress. While chewing on the end of her paper straw, Lynnette looked up at William and smiled.

At six-twenty, William entered Nell's brightly lit dining area and searched for his friends. He heard Niles before he saw him. The group of five were sitting at a table near the back. As William approached, Bob stood and moved over one chair nearer Gwendolyn, leaving space by Lynnette. William sat down.

Lynnette leaned closer and softly said, "Glad you made it, preacher boy."

Bob stood and announced to the table. "Hey! There's a foosball table in the little annex room in the back. You've been challenged."

He pulled Gwendolyn's chair out for her. The two proceeded to the back. Niles and Caroline accepted the challenge and followed.

"So," Lynnette said after a few seconds of silence. "It's just us."

"I guess so. Tell me about yourself, Lynnette."

"My friends call me Netty. I hope you will, too."

"Okay, Netty. Do you go to Belton with Gwendolyn?"

Netty smiled coyly, "No, I'm a student here at Baylor. Will graduate next spring. Studying journalism. That's also Gwen's choice of study."

"And Caroline?"

"She's Gwen's kid sister. You thought she was a college girl?" Netty laughed. "She's only a high school senior."

"Oh, I didn't know. Nice kid. So, journalism? You have classes with Professor White?"

"Yeah, she's the best." Netty raised one eyebrow and smiled. "So, preacher boy, do you play foosball as well as you pitch?"

"Not as well, no. But I do play."

And so it began…William's and Netty's courtship. Slowly at first. Meeting on weekends when games were in town or after baseball practices or after publication meetings or whenever their busy schedules would allow. And then steadily and deliberately…studying at the library or walking alongside Waco Creek; sharing popcorn at the Majestic Theatre and going to church on Sundays. When William kissed Netty for the first time, a small explosion of flutterings rose from his gut and burned all the way down his spine. She was definitely the girl for him.

Mid-June, the 1940 Southwest Conference baseball season ended. The University of Texas won the division; twenty wins and four losses overall; A.M.C., the Agriculture and Mechanical College in College Station, came in second with eleven wins and ten losses. Baylor placed third with eleven wins and nine losses.

After final exams, students packed up their belongings and eagerly headed home for the summer. William was not one of those students. As a pre-seminary student, he was required to participate in student lead revival services held in Baptist churches in town or in cities nearby. The schedule lasted until mid-August.

William had lined up the morning's agenda in great detail. One… he needed a suit. The only one he owned was at least three years old. Two…he wanted to swing by the Elite to tell his friends goodbye for the summer. And three and most important, he needed to pick up his paycheck and ask John Wayne…the café manager not the movie star…. to hold his position for the fall.

William called Netty at home to ask if she'd like to tag along. She lived with her parents, her paternal grandmother, and two younger brothers when classes were not in session. Having her parents living in town proved beneficial whenever dormitory rules required written parental permission for attending functions off campus or attending functions which lasted past curfew.

William pulled his pickup close to the curb in front of the Baker's house. As he walked to the front porch, Netty bounded down the steps toward him. She looked beautiful as always. Her shirtwaist dress of alternating stripes of bright colors—lime green; hot pink and sun yellow—fell three inches below her knees. Her white gloves matched her three-inch white heels.

He leaned down to kiss her. "You look beautiful."

"Not here!" She pulled at his arm. "My grandmother always watches from her bedroom window. She's a spy eager to report wrong-doings to the commander."

William laughed and opened the passenger door for her. She climbed up and slid across the seat closer to him. William sat behind the wheel.

"Now?" he asked.

"No, go around the corner."

"Nah, can't wait that long." He quickly pecked her lips and looked back over his shoulder. "I think we're safe!"

Netty laughed as William headed to Matthis Men's Store. After the purchase of a blue wool suit, he headed to Elite. Netty waited in the pickup. It didn't take William long to talk to Mr. Wayne, get his check and secure his position for the fall. Rick and the other kitchen staff members who were working the early shift wished him well. Some even promised to attend a couple of revival services. Rick teased he wouldn't recognize William without an apron. As William exited the café, it began to rain...a drop here; splatter there. He hurried to his pickup and jumped in.

"Everyone sad to see you go?" Netty asked.

"I guess so. It's only for a couple of months. Darlene wasn't there. Sally will tell her bye for me."

Netty turned her head to look out the side window.

"Darlene's only a friend. You know that, don't you?"

Netty nodded her head but did not turn to look at him. The summer rain beat steadily against the windshield. William turned on the wipers.

"I need to go home," Netty said softly and William nodded.

Netty had hardly spoken two words since leaving the Elite. William pulled up to the curb as the rain continued to pound the vehicle and turned off the engine. Slumping down, he rested his head against the back of the seat. Netty scooted closer. He unfurled a strand of hair she sometimes kept tucked behind her ear.

"Netty, our first service is Wednesday at First Baptist. I can pick you up."

"No, that's okay. Church on Sundays is enough for me. I don't like being at church all the time and I certainly don't understand why you love it so much."

William sat up. "It's not only church. It's God and His Son I love! Their promises of love, mercy, grace, and eternal life. The Bible, God's Words, are printed out for us, speaking to us from the printed page. What was true over 2,000 years ago is just as true today. Truth is always truth."

"See, you're always a preacher boy." She kissed him.

"Aren't you worried about your grandmother?"

Netty's eyes twinkled. "The rain will keep us hidden. I'm going to miss you."

"It's only for the summer."

"But that's a long time!"

William wrapped his arms around her and pulled her close. She rested her head on his shoulder; her hand on his chest. They held each other as the rain spattered against the truck's windows and thunder faintly rolled in the distance.

ALL'S WELL...UNTIL IT ISN'T
1941

L oraine leaned over the handlebars of her bike and pumped her legs harder as she raced her cousin Grant down Main Street's awning-covered walkway. She glanced over her shoulder as she passed TG&Y, the five and dime variety store. Grant was advancing. Loraine veered too close to the benches outside Roger's Hardware Store and almost lost her balance. As she neared her family's drugstore, she noticed an old rusty blue pickup parked at the curb.

"I win!" she cried, pushing her foot backwards against the brake pedal.

Her bike slid to a stop inches from a man and a boy carrying a weighty piece of furniture into the store. The carved oak wood chair secured to a bilevel platform held two leather seats separated by armrests. The lower level held four brass footrests. Under the footrests, two drawers with brass pulls lined the box.

"Sorry," she apologized as Grant skidded up beside her.

"No problem," the man answered. "Cleve! Hold up your end."

Loraine and Grant dismounted their bicycles, rolled them closer to the building's brick wall and kicked down the stands to hold the bikes upright. Grant followed his cousin inside.

Franklin was busy behind the counter waiting on a couple of customers. Loraine sauntered over to the soda counter where her brother Paddy was manning the fountain. When he saw his sister, Paddy placed a glass under a spigot and pulled the lever down. Coca-Cola streamed into the glass and foam gathered at the top. He handed the glass and a straw to Loraine and turned to prepare another drink.

"What are those guys doing out there?" Loraine placed her straw in the cold brown, bubbly liquid and sipped deeply.

Paddy handed Grant a drink and wiped off a wet spot on the counter with the towel he kept draped over his shoulder. "Oh, that's Mr. Johnson and his son. They're setting up a shoeshine business."

"Out there? Is there room?" Grant asked.

"Mr. Johnson thought so. He's the one who persuaded Papa to let him set up shop out there. Offered a portion of his proceeds for rent, but Papa refused. Said he wasn't using that space anyway. Only thing...Mr. Johnson can only operate when the drugstore is open. Seems reasonable. A lot of men pass through here and will more than likely stop to have their shoes shined."

While Paddy continued talking to Grant, Loraine carried her drink to the nearest round table, turned her chair to face the entryway and sat down. She had a clear view of the man and his son as they sorted several smaller boxes they'd carried in earlier. Loraine swirled her straw in the glass and examined the boy.

Cleve...that was what his father called him. He looked about her age...fourteen. Was tall and thin and muscular. Nice features. Dark skin, hair and eyes. A pleasant smile. How long had he been in Oak Hill? Did he live here? She'd not seen him around and was most curious.

It's not like she'd never seen a black person before. Uncle Ernie currently had three black men on his payroll...all carpenters...Emmett Jones, Linus Brown, and Big Boy...the only name she'd ever heard him called. Possibly because the man's arms and legs resembled tree branches...thick and strong. The men were friendly; always returned her greetings whenever she said hello. And according to Uncle Ernie were fine craftsmen and hard workers.

But other than that...the blacks stayed to themselves. Lived in their own community; had their own shopping areas, schools, and churches. She never understood why. And she'd definitely never been attracted to a black boy before. But there he stood. Tall and handsome...Cleve Johnson.

"Loraine! Are you listening?" Grant asked.

"Huh? What?"

"Me and Tommy and Donnie are going to the creek. You coming?"

Loraine glanced out the window. Where was Cleve? Oh, there, standing behind the old blue truck with rusted fenders.

"Yeah, you go ahead. I'll catch up."

"Okay." Grant bustled through the vestibule to retrieve his bike.

Loraine carried the empty glasses to Paddy. "Have fun fishing at the creek."

"I will. Thanks, Paddy."

As she turned from the soda counter, she smoothed out the pleats of her yellow split-skirt and checked that her white blouse was neatly tucked in. She blew an air-kiss to Franklin and walked casually through the vestibule.

"Have a good day, Mr. Johnson. I'm sure I'll see you again."

"I'm sure you will, Miss."

Loraine pulled her bike from the wall and pushed it toward Cleve.

"Hello, I'm Loraine Bailey. My father owns the drugstore."

"Oh, hey. I'm Cleve Johnson."

"My brother tells me your dad is starting a shoeshine business here."

"Yeah." Cleve closed the rusted-out tailgate with a dull bang. "I was just helping set up."

"So you won't be back?" The panic in Loraine's voice betrayed her ruse of simply being friendly.

When Cleve smiled, a small flame ignited somewhere deep inside her chest. Something she'd not experienced, nor expected.

"I've not seen you around. Just move here?" She tightly grasped the bike's handlebars more for her own balance than for keeping the bicycle upright.

"Nah, we live on the north side of town across the railroad tracks."

"Oh, I've not been there."

"No, I guess not." He smiled again that same electric smile.

Loraine looked about hesitantly. "Sorry, I need to go. My cousin and some of his friends are going to the creek to fish. Want to come?"

"That's quite a walk."

"We're cycling." Loraine stepped through her bicycle's frame, held the handlebars in both hands and balanced her left foot on the top pedal. "Well, if you change your mind, we usually meet on Saturday afternoons behind the Branson's place. Cleve...is that your nickname?"

"My name is Cleveland O. Johnson. You see why I prefer Cleve?"

Loraine smiled. "Does the O stand for Ohio?"

"No," Cleve laughed. "O'Dell after my granddad."

"Well it was nice meeting you, Cleveland Ohio O'Dell."

"Nice meeting you….Loraine."

Loraine pushed off and pedaled toward the creek unaware Mr. Johnson had been watching them through the store's plate glass window.

Cleve entered the vestibule and sat down on the stool used to buff shoes. His dad had a small wooden box opened and was arranging shoe polish tins by color...black, dark brown, medium brown, chestut brown, tan.

"Better be careful, boy. You're playing with fire."

"Sir?"

"Stay away from that girl. She could cost me this place. She's trouble for you. Stay clear. Understand?"

"Yes, sir. But we were only talking."

"A black boy talking to a white girl is never good. Trust me on that."

The following weekend, Loraine and Lucy were managing the soda fountain. Paddy had a date that afternoon. A mystery girl. Even with the twins teasing him and badgering him to tell them who she was or at least mention a name, he refused.

Loraine was glum. Mr. Johnson had not opened the stand which meant Cleve wouldn't be coming around. The drugstore would be closing at two. It was ten 'til. Overcome with boredom, she had offered to take out the trash. With trash bags in hand, she passed through the back vestibule and opened the back door. The afternoon was hot and muggy...a usual summer day. She walked across the parking lot, pushed up the lid from one of the two trash barrels, and tossed the bags over the rim. The aroma always made her scrunch up her nose. Mixtures of ashes and decomposed garbage harbored a certain indescribably rancid, unpleasant smell.

"Loraine," someone whispered. Startled, she looked around.

Cleve stepped from behind her father's car parked by the fence. She slammed the lid on the smelly barrel and walked toward him.

"Cleve! What are you doing here?"

"Is it okay?"

"Yes, of course, it is!"

"I want to see you, Loraine."

"Here I am!" she teased.

Cleve smiled. "No, I mean more often….just us. Where can we meet?"

"We're going roller skating tonight."

"I can't go to the rink."

"Okay, well how about the library?"

"Loraine, you're so naïve. I'm not allowed in any of the places you go."

Loraine's brows furrowed. She reached out and touched the sleeve covering his upper arm. "Cleve, I don't understand. Why not?"

"Just the way things are."

"Because of your skin color?"

Cleve nodded matter-of-factly. "Meeting me would mean no one could know. No one….not even your sister."

"You mean…sneak around?"

"It's the only way. If you can't, I understand. I don't want to cause any trouble, Loraine. Honestly, I don't."

Cleve watched Loraine's face intently as she considered his proposal.

"I was just thinking…there's an abandoned house three blocks from the library. On the corner of Post Oak Street. Grant and Tommy and I checked it out one day when we were exploring. Lucy and I volunteer at the library on Thursdays. Meet me there Thursday at four. Go through the alley. The side gate is always unlocked. I'll be waiting on the back porch."

"Okay, I'll see you Thursday."

Lorained turned to go back inside. Cleve caught her elbow. "Are you sure about this? No one can know!"

"Yes, I'm sure! Now you better go. Someone might see you."

****

Oak Hill Skating Rink was the place to be on Saturday nights. Not only for teens but also for young adults and families. According to the teen population, it was the only place to be on Saturday nights…football on Friday nights; church on Sundays. Roller skating had been the craze since 1938. Oak Hill's city manager welcomed the rink as a place for fun and exercise. But the teens only came to socialize.

Lucy and Loraine, who had spent hours primping in front of their bedroom mirror, thanked Paddy for dropping them off and waved as he drove out of the parking lot. As the twins grew older they made a pact to never dress alike as their mother dressed them when they were little girls. Shoes were never considered part of their non-matching agreement…they each wore black-and-white saddle-oxfords and white rolled-down socks.

Arm in arm, they entered the rink. Another crowded Saturday. They hurried to the counter to stand behind four others waiting in line to rent skates. Twenty-five cents didn't seem too extravagant a price to pay for two plus hours of fun.

Since the girls frequented the rink so often, Teddy, the guy who managed the rentals and also the rink's bouncer, knew they would want a girl's skate…white, size six. He placed two pair of roller skates on the counter. Lucy pushed two quarters toward him and smiled sweetly.

"Ready for that couple's dance later, Lucy?" he teased.

"Give it up!" Loraine answered gruffly and grabbed their skates.

"Quit encouraging him," Loraine whispered as they searched for an empty bench to change into their skates. "Over there. Grant and the boys have a spot."

As the girls approached the bench, the boys…Grant, their second cousin, Tommy North, Donnie White, and Arnold Blake…were arguing about which baseball team would win the World Series.

"It'll be the Yankees. Has to be!" Donnie exclaimed. "Joe McCarthy has a good team this year."

"Yeah, Joltin' Joe DiMaggio is on a hitting streak," Arnold agreed and quickly tied the laces on his skates.

"Don't count out the Reds," Tommy argued.

"You guys gonna race tonight?" Donnie asked, changing the subject.

"Yeah," Tommy answered. "I've been practicing!"

"Where?" Donnie teased. "In your dad's auto shop?"

The boys snickered. Tommy playfully punched Donnie's arm.

"Oh, hi! Here, have my seat. I already have on my skates." Arnold, realizing the girls stood behind him, offered his spot on the bench.

"Hey there!" Grant turned from his friends, finally noticing his cousins.

"Hope Pinkey plays some swinging sounds tonight," Tommy added energetically. "Loraine, couple's dance later?"

"Sure," Loraine answered, tightening the laces on her skates. "What's Pinkey's real name anyway?" Loraine asked no one in particular but hoped someone would know the answer.

"Just Pinkey…that's all I know," Tommy answered.

"The lights are flickering. Pinkey's taking his place at the organ. Come on! Meet ya out there!" Grant called over his shoulder as he raced Tommy and Donnie to the skating floor.

"Hurry up, Lucy," Loraine scolded as she too skated out to join the boys.

Lucy removed her saddle-shoes and scooted them underneath the bench. She rolled up the tops of the two pair of white socks she wore and then slipped her foot into the boot of the right skate. She tried to readjust the inner lining, but it seemed bunched under the laces. She tugged harder but the lining didn't budge.

"Here," Arnold offered.

He knelt on his right knee. Reaching for her right foot, he balanced her skate against his left knee. He swiftly relaced the skate, criss-crossed the laces over the metal loops and tied them tightly at the top. After both skates were laced, he stood.

"May I have this….er…skate?" His face reddened.

Amazed by his blue eyes and red hair, Lucy smiled and took his hand.

"I'm not very good," she confessed.

"I'll make sure you don't fall."

As the two waited for a safe opening to join the fast-moving sea of skaters, Pinkey began playing "You are my Sunshine." Lucy skated easily around the wooden floor with Arnold by her side. Beginning their second turn, two older boys who were racing in and around the other skaters sped by too closely. One of the skater's wheels clipped Lucy's back wheel causing her to stumble.

"Eek!" Lucy shrieked; her arms flailed about in the air.

Arnold grabbed her left arm. "Gotcha!" The momentum spun her completely around to face him. He grinned as she gripped his arms.

Embarrassed but grateful, Lucy smiled and released her hold. "Well, I've always wanted to learn to skate backwards. Teach me?"

Still grinning, he skated one step closer and placed his hands on her waist. "Put your hands back on my arms. Now, just skate as I push you back. Ready?"

Lucy followed his instructions. If standing next to him made her nervous, being this close was far more nerve-wracking. Arnold guided her backwards as they skated around in the center of the rink. The masses of other skaters, all going the same direction, circled the outside of their space.

"This reminds me of being stranded in a boat in the middle of a lake while schools of fish swim frantically in circles," Lucy commented. Arnold laughed.

Pinkey played a series of chords that everyone recognized as time to clear the floor. Racing would begin soon. Arnold took Lucy's hand and the two skated to the wall out of the way of the racing but close enough to get a close-up view.

Teddy, clad in a white tee-shirt, black trousers, black skates and wearing a referee's whistle around his neck, skated into the rink. Skating fast with his body slouched low to the floor, he glided around the perimeter twice. He spun in the center of the rink, stopped and blew the whistle.

"Show off!" Arnold grumbled.

Lucy nodded but inwardly disagreed. She was impressed. At nineteen, she knew Teddy was far too old for her. But she could admire his skating skills and good looks just the same.

At the whistle's long-sounding shrill, the boys lined up by age. Boys ten and younger raced first. Boys eleven to thirteen raced next followed by boys fourteen to sixteen. Seventeen and older raced last. Girls could race but seldom would.

Loraine joined Lucy and Arnold to watch the races.

With the first two races over, Grant, Donnie, Tommy and Earl Roberts, who had won three weeks in a row, took their places on the starting line along with three other daring souls. All the racers stood on the toe-stops of their skates waiting for the starting signal. Teddy blew the whistle.

At the whistle's sharp ear-splitting sound, the skaters still standing on their toe-stops ran several steps to get a head start. Pumping their arms and taking long strides, the group skated toward the first turn. Earl pulled ahead early. As they rounded the first turn, Grant pulled away from the pack and skated up five strides behind Earl. Crouching low, Donnie sped past Grant. Skating to the outside, Tommy pulled away from the stragglers and raced toward the lead skater. One more time around to go. The last three skaters desperately tried to keep up.

The onlookers applauded, stomped and yelled encouraging their favorite skater. Pinkey played some song, but no one could hear the organ over the din of loud screams and thunderous noises. Lucy and Loraine clinched hands and screamed as the racers rounded the final turn.

Earl still held the lead, followed closely by Tommy, Donnie and Grant, in that order. The other three were too far behind to make any difference to the outcome of this race. Earl looked over his shoulder to see Tommy two strides behind him. Like a bolt of lightening, Earl flashed across the finish line leaving Tommy second place. Teddy blew the whistle three times. The race was over.

Grant, Tommy and Donnie used their toe-stops to brake and circled back to meet their friends who still stood against the wall. Lucy patted Grant on the back. Donnie pushed playfully against Tommy.

"You beat me!" Donnie teased.

"Great race, Tommy!" Loraine exclaimed. "You almost beat Earl!"

"You *have* been practicing!" Arnold added.

"Next week!" Lucy encouraged. "You'll get him next week!"

The ceiling lights flickered twice announcing time for the girls to choose a partner…ladies' choice…couples only. Half of the ceiling lights were turned off casting dimmed lighting over the rink's skating floor. Lucy clasped Arnold's hand and the two skated to the center of the rink.

Loraine turned to exit the skating floor. Maybe sit down or buy a soda. Before she reached the opening that divided the skating floor from the benches and concessions, Earl skated up and blocked her exit. He extended his arms out to whichever side Loraine tried to pass. Across the rink, Grant elbowed Tommy. Seeing Earl harassing Loraine, the two boys skated toward them.

"Hey, there, Loraine! Where are you going? Don't you want to skate with the best skater here?" Earl smirked.

"Teddy's working!"

"Teddy! Ha! You're cute, Loraine. I'm the one who's won the races four weeks in a row!" Earl boasted. "I'm choosing you out of all the girls here to skate with me. You should feel honored. You owe me a skate!"

"I owe you nothing, Earl Roberts! Let me pass!" Loraine protested.

"Ah, come on! You could be my girl tonight!" Earl persisted.

"Hey!" Grant exclaimed, skating up behind Loraine. "What's going on?"

"None of your business, Grant!" Earl snarled. "Get lost!"

Earl pushed against Grant and Grant pushed back harder. Tommy positioned himself in front of Loraine.

"Loraine, are you causing trouble?" Teddy having seen the exchange from across the rink and as the bouncer there to prevent fights, skated over quickly to stop the fracas from escalating.

"No, I was just asking Tommy to skate with me." Loraine grabbed Tommy's hand and they skated out to join the other skaters.

"Grant, you and Earl separate right now!" Teddy commanded.

"Not leaving until he does!" Grant exclaimed.

"Loraine?" Earl shouted as Teddy escorted him off the skating floor. "You're gonna skate with me! This isn't over!"

****

Thursday afternoon, Maggie dropped the girls off at the library and promised to pick them up at five. Mrs. Nelson, the librarian, waved as Loraine and Lucy entered. The girls proceeded to the back room where the checked-in books were stored. Two empty rolling carts sat against the wall. Loraine filled one cart; Lucy the other. Once the carts were filled, the girls rolled them out to the main floor and filed the books in their appropriate places on the shelves.

Loraine kept checking her wristwatch. She was nervous; certainly not acquainted with this sneaking around business and felt guilty about lying to her sister. Even a lie of omission. But she had carefully planned her escape. At three-forty-five when Lucy read to the children during story time, she'd return her cart to the storage room. Then she'd slip out the back exit unnoticed and unseen. She glanced at her watch again. It was time.

She pushed her empty cart past the "Fiction" aisle and waved at Lucy who sat on a short-legged stool holding a book on her lap. Several children were already there sitting cross-legged on the floor eagerly awaiting for story time to begin.

Loraine's hands were slightly sweaty as she pushed through the back door. Her only thoughts now were of Cleve. She ran toward Post Oak Street then slowed down to a walk....running would look too suspicious. When she neared the alley at the back of the abandoned house, she paused and looked both ways. No one was around. She untied her hair and stuffed the ribbon in her pocket She entered the alley. Honeysuckle vines crawled up and down and over the five-foot fence. Loraine pushed the gate open and waited inside the screened-in porch.

Her nervousness grew. Was she doing the right thing? What would happen if she and Cleve *were* caught together? Would they really get into trouble? Did she select the right dress to wear? She hoped so. She was wearing her sleeveless peach dress. Would he like it? Would he even come? She paced back and forth like a caged tiger. She'd never seen one but had read about them. Why was her mind bouncing about from one random thought to another?

The back gate opened.

Loraine turned around quickly. Cleve stood at the edge of the overgrown lawn and smiled. He looked so dashing....white short-sleeved shirt tucked into black pleated trousers and recently polished black leather shoes. He walked up the sidewalk and stepped up onto the porch.

"You came!" she exclaimed.

"Yes, I said I would."

They stood four-feet apart waiting, watching, wondering what to do next.

Loraine turned and pointed, "There's a swing over there. Want to sit down?"

Cleve followed her and they sat down. Loraine clasped her hands in her lap.

"So," Loraine began, "did you have any trouble getting away?"

"No, you?"

Loraine shook her head, looked down at her hands, then looked back up. "Hmmm, do you have any brothers or sisters?"

"Two younger sisters. They live with my mom in Jefferson."

When Loraine looked puzzled, Cleve explained. "Mama Jo, my grandma, got real sick the summer I turned twelve. My uncle had to work and couldn't take care of her. She's better now but my Pops and I still come during the summer to help around the house. My mom's family is in Jefferson; she prefers to stay there."

"So, you go to school in Jefferson?"

Cleve smiled at her. "Yeah, going back and forth is not so bad. Jefferson High is a great school. Have a lot of friends there. Miss my mom but not my sisters!"

Loraine laughed.

"Just your brother and sister, then?"

Loraine chuckled. "Oh, no! There are eight of us. Lucy and I are the youngest and the only girls. Living in a household of boys, I learned at an early age I had to be on time for dinner if I wanted anything to eat!"

Cleve laughed. "And Grant? Does he live with you?"

"Practically!" Loraine laughed. "He's my uncle's grandson...my second cousin. Grant's parents were missionaries in Germany until forced to evacuate. They're safe. Grateful Grant stayed here with Uncle Ernie and Aunt Elizabeth."

Loraine fidgeted with her hair.

"Are you afraid?"

"Of what?"

"Me?"

"No, of course not. I'm just nervous."

"I can tell. No need to be."

He pushed a wave of hair off her shoulder. "You don't usually wear your hair down. I like it this way."

"You do?"

He scrunched her hair within his fingers and gazed into her eyes. If she'd been a popsicle, she thought, she would have melted right then and there.

She touched his forearm. "Your skin is soft."

"What did you think it would feel like?"

"Oh, I don't know." She gently rubbed the top of his hand. "It's nice."

"Yeah, this is nice."

She looked up into his eyes. "Your eyes are so dark. I get lost in them."

"Really? Yours are like the summer sky…blue and clear. Like an angel's.

"You know for a fact angels have blue eyes?"

Cleve laughed. "You do."

Loraine smiled.

"Loraine?"

"Hmmm?"

"May I kiss you?"

Butterflies somersaulted then pole vaulted within her stomach. "I've never been kissed before."

He leaned forward. She could almost taste his breath. He pressed his lips against hers…gently and lightly. When he sat back, she smiled.

"Loraine, we better get going. I'll leave first. Wait five minutes before you leave. I'll meet you here next Thursday."

The next Thursday lead to the next followed by the next throughout the first two months of summer. Cleve and Loraine made the best of their twenty minutes together. Holding hands as they sat on the swing, he told her about school in Jefferson and being number 24, a running back, for the Lions football team. About how he loved to run and planned to try out for the track team this spring. They talked about their families and how much they loved their grandmothers...his Mama Jo and her Gran. They shared what they wanted to do after graduation. She knew she should go to college. Just didn't know where or what she wanted to study; only knew she should go. He wanted a football scholarship to any university.

They talked about their similarities but most often they talked about their differences. Cleve shared how Mama Jo's Oak Hill across the tracks was an entirely different world from Loraine's Oak Hill. Smaller area, fewer people...an all black community. A handful of men owned cars or pickups and fewer owned property. Most of the houses were rentals. The streets were unpaved. Only a few years back, Oak Hill proper finally provided utilities for the community. Several black entrepreneurs conducted business on their Main Street...Mr. Jamison's barber shop; old man Ivan's grocery and mercantile; Miss Myrtle's café; a general delivery post office; one gas pump; a ten-room schoolhouse for all grades and the church.

Those seeking better wages took the bus into Austin to work but were restricted to the 'Negroes Only' section in the back of the bus. Public restrooms separated not only men from women but also whites from blacks. Water fountains, too, had one for whites and one for blacks. If they went to the movie house in Austin, the balcony was the only place they were allowed. Very few white establishments allowed their patronage at all. But they, the black community of Oak Hill, were a proud people and loved the Lord. They made the best of whatever life cast their way; their faith made stronger in their circumstances.

It was mid-August, a stifling hot, sticky afternoon. Not much of a breeze penetrated the mesh screen on the back porch. Loraine glanced at her watch. Cleve squeezed her hand. It was time. They stood and embraced. The anticipation of seeing each other was worth the week-long wait; but saying goodbye was agonizing.

Every week after Cleve kissed her, he delivered the same instructions. "I'll go first. Wait five minutes before you leave."

Loraine watched Cleve leave through the side gate. She leaned against the fence and plucked a yellow honeysuckle blossom from the vine. Curious she pulled the white sticky stem from its center and sucked the end. It was sweet on her tongue. No wonder bees and hummingbirds fought over the plants.

"Hey! You! Yeah, you! Stop! What are you doing back here?"

Startled, Loraine crouched down and peeked through the slats in the fence. Earl Roberts and two of his buddies were midway down the alley briskly walking toward Cleve. Exiting the alley, Cleve picked up his pace and crossed to the other side of the street.

"Hey! You have no business here!" Earl shouted. "Stop!"

When Cleve did not respond or turn aroud, the trio chased him. One of Earl's cronies stopped long enough to pick up a couple of rocks then followed in pursuit...like wild dogs chasing a defenseless rabbit.

Loraine wanted to yell at them to stop but knew she could not blow her cover. Or cause further trouble for Cleve. She moved to another spot in the fenceline and peered between the slats.

'Run!' she screamed silently. 'Run!'

Cleve looked over his shoulder. The three boys were quickly advancing. He wanted to steer them away from Loraine. He hoped she had heard the shouting and would stay safely hidden in the yard. Rather than turning toward the library, Cleve turned the opposite direction. Loraine could hear the boys shouting as their feet pounded the pavement. She didn't know what to do. She couldn't get help. She and Cleve would be exposed. She squatted behind the fence and waited.

Finally only hearing the sound of chirping birds perched high in the elm tree up above, Loraine opened the gate and hurried back to the library.

Running behind schedule, Maggie picked up the girls at five-thirty. Loraine climbed into the back seat; Lucy sat in the front with their mother.

"Girls, sorry I'm late. We need to run by the store and help your dad close."

Loraine sat up a little straighter. Maybe she could find a way to sneak away and go find Cleve. It had been over an hour. She needed to find him. She disliked Earl Roberts with a seething hatred she didn't know she possessed.

With her mother busy bristling about the store pointing out ways the girls could help, Loraine went to the broom closet pretending to get the broom. To her surprise and delight, Paddy's overalls and UT baseball cap he wore when burning trash hung on a hook next to the mop. She pulled on the overalls, stuffed the ends of her dress inside and fastened the suspenders in place. Bending, she rolled up the pant legs forming a three-inch cuff. Her bicycle was parked in the back vestibule. This could not have turned out more perfectly if she'd planned it beforehand.

Slipping out of the broom closet, she glanced through the plate glass into the store to see if Lucy or her mother were there. Fortunately, they were not. She tucked the ends of her hair up under the baseball cap. Pushing her bike, she quietly headed out the back door.

Swinging her right leg over the bicycle seat, she mounted and pedaled toward the railroad track. She pulled the cap down low, lowered her head and pedaled hard and fast. She had no idea exactly where Cleve lived. He'd mentioned a yellow house, red rosebushes and East 3rd Avenue. East 3rd then was her destination.

Pedaling to the end of Main Street, Loraine turned left toward the railroad tracks. She stopped at the crossing and pushed her bike across the asphalt. At the point the road abruptly tapered off into a dirt road, she remounted. Cycling north she spotted a few buildings on either side of a main roadway. A few pickups and cars were randomly parked in front of the establishments. Must be their downtown...their Main Street, Loraine thought.

Not wanting to be noticed, she steered to the right and traveled east three blocks before turning back to the north. She had no idea where she was going. Panic as well as sweat trickled down her spine. She pedaled faster, frantically searching for street signs. She passed signs for East 2nd

Street, East 2nd Ave, and East 3rd Street. The next street had to be East 3rd Avenue.

She steered her bike onto the street. Narrow houses lined either side of the road. She rode her bike down its center as there were no sidewalks. She looked to the right and then to the left searching for a yellow house. There on the left was a yellow house…but no rosebushes. Loraine slowed. A few houses down on her right sat a yellow house. She passed it by and circled around for a better look. The house had three red rosebushes planted by the porch. But was this the right house? Were there only two yellow houses on this street? Is this where Mama Jo lived?

Loraine pulled her bike to a stop and dismounted. She eyed the house. These small houses she knew were called shotgun houses. Years before, Uncle Ernie and his construction crew had built at least twenty in Buda, a small town eighteen miles south of Oak Hill. She remembered one Sunday afternoon over a plate of fried chicken, Uncle Ernie described the house design. Was a single room wide and three or four rooms deep. The rooms were arranged one directly behind the other…no hallways or wasted space which allowed several to be built on one lot. Uncle Ernie explained why the houses had acquired such an odd name. If standing at the front door, one could fire a shotgun, aim at the back door and not hit a thing.

"Girl, you best come in before you pass out from the heat."

Startled, Loraine jumped when she heard a woman's voice. Her heart pounded as the screendoor slowly screeched opened. An elderly woman well in her eighties held the door open and waited for Loraine to come forward.

"Park your bicycle up here. Watch out! My grass is just now growing good."

Loraine looked down and saw ten 12x12 wooden planks spaced a foot apart forming a sidewalk of sorts. She pushed her bike forward, lifted it over the stoop and leaned it against the side of the house.

"Are you Mama Jo?"

The woman nodded. "Come in, child."

Loraine nervously followed the old woman. She felt like an intruder. When she removed Paddy's baseball cap, her blonde curls tumbled out and rested against her shoulders. The front room was small but cozy. Five square pillows knitted with yellow yarn lined a faded blue sofa that sat under the only window in the room. A radio cabinet sat at an angle in the corner. The family Bible and a red sweater rested in a rocking chair.

Cleve's grandmother seemed as sweet as he had described. Streaks of white coursed through hair that had once been jet black. Her knuckles were gnarled from arthritis; skin wrinkled from age and from working in the sun. She wore a short-sleeved lime green house dress. Blue velveteen houseshoes slapped the bottom of her feet as she shuffled along.

"Would you like a glass of sweet tea to cool yourself?" Mama Jo asked.

"Yes, thank you kindly. Mama Jo? May I call you Mama Jo?"

The woman smiled. Crinkles creased the corners of her dark brown eyes. "Everyone does. Come on. The kitchen is back here."

Loraine followed Mama Jo from the small living room and passed through two bedrooms. The kitchen ended the procession of rooms at the back of the house. Loraine couldn't imagine privacy being be a major concern in a house styled so.

Mama Jo pointed to the kitchen table and Loraine sat down. After pouring the tea into a glass, Cleve's grandmother handed the glass to Loraine.

"Mama Jo?"

"I know why you've come, girl. Cleve told me all about you."

"He did? Where is he, Mama Jo? Is he okay?"

"That sounds like Carver now. You can ask him yourself."

Loraine heard the sound of a vehicle pulling up near the back door. She hadn't noticed the detached garage at the back of the house. She waited apprehensively and impatiently. Who was Carver? Cleve's father? His uncle?

Mama Jo shuffled to the door and opened the screen. Loraine stood, clinching the UT baseball cap nervously in her hands. Two men slowly entered the small kitchen supporting Cleve between them.

"Big Boy?" Loraine gasped as she recognized both men.

The big man smiled sheepishly as he helped Cleve ease into a kitchen chair. Once Cleve was settled, Mr. Johnson glared at her.

"What are you doing here, Miss Loraine?"

"I...I...," she stuttered. "I'm..."

"Carver, she's come to see the boy," Mama Jo calmly answered.

"Well," Mr. Johnson said harshly. "Look at him then!"

"Pop," Cleve uttered, glancing at Loraine. "It's not her fault."

"Yes! Yes! It is! I told you to stay away from her! Look at him, girl!"

Tears trickled down Loraine's cheeks as she looked at Cleve. His left eye was red and swollen shut; his bottom lip split; cheeks bruised and gashed. An abrasion on his forehead had been bandaged. He favored his right side whenever he moved.

"Carver," Mama Jo said sternly. "Why don't you go simmer down in the front room. Larnelle, put the girl's bike in your truck. You can drive her home."

Both men left the kitchen. Mama Jo sat down beside Cleve.

"You okay, sugar? Pastor Thomas fix you up?"

Cleve nodded his head.

Loraine scooted her chair closer to Cleve's and sat down. "What happened?"

Cleve clutched his right side with his left hand. "Earl and the other two chased me eight blocks. I made the mistake of cutting through an alley not knowing it was a dead end. They backed me into a corner and jumped me."

Loraine reached out to touch him. Glancing at Mama Jo, she quickly withdrew her hand and wiped the tears from her cheeks with her fingertips.

"God was watching out for my boy," Mama Jo said. "Carver and Larnelle went out looking for him when he didn't show up at the shoe stand. Carver had an inkling he was with you, child. They found the boys and broke up the fight."

"Cleve," Loraine blubbered. "I'm so sorry. This is my fault."

Cleve extended his left hand. She gently clasped it within hers.

"There'll be no more of that!" Mr. Johnson stormed into the kitchen. Loraine immediatley dropped Cleve's hand as if it were a branding iron.

SEASONS UNDER THE SUN

"Miss Loraine, I mean you no harm. Sorry, if I've frightened you. But, this...you two...has to stop. You see that, don't you?"

Loraine sat as stiffly as a frozen block of ice. Inwardly, her heart was breaking piece by piece as if being struck by a dull axe. Cleve turned his head away.

"Tell her your plan, Carver. She should know," Mama Jo said.

"Why should she?"

"Look at her," Mama Jo instructed. "She's a blubbering mess!"

Mr. Johnson pulled up the only unoccupied chair at the table and sat down. With calmness and authority that allowed no room for questions or debate, he said, "Larnelle is taking Cleve home to his mother Saturday morning. Football starts up in two weeks anyway. Miss Loraine, Cleve won't be coming back next summer or the next. Those boys will be looking for him and will finish what they started."

The back door opened and Larnelle announced, "I'm ready now, Miss Loraine, to take you home."

Mama Jo stood and came around the table. "Come on now, honey."

With tears in her eyes, Loraine stood and looked down at Cleve. Hesitantly he looked up and tried to smile. "Bye, Loraine," he choked.

Mama Jo accompanied Loraine to Larnelle's pickup. "It was nice to meet you, child. Cleve will be okay. He'll heal up good as new. This is best for you both. Larnelle will take you home now."

Loraine hugged Cleve's grandmother and climbed into the truck. Stinging silence was her companion on the drive home. Larnelle pulled his truck near the Bailey's driveway, but didn't enter. He glanced at his passenger. Her cheeks were wet with tears.

"Miss Loraine," he said. "Please, stop crying. I can't stand it!"

Loraine glanced at the large man sitting behind the wheel. His hands as big as saucers; his brown eyes as big and round as a puppy's.

"Thank you for the ride." Loraine opened the door and slid out of the truck.

Big Boy walked around to the back of the truck. With one hand he removed the bicycle and set the wheels on the ground. Loraine took the bike and started pushing it toward the driveway.

"Miss Loraine?"

"Yes?" Loraine turned to face him.

"If you'll be out front here at seven Saturday morning, I'll bring Cleve by."

"Why?" Loraine was confused. "I thought you all wanted him as far away from me as possible! I'm like poison or something worse."

"Yes, 'em. That's true. But I saw my nephew stand up like a man today and take all the blame. It was his idea to go home. Cleve was afraid you'd get in trouble if word got around to your father. Or my brother possibly lose his location at the drugstore. Cause I work for your uncle, I could lose my job. Cleve wanted to leave without your knowing. Who knew you'd be brave enough to come to our house? That was real risky, Miss Loraine."

"I know but I had to see him! Do you know how awful it would be if he just left and I hadn't had a chance to see him or tell him goodbye?"

Big Boy smiled, "Yes, 'em. I'm beginning to. You two needs to say goodbye. Proper like." Embarrassed, Big Boy rubbed the toe of his boot in the dirt.

Loraine dropped her bike to the ground. Before Big Boy could move or realize what was happening, she stood on her tiptoes, grabbed him around the neck and hugged him tightly.

"Ahhh, now, Miss Loraine. This ain't a good idea," he smiled.

"Thank you….do I call you Big Boy or Larnelle?"

"Big Boy will do."

****

Loraine slept fretfully if she slept at all. It was still dark out. She couldn't lie in bed a minute longer. She quietly kicked off the covers and sat on the edge of the bed. Lucy slept soundly. Earlier Friday evening she had hidden clothes and shoes in one of the spare bedrooms. She couldn't risk waking her sister.

Loraine tiptoed across the floor and exited their shared room. She slipped into the bedroom where her clothes were stashed and immediately changed. What does one wear when seeing a special someone for possibly the last time?

Loraine stepped cautiously and slowly down the stairs. Arlo, sleeping on the round braided rug at the foot of the stairs, sat up excitedly as she approached and wagged his tail. If Tip were still alive, Loraine thought, he too would be eagerly waiting at the bottom of the stairs. What a good ole dog Tip had been.

Loraine scrubbed Arolo's head hoping he wouldn't yelp in his excitement seeing her. She opened the front door and commanded the dog to stay, but she could tell he had no intention of remaining in the house. Birds or squirrels or some other unwanted varmit could be lurking in the yard causing all sorts of mischief. Since it was still dark, having a big dog with her as she stood on the road might be beneficial.

Loraine briskly walked to the end of the driveway. Arlo followed. She stood outside the four-foot wooden fence and waited. Arlo sniffed about inspecting each blade of grass or wildflower or wild grape vine growing on or near the fence.

The sky ever so subtly altered in color from midnight black to dusky gray. The stars began to douse their lights. The sun would be rising soon. Loraine paced about anxiously; clinching her hands or readjusting the pleats on her skirt. Her skin prickled when she saw headlights beaming over the hill; the light bounced on the road as the vehicle neared. Her first inkling was to run into the middle of the road and flag it down. Instead, she knew she should wait.

A dark blue 1935 Ford pickup pulled up beside her. Arlo started barking. Loraine commanded him to go home. Finally, the dog reluctantly obeyed. After an agonizing minute, Cleve opened the door and slowly got out. Her heart pounded. The morning light was just enough to faintly see his face.

She opened her mouth but before she could voice any words, he pulled her close. Holding the sides of her face in his hands, he kissed her lips softly and gently. Tears swelled her eyes. Again she started to speak.

"Shhhh, don't say anything." Cleve lowered his head and held her. "Loraine, I will never forget you."

"No! Cleve, don't say it like we'll never see each other again!"

"You know it's true. You and I can never be together." He lifted his head and gazed into her blue eyes. "It's just not possible."

"We'll run away then. Somewhere people don't care about skin color!"

"And where would that be? There's no such place. We can never be. Loraine, you must live your life. And I will live mine."

"No!" Tears fell freely and slid down her cheeks onto his shirt.

"I'd like to hear your pet name for me...one last time."

Loraine smiled weakly and looked up. "Ohio."

He lowered his head and held his forehead against hers. "That's it."

"Cleve, we gotta go," Big Boy announced through the opened window.

Cleve stroked Loraine's cheek with his finger tips. "I'll never forget you. You're my angel. Promise you'll never forget me!"

They kissed each other for the last time...intentionally and sorrowfully. Loraine watched as he climbed into the pickup cab. She nodded her gratitude toward Big Boy. As the truck slowly pulled away, she ran after it. She could see Cleve's reflection in the truck's side mirror. Nearing the end of the fenceline, she stopped.

"Cleve!" she screamed then clamped her hands over her mouth.

Cleve leaned slightly out of the opened window and looked back at her reflection. With his hand outstretched, he waved. A final farewell. Loraine stood in the middle of the road and watched through blurry tear-filled eyes until the truck and her first love disappeared from sight.

BROADCASTS AND NIGHTMARES
1941

Following its typical pattern, time marched steadily onward. September bumped August to one side, tumbled over October and crash landed on top of November. Turning the page on the pertetual calendar, this day marked Thanksgiving Day, November 27, 1941.

As usual, the Baileys were expecting a large crowd. Mostly family, but that too was typical. Art and Rosa sent their regards. Their second child, hopefully a girl this time, was due in December. Neither would risk traveling so far. William had only one day off for the holiday and needing to work on a term paper over the weekend, stayed in Dallas. Clayton, of course, was stationed in Hawaii assigned to the naval battleship *USS Pennsylvania*. He had mailed a witty postcard…a cartoon drawing of a turkey with a black pilgrim's hat on its head and a garland of lilac leis around its neck stretched out on a blanket on the beach. Clayton wrote, "I'm eating Navy beans while you feast on Mama's cooking. Much love and all my best."

Only five from Ernie's and Elizabeth's family would be present this year. Anne and Grayson, of course, in Switzerland waiting for the North American Missionary Board to assist with paperwork and transportation to London. Missionaries were the first group to receive mandates from the Board to leave Germany after Hitler's invasion of Poland. With so many thousands of refugees as well as missionaries fleeing west for safety, the process of returning home had been long and grueling. Anne's last communication via telegram transmitted through the Board was hopeful she and Grayson would be in London soon.

Owen drove in from Wichita Falls where only the month before was part of the construction crew responsible for the completion of Sheppard Army Airforce Base, a training facility on 300 acres of what was previously a cattle ranch. Carter lived at home still and worked with his dad so he would definitely be coming. And then Grant, of course, who felt Oak Hill more his home than any other place he'd ever lived.

In all…thirteen Baileys and five Bonds. And Paddy had invited a guest. So, nineteen for dinner. Maggie fretted over the dining accommodations and recounted the place settings. Finally resolved two highchairs would be needed at the adult table. One for David, Trina's and Sam's son, now three, and one for their baby girl, Polly Annette, who was almost one. Maggie was hopeful Eddie, now ten, wouldn't feel too old for the kid's table. Maggie felt almost giddy thinking about her grandchildren. Five plus one on the way. All well and healthy. So much to be thankful for.

Franklin—dressed in brown pleated trousers and a white dress shirt under a beige cable knit sweater—hurried into the kitchen. "They're beginning to arrive!"

Franklin and Magge hurried to wait on the porch for their family to gather. The house would soon be filled with cheerful voices, laughter, endless teasing, exchangement of ideas while talking all at once, and the atmosphere heightened even more by energetic, high-spirited children.

Embraces and greetings were still underway when Paddy drove up in his bright red 1937 Chevrolet sedan. The car although only four-years-old looked brand new. That was partially due to how much Paddy babied it and more to do with the number of times he waxed it. All eyes turned to watch as Paddy exited the car and opened the passenger door for his guest…Kim Hana Yoshida.

Five-foot-five, petite and slender. Oval shaped face, dark eyes and silky black hair that fell three inches below her shoulders. A beautiful young woman.

"Welcome!" Franklin stepped down the porch steps to greet them.

After introducing Kim to his father, Paddy escorted Kim up the steps to meet his mother. "Mama, this is Kim."

"How lovely to meet you. Paddy...sorry, I think you call him Patrick....has told us about you. I'm looking forward to knowing you better."

"Thank you, Mrs. Bailey. Patrick talks about his family all the time. I'm happy to be meet you. Here," Kim said and offered Maggie a round green tin. "They're Japanese cookies...made from kobacha squash."

Maggie accepted the tin graciously. "Thank you. Come in, my dear."

As Franklin continued introducing Kim to the the family, Patrick pulled his mother to one side. "You did tell the family I was bringing Kim?"

"Yes, as you asked."

"Did you also ask them not to drill her during dinner?"

Maggie laughed and linked her arm within his. "Yes, but, please understand as adults I no longer have control over any of my children. And it is a long day!"

Patrick, nervous about Kim meeting his family, looked even more worried and apprehensive. Maggie laughed, "I'm teasing. It will be fine. They'll be on their best behavior. Let's go eat."

****

"I just don't see how we can stay out of the war much longer," Ernie said after dinner as he and Franklin sat on the top porch step. Patrick, Grant, Owen and Carter played football in the front yard anticipating the NFL playoff game that would be broadcasted over the radio in ten days.

Franklin, smoking his pipe, enhaled deeply and exhaled slowly. "We're already supplying Britain, Russia, and our allies with oil, food, airplanes and other weaponry. Think Roosevelt's Lend-Lease deal will be enough without sending our boys to Europe....placing them in harm's way?"

"Hitler is a maniac. Mussolini and Emperor Hirohito are just as dangerous. All tyrants. Our troops are on high alert. Roosevelt and our leaders must know something. Churchill, although grateful for the Lend-Lease Bill, is biting at the bit for the US to join. Churchill said something about Roosevelt's Bill being the most unsordid act in world history. Because of it Britain could remain strong."

Franklin looked out into the yard as Carter passed the football to Grant. Grant jumped up and caught the overthrown ball then crooked it tightly against his body. Owen and Patrick chased their opponent across the yard. Grant sprinted toward a large painted pumpkin, their make-shift goal line. Owen advanced on the right and plowed over Grant's legs. The two laughed as they tumbled onto the grass. Carter extended his hand pulling Grant to his feet. No score. Back to the huddle.

Before lunch, the two older boys had challenged the two younger ones to a game of football. Not fair, but then the idea of these four young men going to war was not fair either. Suddenly Franklin thought of Clayton, but then relaxed. His son was safe…away from the war… his ship safely anchored in Honolulu's harbor.

Inside the house, Elizabeth, Maggie and Emily were resting in the parlor enjoying a cup of coffee. Their conversation veered away from current events and touched on much lighter subjects…Elizabeth's recent purchase of a Westinghouse two-slice electric toaster; Eddie's constant begging to see Disney's new movie, *Dumbo*; and Maggie's concern over Loraine's mood swings since school started.

"Oh, what time is it?" Maggie glanced at the Grandfather clock in the corner. "Almost five. Guess we should get the desserts ready."

"I'll call the guys." Elizabeth placed her coffee cup on the service tray.

Going outside, she sat down on the first stoop beside Ernie and crooked her arm underneath his. Ernie smiled and patted her hand.

"Ready to accept defeat and have dessert?" Elizabeth called out to the gridiron players. "I brought a chocolate cake. Tia and Kim baked cookies And there're pies, of course."

Carter threw the ball straight up in the air, centered under it and caught it.

"I'm ready! These guys cheat anyway."

"Say that again if you dare!" Patrick grabbed Carter into a playful choke-hold as they followed the others inside.

After Patrick washed up and changed his shirt, he joined Kim and his sisters in the music room. He'd learned years ago not to ask what was discussed within a circle of girls. He sat on the sofa's armrest beside Kim. She smiled up at him.

"You didn't tell us, brother," Loraine began, "that Kim was born in Salinas, California…which makes her a US citizen. Her full name is Kimika Hana. Kimika means noble and Hana means blossom….noble blossom. Kim has two younger sisters…Asami and Akira. Asami means morning beauty. Akira means light. Wouldn't it be grand if our names had another meaning?"

"And Kim has a music scholarship at UT," Lucy added.

"What? I thought you were taking horticulture classes to be a landscape designer," Patrick said somewhat confused.

"I am a girl of many talents," Kim teased. "Time for dessert?"

Holiday traditions, fun with family and loved ones seem to end much too quickly. This day…Thanksgiving 1941…had come to an end. Time to place a check mark on the calendar as completed.

****

Sunday afternoon the front door opened abruptly as Patrick, Owen, and Grant pushed Loraine and Lucy aside and raced to the study. Patrick turned on the radio and kept turning the dial until he heard the broadcast for the New York Giants vs the Brooklyn Dodgers game. The football game was underway.

"The game's started!" Patrick called out. Lucy and Loraine hurried in.

"Franklin," Maggie teased, "I'm surprised church wasn't cancelled! Ham sandwiches for everyone? We can have the roast for supper."

Maggie headed to the kitchen to make sandwiches. She smiled as she glanced at the ten-foot Christmas tree by the stairs. Its twinkling lights of red, green, and gold glistened. The glass decorations were perfectly spaced over the branches. The smell of fir filled the air. The tree skirt was empty but soon would be filled with packages. Christmas was only two weeks away.

"Thanks for letting us come listen to the game, Uncle Franklin," Owen said.

Franklin turned after placing more logs on the fire. "Of course, you boys are always welcome. I'll go help Maggie. Turn up the volume, Patrick, so I can hear."

Franklin and Maggie soon returned to the study with a tea cart. The top shelf held a pitcher of sweetened tea and ham and mayo sandwiches made on either homemade rye or sourdough bread. The bottom shelf held a platter of sugar cookies.

"Grant, turn down the volume, son," Franklin said. "Let's bless our food."

The family joined hands as Franklin prayed. With the prayer voiced, Maggie handed out napkins as sandwiches were eagerly grabbed off the platter. Arlo, sitting next to Owen, stared at the ham sandwich as it traveled from the plate to Owen's mouth and back to the plate. Owen pinched off a corner of the bread and offered it to the dog. Arlo gobbled it down and sat patiently for another bite. Grant turned the radio volume back up.

As Maggie took a bite of her sandwich, an announcement intermingled with static blared from the speakers. "We interrupt this broadcast for an emergency message. This is a live report from Honolulu, Hawaii... 'Hello, NBC. Hello, NBC. This is KTU in Honolulu, Hawaii. I am speaking from the roof of the Advertiser Publishing Company Building. We have witnessed this morning the distant view a brief full battle of Pearl Harbor and the severe bombing of Pearl Harbor by enemy planes, undoubtedly Japanese. The city of Honolulu has also been attacked and considerable damage done. This battle has been going on for nearly three hours. One of the bombs dropped within fifty feet of KTU tower. It is no joke. It is a real war. The public of Honolulu has been advised to keep in their homes and away from the Army and Navy. There has been serious fighting going on in the air and in the sea. The heavy shooting seems to be….We cannot estimate just how much damage has been done, but it has been a very severe attack. The Navy and Army appear now to have the air and the sea under control.'[1]

Maggie's sandwich fell from her saucer and plopped onto the floor. Her face, brandished entirely white, devoid of color. "Clayton," she whispered.

Franklin stood immediately. Lucy scooted to one side as her father sat down and pulled Maggie into his arms. Lucy leaned into his shoulder. Loraine slid off the sofa onto the floor. The boys still sitting on the floor looked shocked and dumbstruck. Gran clinched her hands and bowed her head in prayer.

"What was that?" Patrick stood. "Did Japan attack us? Are we at war?"

"Where's Clayton?" Maggie cried softly.

"Hush, now, he'll send word." Franklin assured her, holding her tightly.

"How?" Lucy cried into the sleeve of his blue sweater.

The phone on the desk rang three times. Patrick answered it. "Hello? Yes, we heard. I don't know exactly where he is. We'll just have to wait. Okay, I will.'

"That was William," Patrick announced to the family.

As soon as the receiver was placed in the cradle, the phone rang again. "Hello?" Patrick answered. "Yes, sir. No, we're not sure. I'll tell them."

Patrick hung up the phone and looked at his cousins. "That was Uncle Ernie. Owen, he asked that you and Grant come home."

The football game was no longer of any importance. The rest of the day was spent listening to the radio in the music room. The telephone in the study rang often enough to make concentrating on news broadcasts difficult. Any word about what was happening now or what was going to happen or Clayton's current location centered everyone's mind. Radio programs continued their regular scheduling as if nothing had happened in Hawaii. For the Baileys, the main interest continued to be news updates about Clayton and very little else.

Gran insisted the family listen to First Lady Eleanor Roosevelt's weekly broadcast. Gran felt it almost a patriotic duty. The First Lady donated her revenue from the broadcasts to charitable causes. Tonight's broadcast was sponsored by the Pan American Coffee Bureau. Surely the President's wife would have words of insight and comfort for the American people.

Then precisely as scheduled a voice recognizable to so many transmitted over the air waves. 'Good evening, ladies and gentlemen, I am speaking to you tonight at a very serious moment in our history. The Cabinet is convening and the leaders in Congress are meeting with the President. The State Department and Army and Navy officials have been with the President all afternoon. In fact, the Japanese ambassador was talking to the president at the very time that Japan's airships were bombing our citizens in Hawaii and the Philippines and sinking one of our transports loaded with lumber on its way to Hawaii. By tomorrow morning the members of Congress will have a full report and be ready for action....'

The First Lady continued...'We know what we have to face and we know that we are ready to face it. I should like to say just a word to the women in the country tonight. I have a boy at sea on a destroyer, for all I know he may be on his way to the Pacific. Two of my children are in coast cities on the Pacific. Many of you all over the country have boys in the services who will now be called upon to go into action. You have friends and families in what has suddenly become a danger zone. You cannot escape anxiety. You cannot escape a clutch of fear at your heart and yet I hope that the certainty of what we have to meet will make you rise above these fears. We must go about our daily business more determined than ever to do the ordinary things as well as we can and when we find a way to do anything more in our communities to help others, to build morale, to give a feeling of security, we must do it. Whatever is asked of us I am sure we can accomplish it. We are the free and unconquerable people of the United States of America.'[2]

The program continued but the Baileys remained still and silently reflected upon the First Lady's words. Franklin and Maggie exchanged glances.

"Things will never be the same again, will they?" Lucy finally muttered.

WAR DECLARED ON JAPAN
1942

Monday December 8ᵗʰ's issue from San Antonio's independent newspaper *The San Antonio Light* carried these top headlines, typed in large bold fonts, plus subheaders:

U.S. DECLARES WAR
3,000 Killed; Wounded in Hawaii Raids
War on Japs Declared by Britain
Japs Raid Manila
Need for Men in US Navy Critical

FDR's "infamy" speech broadcasted at noon was a beacon of hope and resolve for all Americans.

'Yesterday December 7, 1941, a day that will live in infamy, the United States was suddenly and deliberately attacked by naval and air forces of the Empire of Japan…The attack yesterday on the Hawaiian Islands has caused severe damage to American naval and military forces. Very many American lives have been lost. In addition, American ships have been reported torpedoed on the high seas between San Francisco and Honolulu…Hostilities exist. There is no blinking at the fact that our people, our territory, and our interests are in grave danger. With confidence in our armed forces—with the unbounded determination of our people—we will gain the inevitable triumph—so help us God.'[3]

At 4:10pm President Franklin Delano Roosevelt, while wearing a black armband honoring those lost at Pearl Harbor, signed the declaration of war against the Empire of Japan. Three days later the horror intensified as Germany and Italy declared war against the United States. The European war had finally crossed the ocean and knocked forcefully on America's front door. Men between the ages of twenty-one and thirty-six having registered for the draft the year before generated a vast pool of names from which to draw to fill ranks of the U.S. military forces.

Day after day newspapers and radio broadcasts delivered the current news. It was reported that while the Japanese forces attacked Pearl Harbor, they also attacked Hong Kong, Guam, Philippine Islands, Wake Island and Midway Island. The Baileys similar to all other American families crowded around their radios or read the printed page, devouring any news. Fearful but still filled with hope.

Finally, on Monday, December 14th, a telegram from Honolulu was delivered to the Bailey's home. It read: *Safe. No injuries. Keep the faith.*

With a sigh of relief and a prayerful heart, Maggie resumed Christmas preparations. How can one's heart hold joy and fear simultaneously? Only the day before Victoria Camille was born in Kingsville. Art, an overly joyful papa, called from the hospital. He described his baby girl as beautiful and healthy. Rosa was doing well and ready to go home. Juan Alexander, age four, was disappointed he did not get a brother, but Art was certain the boy would be a good big brother. Art wished the family a merry Christmas before ending the call.

The next two weeks passed quickly. Christmas this year seemed not as cheerful and bright as other years. But the meaning of Christmas always remained the same. With the new year heralded in, holidays over, family gatherings concluded, the Christmas tree taken down and decorations stored away, daily life resumed…resumed but much differently, far from its normal course.

****

Patrick hurried across UT campus toward the Liberal Arts Building. Six Texas mountain laurels lined the sidewalk. Their lilac flowers attached like grape clusters on the branches exuded a crisp, clean fragrance. Spring was making her debut.

Entering the classroom, he took his seat on the fourth riser and glanced down where Kim sat diagonally on the row below. She had not arrived. This was the only class they shared and because of their conflicting schedules the only time they could squeeze lunch in afterwards. Puzzled he looked around. As Professor Whatley stood behind the podium, all talking and shuffling about ceased. Class had begun.

As soon as his last class of the afternoon concluded, Art ran across campus to Kim's dorm. Six girls stood outside. One he recognized from English Lit class.

"Karlene?"

"Hey, Patrick!"

"Would you be able to deliver a message to Kim? I need to talk to her. She wasn't in class today. Want to make sure she's not sick. She never misses."

Karlene glanced at her two friends who stood nearby. "You've not heard."

"Heard what?"

"This morning an early radio broadcast announced that the University of Washington and other universities on the west coast have asked all students of Japanese, German or Italian descent to leave those campuses immediately. All first generation Japanese....those born in Japan...are being arrested in California, Washington, and Oregon. They claim it's a safety precaution, but for whom?"

"Seriously?"

"President Roosevelt signed an executive order...9066, if I remember correctly. Since Pearl Harbor, the War Department considers these races of people possible enemies of our country," one of Karlene's friends interjected.

"Kim's not here," another girl said sympathetically.

Patrick took Karlene's elbow. "Where is she? Where did she go?"

"Janet Long, Kim's roommate, came back to their room after her first class and found Kim crying hysterically. She'd packed two suitcases…wanting to go home. Hoping to persuade Kim to stay in Austin where it's safe, Janet took Kim home with her. Oh, Patrick, this is such a terrible situation! I'm still reeling over the fact the U.S. is imprisoning American citizens! We feel so sorry for Kim."

"Do you know where Janet lives? I've got to find Kim!"

"I've been to her house once before for a birthday party. All I remember is she lives on the corner two blocks behind Faubion Grocery on Highway 183 in Cedar Park. There's a large sign with a flying red pegasus in front of the store. Mobile Gas, I think. Anyway, turn there. The limestone house has dark gray trim. You can't miss it. Please, tell Kim I'm so sorry and wish her the best."

Patrick thanked Karlene then raced back across campus to where his car was parked. Twenty-five minutes later as he entered Cedar Park, Patrick slowed down as he approached a small limestone building… Faubion Grocery. The Mobile sign…a flying red pegasus…exactly as Karlene described….stood fifteen-feet high beside a single gas pump. Patrick turned down the gravel-topped road and passed the first block of houses. There on the second corner sat a white limestone with gray trim. The yard was well manicured. Red tulips and orange lilies bloomed in the flowerbed. A five-foot-tall crape myrtle tree covered in clumps of delicate pink blooms stood in the center of the yard.

Patrick parked and got out. He walked up the porch steps and knocked on the door. A pleasant looking woman, possibly in her fifties, wearing a yellow checked housedress, answered the door.

"Yes? May I help you?"

"Yes, ma'am. Is this where Janet Long lives? I'm Patrick Bailey and I'm looking for Kim Yoshida."

"I'm Janet's mother. Yes, please, come in. Janet and Kim are in the kitchen."

Patrick followed Mrs. Long down a narrow hallway to the kitchen. The girls sat huddled together at the kitchen table. Kim was slumped over the table and rested her head on her arms; her dark silky hair fanned out around her shoulders. She was crying. Janet softly patted her back.

"Patrick is here," Mrs. Long announced.

Kim immediately raised her head. She rushed to Patrick and fell against his chest. Her tears turned to sobs as he held her.

"She's been like this all afternoon. There's nothing I can say to comfort her. It's nice to finally meet you, Patrick," Janet said tearfully, her voice shaky.

"Shh, Kim, tell me what happened." Patrick steered her back to the table to sit down. Holding Kim's hand, Patrick again asked, "What's happened?"

"I don't really know," Kim said between sniffles.

"Janet, it's almost five," Mrs. Long stated nervously as she glanced at the clock that hung above the kitchen sink.

"I know, Mama. It'll be okay," Janet answered.

"We've been listening to the radio all afternoon, Patrick." Janet continued, "President Roosevel's order was signed in January but not enforced until now. All Japanese, German and Italian descendants living on the east and west coasts are required to register each family member with the War Department. They have two weeks to handle their affairs and report to a designated control center. Banking accounts have been frozen and property sold at ridiculously cheap rates. They can only bring possessions that can be carried and then will wait for reassignment."

"What?" Patrick interrupted. "Your family? Have you talked to them?"

"No," Kim whined.

"Janet," Mrs. Long said peering out the kitchen window. "I hear your father's truck pulling in."

Patrick heard a door open and close in an adjoining room and the sound of boots being stamped on a rug. Mrs. Long seemed wary as she glanced at Kim.

"Alice, whose car is out front?" a man called out.

The man, Patrick assumed to be Mr. Long, entered in stocking feet; his boots left by the back door. A blue uniform covered in cedar wood dust stretched over his large frame. The left pocket bore the name Cedar Park Mill stitched in gold thread. He placed his black dome-shaped steel lunch box on the counter.

"Alice?" He frowned at the his wife. "What's all this?"

"Daddy, these are my friends from UT...Patrick Bailey and Kim Yoshida. Kim is my roommate." Janet hurriedly introduced her friends.

Mr. Long stared at Kim. "What's *she* doing in my house?"

Kim shrank behind Patrick like a morning glory flower closing at dusk.

"Sir?" Patrick asked.

"Boy, she's Japanese, ain't she? Her kind bombed Pearl Harbor! Know how many boys we lost there?"

"Daddy, surely you don't think Kim's responsible for what happened at Pearl Harbor! She's an American....same as you and me," Janet argued.

"No! Not like you or me! You didn't answer me, Alice. Why are they here? You know I don't like people at the house when I get home from work!"

"They just dropped by," Mrs. Long answered softly. "And were just leaving."

"Yes, we were just leaving," Patrick said resentfully, taking Kim's hand.

Mr. Long ran his eyes over Kim. "Janet, did you say she's your roommate?"

"Yes, Daddy," Janet answered. "I've told you about her."

"Yeah, but you never mentioned her last name. I won't have you rooming with her kind. I'll call the dean and settle this first thing in the morning."

"But, Daddy! Kim's a wonderful person!"

"I work double shifts just to pay for your college. So you can live in a dorm and experience college life like you said you wanted. It's either change your roommate or live at home. Your choice. Now if you don't mind, it's dinner time. Alice, I'm going to clean up. Have dinner on the table. I won't be long." Mr. Long stalked out of the room. Conversation over.

"I'm so sorry," Mrs. Long apologized. "But it's best you leave now. Kim, do you have a place to go?"

"She's going home with me!" Patrick curtly exclaimed.

Patrick took Kim's arm and followed Janet to the front door. Kim's two suitcases sat beside the hallway table. A clear vase of pink asters and a small white lamp sat on the table…a welcoming array most days…just not this one. Patrick picked up the cases as Janet hugged Kim.

"I am so embarrassed by my father's behavior, Kim. He's not usually this way…he's strict, yes, but not so blatantly disrespectful. Patrick, may I have your address? I'd like to keep in touch with Kim."

"General Delivery…Oak Hill," Patrick answered as Janet opened the door. "And, Janet, thanks for looking out for Kim."

Janet followed them down the sidewalk to Patrick's car. With tears in her eyes, Kim turned at the curb to hug her friend. The girls held each other tightly, fearful this was possibly their last encounter. Patrick placed the cases in the trunk. Kim slipped into her seat and waved to Janet as the car pulled away.

When Patrick turned south onto Highway 183, he reached for Kim's hand…small and dainty…her nails covered in polish…pink, her favorite color. Kim tried to smile but she was filled with fear, embarrassment and shame. She'd never experienced such harsh racial criticism as Mr. Long brandished toward her. She was an American. Although her father had been born in Japan and dreamed of taking his family to visit there one day, he never found the opportunity. She had never stepped on Japanese soil nor met either her paternal or maternal grandparents. Her extended knowledge of Japan was only the stories her father shared about when he was a youngster. Mentally exhausted, Kim scooted closer to Patrick and rested her head against his shoulder.

Knowing the drive to Oak Hill would be at least thirty-minutes, Patrick turned on the radio. Frank Sinatra sang "I'll Never Smile Again" on one AM station; "This Land Is Your Land" by Woody Guthrie played on another. Turning the dial quickly searching for a song unrelated to the moment, Patrick finally gave up and turned off the radio. The drive to Oak Hill was cloaked in silence.

Patrick pulled the sedan into his driveway and stopped. His mother and Tia were kneeling in front of the flowerbed by the front porch. When Maggie recognized the car, she placed her container of pansies to one side and stood. Kim sat up and pulled at Patrick's arm.

"Are you sure it's okay my being here?" Kim asked.

Patrick kissed her cheek. "Yes, I'm sure. Wait here a moment, okay?"

Kim nodded and watched Patrick's six-foot-two frame rise from the car and walk toward his mother. Maggie withdrew her gardening gloves and slapped them against the leg of her short-sleeved one-piece cotton coveralls. She and Tia took turns hugging Patrick and then stood together listening intently to what he had to say. Maggie turned toward the car, hurried to the passenger door and opened it.

Extending her hand, Maggie said, "Kim, please come in, my dear. You're most welcome to stay here as long as you need. Let's get you settled."

Patrick took Kim's elbow and led her into the foyer and across the wood floor. They climbed the stairs and walked down the second floor hallway. He opened the door to the bedroom that had once been John's. Funny how rooms are designated as belonging to their original owner regardless how many years that person had moved away or how many times the room redecorated.

Patrick pushed back the curtains emitting the late afternoon sun. Kim ran her fingers over the top of the ornate wooden dresser then turned. Patrick noticed her countenance. She was no longer crying but her beautiful brown eyes were rimmed in red. He stepped closer. She stood on tiptoes and put her arms around his neck as he bent slightly. She hugged him tightly. His kissed her lips softly.

"You'll be okay here, Kim. I promise. I'll take care of you."

Kim smiled and stepped away. She readjusted her light pink cardigan sweater over her gray-and-pink plaid skirt and sat on the edge of the bed.

"May I take a short nap? I promise to be down soon."

"Of course. I'll get your luggage. Sure you're okay?"

Kim nodded and stretched out on the bed. Patrick returned downstairs.

"Patrick! How terribly devastating! Has Kim heard from her family?" Maggie exclaimed, standing at the bottom of the stairs.

"No ma'am. She is distraught and emotionally exhausted. Wanted a nap."

"Of course! I'll call Franklin to see if he knows anyone who can get word to Kim's parents or at least find out where they are."

"Thank you, Mama, for letting Kim stay. You have no idea what cruel racist remarks have been hurled at her today. She's hurt, confused and frightened."

"You're such a caring young man. I'm so proud of you."

Two hours later as the orange sun slid down the gray skies to fade away into the horizon, Kim walked down the stairs looking for Patrick. Arlo met her at the bottom step and led her to the study. Franklin sat in the leather chair behind his desk and listened closely as Patrick, who was perched on the side of the desk, talked on the telephone. Gran was sitting in her chair by the radio with the volume turned low. The twins sat at her feet. Maggie, while relaxing on the sofa, crocheted a pastel yellow baby blanket for Victoria, her newest grandbaby.

When Kim entered the study, Loraine jumped to her feet and hugged Kim tightly. "Kim! Feel better after your nap?"

Maggie placed her crochet thread and needles in the basket sitting beside her and stood. "We've just eaten. Didn't want to disturb you. Patrick is on the phone with John. We did save some dinner for you. The girls will fix you a plate."

Lucy bounded from the floor. The three girls locked arm-in-arm headed to the kitchen. Arlo padded behind them. Loraine placed a plate topped with two pieces of fried chicken and mashed potatoes before her guest. Loraine sat a cup of hot tea and a spoon near the plate. Kim looked so pitifully forlorn.

"Please eat something," Lucy coaxed.

Kim picked up the fork and twisted it around in the mound of potatoes. Without taking a single bite, she put the fork down and sipped the tea.

"I have no idea what you're going through, Kim," Loraine said as Lucy nodded wholeheartedly. "But we are here for you. You know that, don't you?"

"Here." Lucy slid a dessert plate topped with a large slice of chocolate cake toward Kim. "Chocolate always makes me feel better."

Kim nodded and picked up the fork again. She had gobbled down half of the cake when Patrick barged into the kitchen.

"Good news, Kim!" Kim looked fatigued, Patrick noticed, as he sat down across the table from her. He reached out for her hands. "John lived in Sacramento for five years as a grocery warehouse manager. He knows a man who currently manages a warehouse in Salinas. John will call him first thing in the morning. I've given John the names of your father, mother, and sisters. Hopefully, we will have news about them soon."

Tears ran down Kim's cheeks as she nodded weakly.

"How's that cake? Got anymore, little sis?" Patrick asked as Lucy jumped up to serve him.

Soon the four chocolate lovers sat at the kitchen table consuming chocolate cake drizzled with dark chocolate icing. Kim eagerly devoured a second piece, forgetting her troubles if only briefly.

With the dishes washed, dried, and put away, the chocolate connoisseurs plus Arlo returned to the study. Gran had turned the radio dial to CBS. Was time for *Fibber McGee and Molly*. Everyone settled down to hear an hour of comedy…something everyone cherished and needed desperately…a little frivolity to cast aside anxiety and worries.

During the end of the script before Fibber opened his closet door and a crash sounded over the radio speakers, Lucy exclaimed, "Don't open that door, McGee!"

Everyone laughed then chanted together, "'Gotta straighten out that closet one of these days.'"

"Don't know why that's so funny!" Gran laughed. "I laugh everytime!"

"School day tomorrow. Time for bed," Maggie announced to her daughters.

"Time for me to call it a day, too," Gran said, using the arms of her chair to push up slowly and stand.

"Come on, Kim. We'll walk you up," Lucy offered.

Patrick walked Kim to the stairs and kissed her cheek. "I have a ten o'clock class in the morning but can skip it and stay home with you."

"No, Patrick, don't do that. I'll be fine."

Patrick watched until Gran, Kim and his sisters had safely climbed the stairs. As he turned, Franklin was standing in the doorway of the study.

"Son, your mother and I would like to talk to you. Have a minute?"

Patrick followed his father into the study.

"Son," Franklin began. "Your mother and I are concerned about this situation. Kim is a wonderful young lady. We will do everything we can to help find her family. But you know there's a possibility there may be nothing we can do. We will never oust Kim from our house but the law is the law. Things may go sideways…for the worse rather than for the better."

"I know but what else am I to do? She means a great deal to me."

"I know. Just be careful," Franklin patted his son on the back.

Fully awake after midnight, Patrick continued to toss and turn, worrying and fretting over Kim. What will happen to her? Was her name submitted to the War Department? Where is her family now? Has her father been arrested? If so, where are her mother and sisters? If this upset him, how must Kim be coping?

Patrick got out of bed and opened the top drawer of his six-drawer oakwood chest. He took out a pair of blue striped pajama bottoms and pulled them up over his boxers. Tucking in his white cotton undershirt, he left his bedroom. John's room was two doors down the hall. He leaned an ear against the door and could hear muffled crying. He eased the door open.

The lamp on the bedside table was on. Kim was lying on her right side in a fetal position with the blue bedspread pulled over her head. When the door opened, Kim sat up quickly.

"It's just me," he whispered.

"Patrick!" Kim held out her hand as he approached the bed.

He sat down beside her and smirked as the bedspread fell into her lap.

"What?" she asked quizzically.

With a grin on his face, Patrick pointed at her sleeveless white cotton nightgown. Red-headed Raggedy Ann dolls of various sizes were printed overall.

"Don't laugh at my gown! I love Raggedy Ann!"

"I see that…you do look adorable! I came to check on you. I couldn't sleep and knew you couldn't either."

"Stay with me?"

"Kim, you know I can't do that. It's not proper."

"No, not like that. Just hold me until I go to sleep."

Patrick nodded. She held up the sheets for him to slip inside, but Patrick settled against the bed pillow on top of the covers. He leaned slightly to turn off the lamp. Kim rolled closer. He put his arm around her as she leaned against his shoulder and stretched her arm across his chest.

"Patrick?"

"Hmm?"

"Thank you."

"For what?"

"For coming for me today."

He held her snuggly as they lay in the dark. She was so close. Her hair tickled his chin. She smelled so good…some floral scented perfume. He could feel her heart pounding against his chest and wondered if she could feel his. Sheathed in stillness and totally consoled, sleep soon consumed them both.

****

The following morning when Kim came downstairs, the house was quiet. Everyone seemed to have gone for the day. Even Arlo was not under foot. As Kim pushed through the kitchen door, she found Tia washing breakfast dishes and humming a song Kim didn't recognize.

"Good morning, Tia."

Tia smiled and wiped her wet hands on a dish towel. "Good morning, Kim. Sleep well? Have a seat. I kept your breakfast warm."

"Yes, thank you. Is everyone gone? I hadn't intended to sleep so long. You didn't have to save another meal for me! I don't want to be a bother!" Kim sat down.

"You're not a bother. Coffee?" Tia placed a plate of crisp bacon, scrambled eggs and toast on the table. "When you've finished eating, take your coffee out to the gazebo. It's a lovely place to relax and enjoy the morning. Patrick asked me to tell you he'd be home for lunch."

After eating, Kim followed Tia's instructions and stepped outside to face the brisk morning. Arlo bounded up to meet her.

"There you are!" Kim said, rubbing the dog's head.

Entering the gazebo, Kim sat down on a bench. She pulled her white cardigan more securely about her. The view was indeed beautiful and soothing. How lucky, Kim thought, Patrick was to have grown up here…fishing at the creek; climbing oak trees; swinging from a rope; riding horses or being chased by his dog. The more she thought of Patrick's childhood, the more she was reminded of hers. She placed her cup on the bench and left the gazebo.

Maybe a walk would clear her mind. She walked through the barn and remembered Patrick saying only three horses were stabled there. The barn was empty. The horses, too, must be out doing whatever horses do every day.

She continued walking past a stone cottage and followed the path beside the house until it abutted a fenced-off area…a garden. She breathed in the smell of freshly turned soil. A man wearing a large straw hat was bent over a row of new plants that had pushed up through the dirt to peek around.

"Hello?"

The man stood, removed his hat and said, "Buenos días."

"My name is Kim. Do you speak English?"

"Yes," the man laughed. "I'm Luis Santiago. Santos….Tia's husband."

"Oh! I'm sorry. I'm asked all the time if I speak English. People just assume I don't. So nice to meet you. What's growing there? Looks like brussels sprouts."

Santos smiled. "Yes, they are. Are you a gardener?"

"My father is or was in California. I see a bucket of seeds there. May I help?"

"Yes, of course."

Kim looked down at her dress and white sweater. "Wait until I've changed?"

Santos smiled. "Okay, I'll take a little break and drink my morning coffee."

Kim grinned. She could hear Santos chuckling as she raced back toward the house. Fifteen minutes later Kim reappeared. With Tia's help, she'd borrowed a pair of Patrick's denim overalls and a long-sleeved red plaid shirt. Both the hem of the pants and the shirt sleeves were rolled up to fit her petite body. Tia's gardening boots and straw hat fit her perfectly. And the gardening gloves she'd also borrowed from Tia fit securely in Kim's back pocket.

"How do I look?" Kim asked twirling about, modeling for Santos.

"Buena," Santos laughed. "A real gardener."

"Where do we start?"

"Beet seeds...this bucket red and this one yellow. Fill those two rows over there. Then I have several tomato plants and a bucket of carrot seeds."

Kim took the small buckets of seeds and a trowel to the loosened mound of soil Santos had pointed out. Compost had already been mixed in. Kim felt so at home planting the seeds. Remembering what her father taught her, the seeds needed to be planted ¾ inch deep and spaced an inch apart. She covered the seeds lightly with soil and patted the earth down with her gloved hands.

So absorbed in her work, Kim hadn't realized the time until she heard a familiar voice. "Santos? Got a new hand?"

"Yes, a very good worker," Santos answered.

Kim looked up from her squatted position. "Patrick!"

Patrick extended his hand. Kim removed her glove and allowed him to pull her up. He grinned as he pushed up the rim of her straw hat to better see her face.

"Nice outfit. New?"

Kim blushed. "Tia got them from your room. I didn't go snooping around if that what you're thinking! What's in your basket?"

"Tia made sandwiches for us. Santos, Tia has yours in the cottage."

"Better go then if Tia calls." Santos pulled off his hat and wiped his forehead with the handkerchief kept in the front pocket of his overalls. "Thank you, señorita."

"I had a wonderful time, Santos. My father once told me I was a natural gardener. I reminded him of a Japanese folklore story. Was about a princess who as a baby was found within a stalk of bamboo by an old bamboo cutter. She had been sent to earth from the moon to learn a moral lesson."

Santos nodded and waved as he trudged off toward his cottage.

Patrick took Kim's hand and led her to the edge of the creek. They sat down on the grass and he opened the basket. The water in the creek was running fast, bubbling and churning over the rocks in its shallow path. She removed her hat and shook out her hair. Patrick watched as she ate an egg salad sandwich. She wiped the corners of her mouth thinking he was staring at a smear of mayo.

"Kim, I care for you very much and have an answer to our problems."

"Our problems? My situation is not your problem."

"I know this may seem sudden and possibly not the right moment, but will you marry me and stay here with me until the war is over? After the war…and that shouldn't be too long now that the U.S. is involved… our whole future is ahead of us. The sky holds no limits for us."

Kim stared at him for a few seconds and then shook her head slowly from side to side. "Patrick, getting married isn't the solution. I'm Japanese American! I have no idea what my future holds and neither do you!"

"I know whatever happens will be a challenge, but I want to take care of you; to be with you. I love you! Did you not hear me? I'm very serious, Kim. I would have asked you to marry me even if there wasn't a war going on. If I'm called up, you can live here with my folks until I come home. You'll be safe!"

"You really can't honestly promise me any of those things!" She stood and climbed up the grassy knoll.

"Wait!" He picked up the basket and took her hand.

Hand-in-hand….they walked to the house….both deep in thought.

One evening a week later Kim stretched out on the sofa in the music room listening to Lucy practice the composition she'd written for her upcoming spring recital. The melody was slow; the crescendos soothing. Kim closed her eyes and let the music drift over her and lift her spirits.

"Kim! John's on the phone for you!" Patrick hastily entered the room.

Startled Kim stared up at him. Unable to move. Fear gripped her heart. She finally stood; her body shaking. Patrick walked with her to the study. Franklin was talking with John on the phone while they waited for Kim. When Patrick and Kim entered, Franklin held out the receiver toward her.

Apprehensively, she placed the earpiece against her ear. "Hello?"

"Kim? Hello! This is John. I think Patrick told you I had a colleague in Salinas who has been helping us look for your family?"

"Yes….yes, he did."

"Ralph Morris is his name. Ralph just called and said his friend who works for the War Department was able to obtain a listing of all the Japanese families who registered in Salinas…Hiroto and Sakura Yoshida. Are they your parents? Asami and Akira your sisters?"

"Yes," Kim's voice trembled.

"Your mother and sisters are to report to an assembly center at the Salinas Rodeo Grounds in one week. They'll be transferred elsewhere but Ralph doesn't know when or where."

"And my father?"

"I'm sorry. I don't know. That's all Ralph found out. But I promise he'll keep looking! I'll let you know as soon I hear anything. Okay? Stay strong, Kim. You're in good hands there with my brother and my folks. If there's anything Emily or I can do for you, please let us know."

"Thank you, John." Trembling, Kim handed the phone back to Franklin.

As Franklin said goodbye and hung up the phone, Kim turned and slowly walked toward the stairs. Patrick stepped behind her with intentions to follow.

Franklin caught his arm. "Give her some time to sort this out on her own."

"Sort through what?"

"Sit down, son. I'll tell you what John told me."

The next morning's routine began with chores, work and school as usual. Almost as if no one realized there really was a war going on! Patrick kissed Kim goodbye then climbed behind the wheel of his car. Had an early class and was also tasked taking the twins to Austin High. Maggie was busy organizing some sort of war-effort drive at the church…collecting tin cans, old fur coats, metal objects of all sorts, nylons, old rubber tires…so much to do. As he drove the car down the drive, he stopped at the road and peered into the rearview mirror. Kim stood on the porch, waved and blew a kiss. Patrick felt contentment course through his veins.

Not wanting to waste another minute away from Kim, Patrick ditched his last class. Between classes he had called the Justice of the Peace from the Student Union and scheduled a marriage ceremony for Thursday at two. Kim had not said yes, but she had not refused either. He hoped this would be just the little nudge she needed. Mrs. Kimika Hana Yoshida Bailey…he liked the sound of that….and repeated it three more times. Patrick pushed down on the accelerator and sped home. Turning into the drive, he stopped the car with a screech and jumped out. He ran up the steps and opened the door.

"Kim?" he called directing his voice upward toward the stairs. Not hearing a response, he checked each room downstairs. No one, not even Tia, was to be found. Patrick charged up the back stairs and ran down the hallway to Kim's room. He knocked faintly at the door.

"Kim?" He knocked again more forcefully. "Sweetheart?"

When she didn't answer, he slowly opened the door. The room was tidy and neat, too neat. Frantically he opened the closet…only empty wooden hangers hung on the rod. Kneeling, he looked under the bed. Kim's cases were gone. As Patrick stood, something caught his eye…a yellow envelope leaned against the pillow.

"No! no! no!" He groaned and clinched the envelope before mustering courage to open it. Taking a deep breath, he unfolded the letter and read:

Patrick, my love,

By the time you read this I will be on a train miles away. I'm going home. I know you won't understand but I cannot desert my family. I would feel like a traitor if I accepted your marriage proposal. If I stayed, I would be safe and cherished and have all the love and comforts I've always dreamed while my family faces unknown terrors. I would never want you pulled into my world because you think it honorable or your gentlemanly duty. I know you love me and knowing that is why I must leave. Please, promise me you won't try to find me. You have given me a glimpse of how our lives would have been. You will always be my first love—fierce, noble, compassionate and true. Please search your heart to find someone who loves you much more than I.

Patrick stood slowly. Kim's letter tumbled from his hands and swirled leisurely in the air ultimately landing on the floor at the foot of the bed. He screamed at the top of his lungs and kicked at the bed. He called out Kim's name. Stifling intense anger, he charged down the stairs and out the front door. The door banged behind him. He climbed into his car and started the engine. He needed to clear his head. He backed around and headed out. Destination unknown. Just needed time to let his raging heart cool down. How could two simple pieces of yellow stationery be so explosive and emotionally painful? Hopeful the sound of the tires humming against the pavement would alleviate his hurt and disappointment, Patrick pushed his foot down harder on the gas pedal.

ON THE HOME FRONT
1942

"**M**aggie?"

"In here, Elizabeth. We're in the library."

Elizabeth, her face ashen, stepped into the library. Maggie and Gran sorted through old clothes and coats stacked on the oak table. Two piles lay separated on the floor. One to give to the war-effort collection center to use for making uniforms, tents and bandages; the other set aside to remove buttons and metal fasteners and other decorations before donating them to the cause.

"Elizabeth! What's wrong? You look so pale," Maggie said, pulling out a chair for her sister-in-law.

Elizabeth sat down. She looked up and tears trickled down her cheeks. She held up an envelope with an official Selective Services logo stamped at the top. The small round symbol held a picture of a bald eagle on a dark blue background. The eagle held a banner in its beak bearing the motto "E Pluribus Unum"—out of one, many. Thirteen white stars perched above its head; a shield with the letters SSS stretched across its breast; in its right talon a bundle of thirteen white arrows; in its left a green olive branch.

"Elizabeth?" Maggie asked anxiously.

"It's Owen's. He reports to the Army Air Force recruitment center in Amarillo the end of May. Oh, Maggie, our boy will be..."

"I'll get some coffee," Gran said and left the room.

Maggie put her arms around Elizabeth to console her. "Before this is over, I'm sure more of our boys will be called into service. William volunteered yesterday as a chaplain. He reports in June."

"Oh! I hadn't heard!" Elizabeth gripped Maggie's hand. "And Patrick? Have you heard from him?"

Maggie sat next to Elizabeth, pulled a letter from her apron pocket and handed it over. Elizabeth took it hesitantly and then unfolded the sheet of notepaper and read silently:

Dear Mama and Papa,

I have arrived safely in Salinas. Am staying with Mr. Morris and his family. I was not allowed inside the Rodeo Grounds. There are so many Japanese American families here. One count was over 3,500 people. The area is secured with barbed wire. Guard towers are being erected at each corner. So tragic the way these innocent people of all ages are being treated. It seems Kim's family is no longer here. I don't know if Kim made it here since travel for Japanese is restricted. But knowing Kim, I feel certain she did. Still no word about her father. From Salinas families will be sent further inland…Arizona, Utah, Idaho, or even a few designated places in Texas—Seagoville, Crystal City, Kenedy, Fort Bliss in El Paso and Dodd Field in San Antonio.

I understand why you tried to persuade me not to come. Even Kim asked me not to. But I just couldn't stay home and wonder every day what happened to her. I've contacted UT and have withdrawn from my classes. School just doesn't seem important to me right now. I'll stay here until all of my efforts are exhausted. I've not given up hope.

Love to you both and to the family,

Patrick

Elizabeth handed the letter back to Maggie. The two women gazed at each other. Words were unnecessary for two mothers who knew undoubtedly the sleepless nights, fears and anxieties they would soon face. Maggie reached out for Elizabeth and the two were clinched in an embrace when Gran returned with a coffee service.

"Franklin and the girls just arrived." Gran placed the tray on the table.

Maggie poured three cups of coffee.

"Elizabeth, so nice to see you," Franklin said as he joined the ladies. "We stopped by the mercantile after school. The girls wanted to make a banner and use blue stars to represent each of our family members who are serving. The banner will be displayed in the drugstore window. I think we bought enough flannel and gold cord. I also picked up our ration books and gas stickers. The line at the courthouse wasn't that long. Do you have yours, Elizabeth?"

"Ernie picked ours up yesterday. He was given a "B" gas rationing sticker for his truck. Told me "B" stickers are for essential driving."

"I have a "C" sticker. Guess druggists are placed in the same category as ministers and doctors. Limitless supply until something drastic happens."

"I read "A" stickers only allow four gallons of gas per week. There's a gas shortage on the east coast," Gran said and then chuckled. "If that happens here, I'll wish I'd learned to ride a bicycle!"

Franklin laughed then saw the letter on the table. "Oh, what's that? Selective Service? Whose is it?"

"Owen's."

Franklin took Elizabeth's hand and squeezed it. "And here I've been going on about gas stickers, ration cards and banners. We will add Owen to our church prayer list of our young people who are serving. You've heard about William?"

Elizabeth nodded.

"Oh," Franklin interjected. "I almost forgot! Sam tells me Ernie and Bond Construction have a project coming up in Waco. The War Department leased some acreage to build Blackland Army Airfield to use as a glider airplane training facility. The civil building plans sound impressive—barracks, a mess hall, a church, hospital, administration buildings, and of course plane hangars and a control tower. Sam said they'll be away until the project is completed. You're welcome to stay with us if you or Carter or Grant get lonely."

"Carter's going with Ernie," Elizabeth said sorrowfully. "Grant and I should be fine. But thank you, Franklin, for your offer."

A week later after dinner, the phone in the study rang sharply. Franklin, who'd been shuffling through house bills, picked up the receiver on the third ring.

"Hello?"

"Papa, it's John."

"Son, hello. So good to hear from you. Any news on Kim or her family?"

"Nothing more than they're no longer in Salinas. That's not why I'm calling."

"Everything alright? Emily and Eddie okay?"

"Yes, well...they've been better. Papa, I received my induction letter today. I report to Childress Army Airfield next month on the 15th."

Franklin's heart caught in his throat...took him a second to respond. "Okay, son. You'll be serving right along with William, Clayton, Dottie and Owen. Your country needs all of you now. I know it won't be easy leaving Emily and Eddie. Your mother and I will watch out for them."

"Owen? I hadn't heard."

"Son? I'm proud of you. I pray God keeps you safe."

"Thanks, Papa. Will you tell Mama? I don't think I can."

"Yes, son, I will. I love you."

"Love you, too, Papa."

Franklin hung up the phone and just stared across the room...his mind void of thought. As Maggie, Gran and the girls filed into the study to listen to the radio before bedtime, Franklin forced himself to act as if he'd not talked to John. He wanted to tell Maggie first...later that night...alone.

Gran turned on the radio and dialed the tuner to NBC. *The Bob Hope Show* was starting. She sat down in her chair and propped her feet on the ottoman. Arlo curled on the rug at her feet. Loraine and Lucy sat cross-legged on the floor and laughed whole-heartedly during Bob Hope's first comedy routine.

Franklin lit his pipe. Maggie sat on the sofa and eyed her husband. He didn't seem himself. Was fine at dinner. His mind must be adrift with work-related matters. She turned her attention back to the show as the next skit began.

Bob Hope began, "Boy! Have prices gone up! I went to the market and asked the butcher for a ten-pound turkey. He said, 'Ok, how do you want that financed?'"

Laughter from the live radio audience spilled over the speakers.

"That must be an old joke!" Lucy remarked, "Can't get any kind of meat now without seven ration stamps! Right, Mama?"

Maggie nodded. When the program ended, everyone said their 'good nights' and proceeded upstairs to bed.

"Coming, Franklin?" Maggie asked at the foot of the stairs.

"Yes, sweetheart, in a minute. I'll take Arlo out first."

Franklin opened the front door. Arlo, nose pointed upward, bounded down the porch steps into the black night. Franklin followed the dog to the end of the sidewalk and stopped. He looked up at the sky. The stars….millions of them…twinkled like pinpricks against the black cloudless sky.

"Lord," he prayed. "I know you created these stars and call them each by name. You are the Creator of all things! If You can name billions of stars and know the number of hairs on my head, I know You will watch over my sons and nephew in the days and months and possibly years to come. They are in Your hands…but then I suppose they have always been."

VICTORY CORPS
AND ARIZONA
1942

Sunday afternoon a week later, the twins and their guests...Arnold and Grant...sat on the front porch. Although being a cousin, Grant was more a resident than a guest. The boys had come home with the Baileys after church. The teens discussed current events... national events first and then those more close to home. Lucy sat with Arnie on the swing; Loraine on the top step; Grant the second.

"When are you joining the Victory Corps, Arnie?" Grant asked enthusiastically. "So far it's a lot of discipline! Push-ups, pull-ups, running, discus throwing. We're getting ready for the competition in Houston in December."

"Plan to next week. Had to wait for my dad's approval. He thought football games and football practice were enough physical fitness."

Grant laughed. "Yeah, you'd think so. My baseball coach read an article to us from the United States Office of Education. States before the war high schoolers spent two to three hours a week in physical fitness training. Now with this new initiative and with the war going on, high schoolers will spend five hours a week. Also suggested these five hours be in addition to school-based athletic sports. The purpose is to prepare boys for military training. To build strength, stamina, and endurance while learning to work as a team."

"There're so many more classes to choose from, too. I'm excited about riflery and code navigation," Loraine said.

"Yeah, I'm taking shorthand and first aid," Lucy added.

"Wait!" Grant barked turning to Loraine. "You're taking riflery?"

Loraine frowned and crossed her arms across her chest readying for a fight. "Yeah, so what? Think girls can't shoot?"

Grant smirked, "Nah, I know *you* can. When we go dove hunting, you bring down more birds than any of us! Hey, how's the football team this year, Arnie?"

"Oh, the Maroons are slated for first again this year. We're undefeated. Wanna keep it that way! Funny how high schools are allowed to still play with so many gas rationing restrictions. The coaches were given "B" windshield stickers for necessary driving…eight gallons of gas a week which is about 80 miles of driving. Good thing our games are not far," Arnie laughed.

"The other day Gran shared a newspaper article she'd read about a small town high school. Avid fans there who owned two vehicles offered one of their cars to the school for transporting players and coaches to games," Loraine laughed.

"Gotta love Texas football!" Grant exclaimed.

The four laughed boisterously as a red sedan pulled into the driveway.

"Isn't that Patrick's car?" Arnie asked Lucy. "How long has he been gone?"

"Oh, close to four months."

Patrick got out of his car and trotted up the porch steps. "Hey, there. You guys look like trouble fixin' to hatch!"

"Patrick, there's a letter for you on the table in the vestibule," Loraine said.

"Its return address is Cedar Park. Know any one in Cedar Park?" Lucy asked.

Patrick hesitated a moment then quickly replied, "Yeah…yeah, I do."

Unwilling to answer any further questions, Patrick hurriedly escaped from his inquisitive sisters. He thumbed through the mail his mother kept in a basket on the hallway table. The letter addressed to him was near the bottom. He lifted it carefully as if it were handblown glass. Patrick gripped the envelope tightly and left the house through the French doors in the sunroom. He needed privacy. He walked purposefully to the creek and eased down under an oak tree. The oak's spreading branches offered a covering of solitude to compliment the warm autumn afternoon.

Patrick removed the letter from its envelope. A note was attached:

Patrick,

I received this letter from Kim. Even though she asked that I not share its contents which would surely cause much concern and heartbreak for you, I thought otherwise. You'd want to know.

Janet

Patrick unfolded the three page letter and immediately recognized Kim's handwriting. His eyes blurred as he read:

Janet,

I am finally able to write to you. I trust this letter finds you happily enjoying your fall semester. I mailed the letter to the attention of our resident hall director. I dared not send it to your home. I did not want to cause any more trouble for you.

My life has turned into a ghastly nightmare. When I arrived in Salinas, I had no trouble finding the rodeo grounds. In fact, I was escorted to the grounds from the train station along with a couple of German families who were on the train with me. We were taken to the holding center and our names placed on the War Department's alien registry. I think my parents assumed I would stay in Texas.

It took three days to find my mother and sisters in the camp. My mother, even though she fussed at me for coming, was eventually grateful I did. My father was arrested because he had been born in Japan. Under U.S. Immigration Laws he was never allowed to become a U.S. citizen. We are still uncertain where he is. My mother, too, was born in Japan. Because she had young children and I suppose not considered a threat to the U.S., was not arrested.

After living in make-shift tents, a large group of us were transported by train to Poston, Arizona. If you thought Texas summers were hot, let me say they are a welcomed cool breeze compared to desert heat. My mother, sisters and I were placed in the second grouping of three camps. Each camp is exactly three miles apart and three miles from the Colorado River which is just outside our camp's barbed-wired perimeter.

We understand these three camps were built on the Colorado River Indian Reservation. The Indian Tribal Council objected to our being treated as they had and wanted nothing to do with our internment. The army officials overruled the Bureau of Indian Affairs so here we are.

The internees jokingly named the camps Roastin', Toastin', and Dustin'. I live in Toastin' which sounds homier than Poston Camp 2.

Our barracks is divided into six apartments. Each compartment has sleeping cots, a wood-burning stove and an overhead light. The restrooms, showers, laundry barracks, and mess halls are located in different areas around camp and thankfully within easy walking distance.

I teach music at the children's school to a class of 30 ten-year-olds. There are so many of us here with valuable skills and talents. We just find something we know how to do and do it. Whatever our trades were on the outside, we have incorporated them here on the inside.

Don't misunderstand. Our living conditions are far from ideal but we are complacent, trying to demonstrate our loyalty to the United States by complying with her rules. I've heard we will be interned for the duration of the war however long that will be. We remain hopeful that won't be too long.

Patrick's letter left for me at the Salinas center was forwarded to me here. In his letter he promised to search every camp until he found me. What if he had found me? What then? Nothing would happen. Nothing could change.

I hurt him deeply. Please, Janet, do not tell Patrick where I am. If you should see him at school, just tell him I am well and wish him my very best. Knowing he has moved on and is happy will make me equally happy.

I'll always remain your dearest friend,

Kim

Patrick wadded the sheets of paper in a ball and thought of tossing them into the creek but then changed his mind. He dropped the wad on the ground between his legs and leaned back against the tree. Drawing up his legs, he rested his hands on his knees and closed his eyes. His only thoughts were of Kim. He groaned inwardly thinking of her and the undesirable living conditions under which she now lived. From the outside of the compound fences, he had seen for himself the living conditions in Salinas and also the camp in Utah. He would never forget the sadly defeated faces and undisguised broken spirits of the people there.

"Patrick?" At the sound of his name, Patrick's eyes jolted open.

"May I join you?" Loraine asked.

"Free country...or well, it used to be."

Loraine eased down beside him and noticed the tightly crunched ball of paper on the ground. She picked up a stone and tossed it toward the trickling water. The stone bounced over a mound of tall grass, plunged into the shallows and was quickly swallowed up in a large gurgle.

"Never good at skimmimg stones. Better with a rifle."

Patrick smiled. "Easier if you're standing."

"Why is it society rather than our hearts choose whom we are to love?"

Patrick regarded her carefully. "That's quite profound for a kid."

"I'm hardly a kid any more."

"Hmmm, guess not. Speaking from experience?"

"Maybe."

"Want to talk about it?"

"No. How about you?"

"No," Patrick laughed. "Guess we share similar miseries then."

Loraine leaned against her brother's shoulder as he put his arm around her. Sitting under the tree, they remained another thirty minutes wallowing wordlessly; drowning in their own self-pity and heartache.

INDUCTIONS AND
MAIL SERVICE
1942

Franklin rushed into the music room where Maggie was sitting on the sofa darning a pair of socks. He hurried to the phone sitting on the end table and picked it up.

"Art's on the line."

Maggie rose quickly and listened as Franklin held the receiver between them.

"Gran and the girls are on the line in the study," Franklin said. "Go ahead, son, we are all here. Except for Patrick. He'll be in later."

"Hello, family!" Art's voice was strong and clear.

"How are you?" Maggie asked. "And Rosa and the children?"

"We are well. Alex and Vicky are growing like little dandelion weeds."

"And the De Leóns?" Franklin asked.

"Yes, yes, everyone here is fine. I'm calling 'cause I wanted to tell you this over the phone rather than in a letter. Texas Congressman Richard Kleberg...you remember meeting him at our wedding?"

"Yes," Franklin replied. "Of course."

"Well, Congressman Kleberg and U.S. Congressman Lyndon Johnson petitioned Roosevelt in 1940 when Germany took over France to use land on the Corpus Christi Bay as a naval air training station. The flat terrain and the suitable all-year-round weather are perfect for pilot training. The first graduating pilots received their wings in November last year."

"Seems a reasonable plan," Franklin interjected. Maggie raised her brows curiously. Franklin shrugged his shoulders in response.

"The War Department is also using the unimproved land on Ward Island. Their purpose is unclear. The Coast Guard is acquiring horses for all U.S. beaches. Seems an odd request for seafarers but must be important. King Ranch is leasing some of their stock to the cause and Congressman Kleberg has arranged for me and Rosa's younger brother, Roman, to volunteer with the Coast Guard on Padre Island to protect his investment."

"What?" Maggie blurted. "You're joining the Coast Guard?"

"Yes, Mama, but only as a beach patrol volunteer. I'll be in Corpus. Still near Rosa and the kids."

Maggie gripped Franklin's arm.

"What color will your uniform be?" Lucy asked.

Loraine elbowed her sister and whispered, "That's hardly important!"

"I'm not sure," Art laughed. "I'll send a picture."

"Yes, do! We'll put it on the map in the library. We have push pins indicating where everyone is located and will add another blue star to our service banner," Loraine added excitedly.

"Do you even know how to swim?" Lucy teased.

Art laughed, "Probably not as well as I should. Not much practice here."

"And how is Rosa coping?" Maggie asked.

"As you can imagine. Thankfully she has her family close by. Roman and I leave for Port Arthur in three days for three-weeks of volunteer patrol training. Just wanted to tell each of you how much I love you. When I have a mailing address, I'll let you know."

"Goodbye, Art. We love you," the twins replied in unison.

"Grandson, take care of you," Gran, eyes glistening, said with a smile.

"Son, your mother and I love you very much. Our thoughts and prayers are with you always," Franklin said as Maggie gripped his arm.

"I love you, Art," Maggie finally sputtered as the other line clicked off.

****

"Maggie? The mail has come." Franklin carried a small package under his arm and a handful of letters in his hand as he backed through the kitchen door.

He placed the bundles on the table. Maggie, Tia and the girls were making Christmas wreaths out of pine branches and red ribbon. Lucy reached out to snatch a letter to see where it was from, but pulled her hand back when her father frowned.

Maggie leafed through the letters and pulled out a mustard-brown colored envelope. "Oh, how I dread these colored envelopes from the War and Navy Department! What does this mean, Franklin?" Maggie held up the envelope.

"Let me see. Oh, V-Mail Service…short for Victory Mail. It's what the Armed Services requests for guaranteed mail delivery to servicemen overseas. There are special forms at the post office. The letters have to be typed or printed. Then they're microfilmed. The film is transported to the appropriate military station to be reproduced and delivered to the addressee. Cuts down on the volumes of letters being transported on our aircrafts. Frees more space for supplies and men."

"Who's it from?" Lucy asked impatiently.

"It's from Clayton!" Maggie smiled brightly. "I'll read it."

Ahoy!

Thinking of you all. Must be Christmas time there. I miss the smell of pine and all the family festivities. Mostly I miss the cakes, pies, and cookies! Can't tell you where I am or the name of my ship. Just know I'm surrounded by water! According to this new mail delivery service, you may send packages only if I specifically request something.

So please send white socks, peppermints, sugar cookies and
pictures! The package is for the girls. Happy birthday to
my little munchkins. Missing you all terribly and Merry
Christmas!

Your favorite sailor, Clayton

"That's ours?" Loraine asked excitedly.

Franklin pushed the box closer to the girls. Lucy glanced at her
sister. Then together the girls ripped at the sides of the brown-paper
wrapping. Loraine popped open the top of the box and peeked inside.
Amused, she turned the box toward Lucy. Grinning broadly, Lucy
pulled out two white sailor hats.

"Happy birthday to me! I'm wearing mine to the Christmas dance!"
Lucy exclaimed as she placed a white hat…rolled brim with a high-
domed top…on the side of her head. Loraine giggled.

****

Dear William,

I got your address from Netty. I just couldn't let the season pass without
wishing you a Merry Christmas and a Happy New Year!

My semester exams are over and am confident I did well. I'm
attending Mary Hardin-Baylor rather than your beloved Baylor. Am
I considered a traitor? Purple looks better against my red hair than
does gold. Hard to believe I'm almost through.

I'm sure Netty told you Gwen and Bob eloped November 15th.
When Bob received his induction letter from the Army Airforce,
the two were married that very afternoon. My parents disapproved.
Thought they should have waited until after the war. But if you
could see those two together, getting married was the right thing.
Bob leaves for boot camp in February. Niles, not wanting to be the
last man standing, joined the Navy. He leaves for basics around the
same time.

So does the War Department really read all of these V-mail letters before they're filmed? I'll be mindful of what I say.

Take care, William
Caroline Hawkins

****

Dearest Uncle Franklin and Aunt Maggie,

Well, here I am. Finally settled into pre-flight training school in Lubbock. Flat as a pancake here. Nothing to see for miles and miles except acres and acres of cotton and sorghum fields. Sometimes an occasional tumbleweed pushed by whirlwinds of stinging red dirt skitters by to some unknown destination. But I must admit...the night sky is incredible. Almost like living within a snowglobe of twinkling stars. The residents are incredibly friendly and welcoming.

With housing being scarce, we've been put up in two of the men's dormitories, Sneed Hall and West Hall, on the Texas Technological campus. I'm in Sneed. The building is a three-story brick with a Spanish tile roof. Reminds me of Rosa's house in Kingsville. I share my room with a guy from Arkansas whose name is Bennett but prefers to be called Bullet. Nice guy. Funny, too. We each have a long twin bed, a desk for studying, and a chest for clothes. At least I don't have to worry about my big feet hanging off the end of the mattress. Our dorm buildings have been roped off with signs that read "Posted Military Training Site. No Trespassing." Makes us feel eery and special all at the same time.

Exercise is key. We march everywhere—around campus; to and from classes; up and down the red-bricked streets of downtown and even run in formation along a railroad track near campus that stretches for miles. At least there's no uphill marching. Physical training is absurb but necessary.

Due to the number of male students and professors leaving to join the armed services, the students and professors here are mostly female. The college students have been instructed not to mingle with us. Our classes are timed so that we don't even see other students between classes. Feels like we're the only ones here.

The army-air force doesn't have enough military pilot instructors available to train new cadets so civilian instructors were hired. Some of the cadets train at Breedlove Field on 50th Street. The rest of us train at Dagley Field on 34th Street. The city is easy to navigate....streets run perpendicular north to south and east to west. Lubbock's founding fathers used a foolproof grid...that's for certain.

I have four more months of training before I graduate. The first month is completed. I'm studying hard to pass these pre-training class courses. My end goal...getting my wings. Can't wait to climb into the cockpit and see the cotton fields and the canyon north of town from the air.

The canyon is called Yellow House and is rich in history. Goes back to the real cowboys and Indian days. Well actually buffalo hunter days. There was a big skirmish between the hunters and the Indians in the canyon. According to the buffalo hunters, raids by the Indians were unprovoked. The Indians were just protecting their livelihood.... the buffalo. War...one side against the other for whatever the supposed great cause....is hardly anything new.

There's also a glider training facility here at South Plains Army Airfield. I understand the gliders are made in Waco! The gliders, as you'd suppose, are non-motorized and weigh 3,900 pounds. Each can carry 9,000 pounds. A tow plane hauls them in the air and releases them to complete their mission. Imagine the enemies' surprise when supplies and men are landed silently behind their lines.

It's almost chowtime and study hall is in an hour. So I must end this letter. Was relieved and thankful to hear Grayson and Annie are finally home!

Flying high, Owen

****

Maggie lay on her back staring at the ceiling. Unable to sleep, she counted imaginary sheep. Once the wooly animals jumped over the fictional white picket fence, they suddenly morphed into faceless soldiers and airmen. But they weren't faceless. Each bore the face of one of her sons or her niece or her nephew. She rolled to her side and punched the pillow with her fist.

"Maggie?" Franklin whispered. "Sweetheart? Can't sleep? It's going to be all right. Our boys will be okay."

Maggie sniffled. "Patrick's leaving tomorrow to go with Ernie, Sam and Carter to Lackland Field in San Antonio."

"Yes, but only until the barracks and mess halls are built."

"All our boys…Franklin…all of them. Only the girls remain."

"Maggie, don't fret so. We must stay strong and not lose hope."

Franklin held Maggie until she fell asleep. He must stay strong for her above all else. His fear and anxiety would take a back seat. A hymn suddenly filled his thoughts. "Onward Christian Soldiers." How did it go? He began to sing softly.

'Onward Christian soldiers, marching as to war. With the cross of Jesus going on before; Christ, the royal Master, leads against the foe; Forward into battle, see his banners go…..' With God's help, he must become that kind of brave soldier on the home front.

COAST GUARD PADRE ISLAND *1943*

The Willys Overland four-wheel-drive jeep bounced, jerked and jostled over and across the sand dunes. The driver snickered as the passenger in the back held tightly to the bar used for attaching an overhead canvas. The rider braced the bar in a death-grip as if his life depended on it. And perhaps it did. Loose sand kicked up under the tires as the driver shifted into the next highest gear. The jeep practically flew over the next dune, descended toward the hardpacked sand and came to an abrupt stop near a wooden structure built on four-foot stilts.

A young man dressed in blue trousers and a khaki short-sleeved shirt hurried down the hut's steps and ran toward the jeep.

"You made it!" he exclaimed. "Hey, Skinny, why did you come over the dunes and not use the road?"

"Thought you said he was a bronc rider. Wanted him to feel at home!"

The passenger disembarked and pulled his duffle bag and bedroll from the jeep's floorboard. The driver slid from behind the wheel and readjusted his navy-blue Coast Guard hat over his blonde windblown hair.

"Sure you didn't put Skinny up to it?" The passenger asked with a grin.

The young man grabbed the newcomer around the neck. "Good to see ya, Roman!"

"You, too, Art! Nice surroundings!"

"Yeah, the beach is the best! Did you meet Skinny?"

"Avery Tanner." Skinny nodded toward Roman and chuckled. "Sure you're a bronc rider?"

"Roman De León. Yeah, I am a bronc rider and you gave me a good ride!"

"I'll leave you two lovebirds. Need some shuteye. I have night duty. Show him around, will ya, Mozart? See ya later, Bronco."

"You bet. Thanks for bringing Roman down, Skinny."

Stretching six-foot-five on long, gangly legs, Tanner, looked as if his torso might also sit on stilts. He ran up the four steps to his quarters hoping for some sleep before his scheduled night duty began.

"Mozart?" Roman asked.

"Yeah…you know…Art…Mozart." Art grinned. "Everyone here has a nickname. Hopalong shares that half of the hut with Skinny. Hopalong's name is Hugh Cassidy…thus…"

"Hopalong!" Roman laughed.

"Later you'll meet Curly. The man can't claim a single hair on his head! Shaves it every other day! What a card! He'll bring our mares over tomorrow."

"Where are the horses? Any of them from the Ranch?"

"The four we handle are. They're housed in make-shift stables built on the other side of the dunes. Each stable houses four horses…two day shift, two night shift. Same number as the men in each hut. The huts are situated six miles apart. Telephone lines connect each hut allowing quick responses to alarms, shipwreck survivors, or U-boat sightings."

"Shipwreck survivors? You're serious?"

"Yeah, there's been a couple of rescues at Port Arthur and further north on Padre. The German boats sit in the water like alligators with only their eyes visible above the waterline patiently waiting for innocent prey. The Germans torpedo our cargo ships filled with oil or gasoline in broad daylight as the ships leave port. That's not broadcasted to the public. Don't want to cause panic. Come on. Let me show you to your living quarters for the next eight months."

Roman followed Art into the hut. The structure was built like a duplex. Each compartment held a bunk and a small closet for each man; a kitchenette with table and chairs; and two lounging chairs. The windows had drop-down coverings that were usually propped open with dowel rods. Showers were accessible at the stables. Outside a canopy stretched across one side of the hut and was attached to a six-foot fence where the jeep was sheltered when not in use.

"This is your bed and closet. Your uniform is hung there. It must be worn when you're on duty. I laughed at myself when I first put mine on. Stow your gear and I'll take you to see the horses."

Art and Roman headed toward the stables and topped the dunes easily. Tall green grasses stood together in clumps at the tops of the dunes. Their long feathery spikes blowing side-to-side in the breeze were filled with seed heads and looked similar to wheat plants. Low-growing ground cover showcasing small pink flowers on grayish-green succulent leaves snaked across the loose sand.

"Curly?" Art called when they reached the covered stables. "Want you to meet my brother-in-law."

A man's bald head appeared over the last stall's railing where he busily brushed a reddish-brown chestnut mare. Curly exited the stall and his absence of hair was replaced with a self-assurance that oozed from his sweaty, muscular arms.

Curly extended his hand. "Mason Irons. Glad to meet ya."

"Roman De León."

"Mason is a Seaman in the Coast Guard. But insists we not call him Seaman Irons. Just wants to be one of us. Hugh Cassidy is also a Seaman...we along with Skinny are volunteers." Art explained.

"You'll be on patrol with Art beginning tomorrow 0600. Fourteen hour shifts. There's a rifle, binoculars, water canteen and HT in your quarters."

"HT?" Roman asked, embarrassed he was unfamiliar with the item.

"Oh, a hand-talkie. We use it to communicate back to the main

Coast Guard station at Port Aransas," Art explained. "We'll ride together for the first few days. Then ride solo afterwards."

"Oh, you need to meet your riding partner." Curly turned toward the stables.

"Tiny?" Curly called, taking long strides toward the first enclosure.

"Tiny?" Roman asked curiously. "Art, I thought you were my partner."

Art laughed as he watched Roman's eyes enlarge in surprise. A dog, or perhaps a small colt, unfurled her long legs and stood. The dog, who measured three-feet tall from the pads of her front paws to the top of her head, strolled gracefully through the gate. Her color was mottled black; her countenance regal. The dog snuggled under Curly's elbow and looked up waiting for a command.

"Tiny," Curly said, "meet Roman."

The Great Dane walked up to Roman, sat and extended her front foreleg.

"What? She wants to shake hands?" Roman guffawed. He took the dog's paw and shook it. "Hello, girl."

Curly smiled broadly. "This dog will be your four-footed guard to accompany you on patrols. She's well trained. I know that for a fact. I trained her."

Roman patted the dog's massive head. Her long, black silky ears bore splotches of white over each tip like salt sprinkled freely from a salt-shaker.

"Better get a good meal at the station and get some sleep. You start early. I'll bring Greta Garbo and Bette Davis over in the morning."

Roman looked about quizzically. Art laughed. "Our mounts. Greta is the chestnut; Bette there in the fourth stall, a bay."

"So I suppose it's hopeless to ask for a Dolores del Rio or Maria Félix?"

Art clapped Roman's back robustly. "Yes, hermano, that would be!"

As the two walked toward the mess hall, a plane banked overhead, lowering in altitude as it directed its flight path toward Padre Island.

"Wow! He's kinda close, isn't he?" Roman asked, shading his eyes to observe the four-engine plane.

"You'll get use to them. It's a B-17…Boeing makes them. The planes have practice bombing targets further south on the island."

"No kidding! Real bombs?"

"Not big ones! Marty, one of the crewman I had dinner with last week…a tail gunner…said the targets are spaced five miles apart. They're large white bull's eyes of concentric circles constructed with white rocks and spaced 100 yards apart. The bombs are only powerful enough for the pilots to check their accuracy. Some of the bombs are only filled with water and sand. Marty said the Mark IV bomb is most often used. Only nine inches long with a 40-gauge shotgun shell in its nose."

"I never thought about where pilots learned to drop bombs with skilled accuracy! And I never imagined it would be so close to home!"

"Yeah, I know! Learned a lot from Marty and his buddies. I didn't know that each plane has up to a ten-man crew including the bombardier, navigator, radio man and two pilots. He was funny laughing about how after each bomb run, a ground crew has to rebuild or repair the damaged target. The navy personnel are housed at the Caffey Barracks if you ever want to meet them. Interesting guys."

The next morning before the sun had stirred the calm ocean ripples into rolling swells, Roman and Art emerged from their side of the duplex. They each donned the standard navy blue Coast Guard uniform. Trousers and matching long-sleeved billowy cotton shirts. Similar to naval uniforms, the collars were large, draped over their shoulders and rested against their backs. The two ends of a navy-colored silk tie streamed down from their necklines. Buckskin-colored leggings covered their black boots. Unlike the sailor's white hats, the Coast Guard's hats were navy blue with a flat, billowing-looking top. 'U.S. Coast Guard' stitched in white across the breadth of the wide band identified the armed service.

Greta and Bette were saddled and waiting. Tiny stood rigidly beside the horses as if standing at attention, eager to begin patrol. Roman and Art loaded their gear and mounted the horses….Art on Greta; Roman astride Bette. Art pulled Greta's reins to the right to travel south and

Roman followed. Roman looked down and smiled. Tiny plodded along beside Bette; their gaits synchronized motion.

Patrolling hour on end underneath the blazing hot sun required copious amounts of water and more importantly…patience. Every six miles or so, the riders dismounted. Fresh water readily available at each hut was a relief and a necessity. Roman pulled both sets of binoculars from the saddle bags while Art filled their canteens with fresh water. The animals quenched their thirsts at the water trough.

Art removed his sunglasses and scanned the horizon through the binoculars Roman handed him. The sun's unmerciful brilliance cast blinding pulses of light upon the waves. Hard to see anything clearly without squinting. He replaced his sunglasses and regretted not having his cowboy hat to shade his face and eyes.

His brother-in-law, too, was watching the horizon through binoculars. But Roman's interest centered on a black osprey as it dove head first into the waves. The bird tightly folded its wings up against its body forming a silhouette any Olympic high-diver might emulate. At thirty-feet or more in the air, the osprey dove toward the water. A death dive…a missile projectory. At the last second with outstretched talons, the bird plunged under the rolling waves. A few seconds later the victor erupted from the foamy wave with a captured fish wriggling within its claws. Spreading its massive wings, the bird flew away.

Roman grinned. "Wow! That was something! Wish it were as easy for us to detect U-boats as it is for those birds to spot fish!"

"Our jobs would definitely be much easier!" Art agreed.

"What is it the U-boat is called in German?"

"Unterseeboot," Art answered and then laughed.

"Yeah, that's it! Under the sea boat! I should've remembered that! I was amazed when I learned a German submarine travels 13,000 nautical miles without refueling, has massive aircraft guns, and houses 22 torpedos."

"That's why we're on the lookout for them!" Art exclaimed.

"Oh, wait! What's that long-legged bird there at the edge of the water?"

"A heron, I believe."

"Amazing!" Roman grinned.

Art returned a smile and thought how the ocean must seem strange and somewhat foreign to this man who grew up on flat terrain covered in cacti and mesquite trees. And the Rio Grande the only large body of water to be seen for miles. But then, how could a river, even if 1,900 miles in length, be possibly comparable to the ocean?

A couple days later, Curly entered the hut where Roman and Art were resting after dinner. A male Great Dane trotted obediently by the Seaman's side.

"Boys! Want you to meet Archie! He's Tiny's brother. Art, he'll be accompanying you on patrol tonight."

The massive dog with inquisitive dark brown eyes inspected the two men lying in their bunks. He shook his massive head as if he understood exactly what Curly said. Archie was solid black. Unlike Tiny, not a spot or sliver of white was found on his body. And he stood at least four inches taller and weighed ten pounds heavier. Tiny, who was sprawled underneath Roman's bunk, eased herself out and curiously approached her brother. The dogs sniffed each other amicably.

Art rolled off his bed and knelt in front of the big dog. In this position, they sat eye to eye. Art scruffed Archie's ears. "Well, hello there, big guy. Coming with me tonight? I'll have to put a bell around your neck. You'll be hard to see."

As Art leaned slightly, but much too closely, Archie graciously bequeathed one large, obligatory slurpy swipe of his wet tongue across his new handler's face.

"Hey!" Roman laughed. "Not on your first date!"

Curly laughed and slapped his leg. "Okay, suit up. Your shift starts in fifteen. Your ladies are waiting outside."

With that being as close to an order as Curly ever commanded, Art and Roman put on their uniforms. With gear loaded, Art rode south with Archie. Tiny and Roman headed north. Art looked forward to every minute of night duty.

Around twenty-three hundred, or 11:00pm, Art pulled Greta to a halt and dismounted. Archie stood at attention awaiting a command. Art rubbed the dog's head and slipped the reins over Greta's head.

Leading Greta by her reins, Art strolled down the beach to stretch his legs. Archie walked beside him step-for-step as if the two were best friends or at least, colleagues. The moon's light reflected off the ocean's waves. Art closed his eyes and listened to the water as its low tumblings gathered into a wave, crescendoed in sound, and crashed against the shore. He opened his eyes in time to see the foamy water quickly receding leaving bubbles and small living crustaceans in its wake.

Art breathed in deeply. Majestic…was the only adjective he could think of to adequately describe the vastness of the ocean. It should never be described nor considered an inanimate object. It had a life of its own. Always moving, churning, rising, falling, receding, rumbling, carrying oxygen, life and sustenance for God's living creatures….high above and far beneath the depths below. And it provided transportation from continent to continent….transportation! Art cast his daydreaming aside and concentrated on the waters. Nothing out of the ordinary.

Art mounted Greta and turned north. After riding slowly for thirty-minutes, he saw flickers of light on the horizon. Before he could determine its origin, a voice sounded on his HT.

"Station One to Station Eight…come in…over."

"Station Eight…over."

"Alert! I repeat alert! Station One sighting! Alert!"

"Alert received. Over and out."

Art tied his HT onto the saddle horn and removed his rifle from the scabbard which hung from the saddle. His muscles tensed as he viewed the horizon with his binoculars more closely. Station One was Port Aransas. A U-boat had been spotted. Port Aransas sat on the mouth of Corpus Christi Bay less than forty miles away. There could be more submarines out there! Germans this close could send skiffs ashore on reconnaissance scouting missions.

The moon cast enough light to see dark shadows skimming across the waves. Using the binoculars, Art scanned the perimeter again paying more attention to the waves rolling in from the third sandbar—a build-up of course sediment deposited by the waves and aligned in varied distances from shore.

Almost two hours elapsed before Art glimpsed flashes of light coming from Aransas Pass to the north. The light seemed almost pulsating...short beads of light followed by longer ones. A blinker-tube? The navy used gun-like blinker tubes to communicate in morse code from ship to shore. The tube which also had a mounted scope was attached to a gun stock and easily braced against a shoulder. The signal man pulled the string mounted on the aluminum tube quickly for a dot; a longer pull for a dash. Pauses were used to separate letters.

Art studied the light and tried to recall what few letters he knew of morse code. He pulled up his binoculars and repeated the letters to his companions. Archie sniffed the air as if he, too, could decifer morse code.

"Dash—dot—dash—dot...space. That, I believe, Archie, is a C; dot—dash—dot—dot...space. L; dot..space...an E; not sure about the last two letters, boy," Art apologized to Archie whose nose still pointed north.

A sound of static rang from the HT hanging over the saddle horn. Art immediately picked it up.

"Station One to Station Eight...come in. Over."

Art replied, "Station Eight. Come in Station One...over."

"All clear. I repeat all clear. Over."

"Received. All clear. Over and out."

Art checked the time on his wristwatch...0530. Wasn't really necessary to look at his watch to know the time; the sun's rays crept over the invisible line where the ocean links with the sky and slowly streaked the cobalt blue expanse with warm hues of pale oranges and pastel blues. Two hours still remained on his shift. Art pulled Greta's reins to the right, kicked her sides lightly and the horse loped south on the hardened shoreline sands. Archie ran beside them; his ears flapping against his head. As if needing reassurance, the dog glanced up three times at the rider who sat completely at ease in the saddle.

"Good job tonight, Arch!" The dog shook his head in approval.

With their shift concluded, Art and his two-animal patrol team headed back to camp. Roman, Skinny, and Hopalong soon joined them. With an all alert signal, all four men were called out on patrol.

Skinny's and Hopalong's canine patrol partners were two male German shepherds....Popeye and Bluto.

"What a night!" Roman announced removing his hat and sitting on the bottom step of his hut.

"Anybody hear what happened?" Hopalong asked.

All four men turned their heads as a motor vehicle advanced steadily toward them. Curly braked the jeep with a screech and got out.

"Great work tonight, men!" Curly's voice was still adrenaline-filled from the evening's event.

"What happened?" Skinny asked.

"Talked to the Seaman in charge at Station One. Smoke was seen offshore about hundred-fifty feet out. Seems the Germans were using smoke bombs to communicate. The Coast Guard immediately sent out their clipper that docks at the port and is always ready to sail. The U-boats slipped away but there were four Germans found trying to hide a skiff in the dunes. They were arrested by the Guard."

"That was a close one!" Hopalong exclaimed. "The Gulf of Mexico is a large body of water....the largest gulf in the world! Who would ever think the Germans could get this close inward. What were they up to, I wonder?"

"Just casing the coastlines and the port; counting oil tankers; seeing best places to send in spies," Skinny answered.

"The mayors and city officials up and down the coast from Aransas Pass to Brownsville have been reminded to warn their residents about mandatory blackouts....turning off all lights at night. Even a car's headlight or a simple lamp by a window is like a welcoming beacon to those devils sitting out in the ocean," Curly expounded. "I'm driving my jeep up and down the coastline for a couple more hours. You four... get some shuteye after you stable these horses. Stay alert! Tomorrow's a new day."

LETTERS FROM HOME
1944

Dear William,

I wanted you to be the first to know I have accepted a 5th grade teaching position at Nolanville Elementary School. Located in...where else? The small community of Nolanville. If you're driving down their main street and happen to blink or sneeze, you'd miss the entire four blocks of downtown! I will stay in Belton and continue renting a house with my college roommate Glenna Harper. I'll be teaching two reading classes and three music classes. I'm over-the-rainbow excited.

Have received two letters from Niles. Reports he is doing well. Says he keeps his head down and the decks spotlessly clean. Bob is somewhere in Italy. He doesn't tell Gwen much. Guess, it's better we don't know although movie theaters bombard us with action-packed news reels. It's hard enough to read newspaper articles about what's going on rather than actually seeing them. We worry enough about our servicemen without seeing those clips. You are included in our little worry club.

Gwen and I are invited at least twice a month to Emily's for Sunday dinner. I see Eddie often. He's growing taller and is quite the checker player. I must admit I struggle to keep up with him. He always seems to be three plays ahead of me.

Write when you can. I look forward to hearing from you.
Your friend,
Caroline

****

My love,

It's eleven here. I'm lying in bed reading. Helps keep my mind occupied with other things other than worrying about you.

I'm fairly busy at work. Regular stuff….headaches, cramps, sprains, sore throats, colds, heartbreaks. What other ailments might be expected at a women's college? I see Olivia Crandall almost every day. I treasure her friendship. My recently acquired friendships with Gwen Hawkins Clemson and Caroline Hawkins have also attributed to my not going completely bonkers. Eddie has developed an attachment to Caroline. She shares his love of sports, checkers, and hot dogs.

Can you believe our baby is thirteen? I certainly cannot! An eighth grader! He has tried out for the baseball team and I'm certain he will be selected. But then I'm only his mom!

Oh, John, I miss you so terribly. Especially at night. My bed is so empty without you. I hope you are safe and at least have a warm place to sleep. I'm trying to stay strong as you've asked, but some days are just too difficult.

Counting the days 'til your return.
I love you dearly,
Emily

****

Daddy,

I asked Mom not to seal her envelope until I had finished my letter. I guess she told you I tried out for third baseman. Coach Henderson said I have a good chance. Belton Junior High had a so-so team last year so I hope to make a difference. Uncle Patrick helps with my batting.

Mom tries. But the balls she pitches bounce before reaching the plate. She needs practice! Don't tell her I said that.

With so many major league baseballers and managers entering the war, a new league of women-only teams started up last year. I listen to their games on the radio. I like the Milwaukee Chicks, the Racine Belles, and the Rockford Peaches. One twenty-two-year-old from California, Annabelle Lee, pitches for the Minneapolis Millerettes. She pitches left-handed, uses an underhand fast pitch and a knuckleball. Would love to see her play in person. But all the games are played on the east coast.

School is fine. I like all my teachers especially my English teacher, Miss Alderson. Coach Henderson teaches science. No nonsense with him on or off the field. There's this one girl, Cathy Richards, who sits by me in math class. Her hair smells nice. She has freckles on her nose. I think she likes me!

I miss you, Daddy. Sandy is sitting beside me and wagged her stumpy tail. Misses you, too.

Your son, Eddie

****

Hello Art,

I'm writing to you because I know you above all our other brothers will appreciate my new weekend interest. I've peeked your curiosity, haven't I?

Remember the creek that runs along Oak Hill? Archie Patton, the owner of that stretch of land, turned a portion of it into a race track. Started out for mule or donkey racing. Then dog racing and jalopy racing. Now it's quarter-horse racing.

My friend, Tommy North, took me to see the races and they were so exciting! With no lights out there, they run only on afternoons. The track is open from March to September. Three or four horses at a time race on a quarter-mile oval track. After watching the races, I was certain Honey could outrun any horse on the track. Grant encouraged me to sign up. Santos designed a racing saddle for me and is giving me well-needed riding tips. I race on Sundays and have won three weekends in a row.

Mother, of course, thinks racing is not a lady-like undertaking especially on Sundays. She insists Lucy and I start thinking about college and what we want to study. I tease her that I plan to live with you and Rosa in Kingsville and work on the Ranch. She just frowns. I have no idea what I want to do the rest of my life.

Hope you are doing well.

Love you, big brother,

Your horse-race-loving baby sister, Loraine

****

Dear Clayton,

I'm writing from my English class. Supposed to be studying a 50-word vocabulary list, but writing to you is more fun.

Carter just received his induction letter into the Navy. Aunt Elizabeth is beside herself with worry. This of course means another pin to add to our map and another blue star to our banner.

Doc Lawrence works at the hospital in Temple twice a month. Because of the shortage of army hospitals, McCloskey General was designated an amputee rehabilitation center. Grayson and Anne volunteer three days a week. Grayson serves as a chaplain and Anne helps in food service. The hospital grounds are like a small city...fifty-four buildings connected by covered walkways.

Doc encouraged me to come with him on Saturdays to play piano in one of the physical therapy rooms. Said my playing would be great therapy for the recuperating soldiers. I only play upbeat songs. These men have enough sorrow and distress in their lives without hearing some sappy love-found-love-loss piece.

There's this one Army private who would often linger after PT and wheel his wheelchair near the piano. Introduced himself as Stumpy. Had lost his right leg from the knee down. He'd sing along as I played. His voice was as loud as the smile stretched across his face. His favorite song was "Mairzy Doats." You know…mares eats oats; does eat oats; little lambs eat ivy; kids will eat ivy, too; wouldn't you?…that song? Stumpy would sometimes lead four or five soldiers in a musical round. Loved hearing his vocal accompaniment (side note…that's a word on my vocabulary list.) Guess I should close now. Mrs. Armstrong keeps peering over the bridge of her glasses at me. Someday those glasses are going to slide right off!

Stay safe.

Love you, Clayton,

Your loving sister, Lucy

MAIL CALL
1944

Thursday mid-morning aboard the *USAHS (United States Army Hospital Ship) Thistle*, a soft knuckle-rapping sounded on the chaplain's compartment door.

"Padre?" a man called.

"Come in, Seaman." William, sitting at his desk, turned to greet his visitor.

"Mail call, sir." The sailor opened the door; a package tucked under his arm; a canvas letter bag slung over his shoulder. "The package is yours."

William stood. "Wonderful! Hopefully, Gran sent more homemade cookies."

"Yes, sir. The return address is Belton. Is that your home town?"

"No, Oak Hill. Let me see." William took the package and popped the top open. The box was filled with letters.

"Thank you, Seaman Gibson."

"Yes, sir. Shall I close the door?"

"Yes, thank you." William removed the top letter on the stack and sat back down. He glanced at the signature line....Caroline. He leaned back in his chair and a smile materialized as he rearranged the pages. Another letter from Caroline. He received more letters from her than any of his family members...except his mother, of course. He quickly read:

"William,

Surprise! These letters are from my students. Please distribute them to the young men under your care. Many of my students have family members serving abroad and know how important receiving letters from home can be for a lonely soldier or sailor. Writing and sending the letters actually was their idea. I've included photos of each class and have written their names on the back.

Yours always, Caroline"

William shuffled through the photos and held one up to see more closely. Fifteen faces smiled back at him. There to the right side of the group stood Caroline. William stared at her. Had she always been this lovely? He must have forgotten. He placed the photos on the desk and chided himself for his thoughts about her. Netty was his true love...if only she would write.

Curious, William selected a random letter from the box, unfolded it and read.

"Dear Serviceman,

My name is Lillie Clark. I am eleven years old and live in Nolanville, Texas. I am in the fifth grade. Caroline Hawkins is my music teacher. She agreed to collect the letters from my classmates and mail them to her friend, Lt. Bailey.

My father is in the navy, too. But I don't know the name of his ship. His name is Quinton Clark. If you should ever meet him, tell him his little Lillie says hello."

William replaced the letter and stood. He swept his coat from the back of his chair and hastily buttoned it on. Standing in front of the mirror attached to the back of his door, he adjusted the sleeves of his navy-blue jacket...two gold one-half-inch braids spaced evenly apart marked his rank as lieutenant; a gold cross affixed at a slight angle above the top stripe identified his chaplaincy. Grabbing the box and his Bible, William left his cabin. Hurrying down the corridor, he stopped at the mailroom. Two sailors were sorting newly received mail into the built-in bins on the wall. Seaman Gibson sorted packages on a table centered in the room.

"Padre?" Seaman Gibson looked up. "May I help you, sir?"

"Seaman, are there men aboard the ship who do not receive mail?"

Seaman Gibson looked perplexed. "A few I imagine."

"Would you check? I'd like to give them a letter from this box. If you could get me those names, I'll stop back by after chapel tomorrow to pick them up."

"Aye aye, Lieutenant. I'll have them for you."

William left the mailroom in a much brighter mood with almost a skip in his step as he whistled a nonsensical tune. Hearing from Caroline's students was exactly the morale boost these men needed. What was more uplifting than the innocence of childhood? William pressed his Bible to his chest...hopefully, reading a passage from the Bible would do for now.

After his short sermonette and midway through his closing prayer, a sailor rushed hastily into the chapel. The seven sailors sitting in straight-back chairs turned to see the source of the disturbance.

"A transport is arriving, sir. Captain Harvard requests your presence. I am to accompany you."

"May I conclude my prayer?" William asked the young sailor. The sailor nodded, removed his cap and stood reverently.

"Father, with the news of these newly arrivals our hearts are heavy. Be with the doctors, nurses and medical staff as they attend the wounded. Cover these injured men with Your healing hand. Brighten our spirits with Your hope and love. Amen. Dismissed."

Later that evening at dusk, William stood on the deck of the ship and leaned his forearms on the railing. The breeze blowing off the Atlantic Ocean chilled his face. The water broiled underneath the ship as the vessel cut a foamy wake through the ocean's current. William's eyes were drawn upward. Long-feathery whisps of bright orange and charcoal gray clouds shuffled past in the wind. The sky looked as if God had dropped His palette of paints. The colors on the opposite side of the colorwheel not usually assigned to the sky's array of robin-egg or cobalt blues had slipped off. God's majestic beauty...the sky. William closed his eyes and prayed.

The latest transport of fifty-two injured men from North Africa filled William's thoughts. He had personally met eighteen of them at their bedside earlier. Thirty scheduled for visitation over the next three days. Four required extensive surgery and were taken by gurneys immediately to the operating theatre aboard ship. William would visit with them after they were able to have visitors.

War...so brutal...so vicious...souls lost...bodies torn...spirits crushed. But he was determined to bring these young men...and they were young...aged eighteen to twenty-five...a smiling face, a cheerful word, and most importantly God's reassurance of hope and healing.

Fatigued from talking to and praying with patients in the compartment known as Ward 3, William returned to his private quarters the next day at 1400 hours...army time...4 bells...navy time. He removed his jacket and shoes and stretched out on his bunk. Had exactly one hour before afternoon chapel. He closed his eyes. The ship's smooth movement relaxed him and drowsiness overtook him.

Dreams of Netty invaded his mind. He dreamt she was waiting for him at the Brooklyn Port. He could see her waiting there on the pier... her long brunette hair whipping about in the wind. She was running to him; her arms opened wide.

"Padre? Are you in, sir?" a voice preceded a soft knock at the door.

"Enter," William said, sitting up, reluctantly leaving his dream on the pillow.

"Sorry to bother, Padre. I have that list you asked for." Seaman Gibson handed William two sheets of paper.

"I had no idea there were so many. Would you distribute these letters to the first fifty men listed here?" William held up the box.

"Of course. Padre, you missed mail call this morning. Here's a letter for you. It's not from Belton this time." The young man grinned and closed the door.

William stared at the envelope. The return address was stamped Virginia. He didn't know anyone from there. A sailor or soldier he had previously met aboard the ship perhaps? He removed the pocket knife from his desk and sliced the top of the envelope. Its contents held a single page...two short paragraphs. Typewritten not handwritten. Curiously William began to read:

"William,

This letter is long overdue. You should know I met a doctor at a USO dance in Dallas. His name is Captain Trevor Hastings. He was transferred to the Naval Medical Center in Portsmouth, Virginia. I followed him and we were married six weeks later.

I know this comes as a shock to you. For that I am truly sorry. But you must have known I could never be a minister's wife. I know you well enough to know you'd not give up being a 'preacher boy' for me. I hope one day you'll be able to forgive me. There is a girl out there who will share your passion. It's just not me.

Lynnette"

Couldn't be true! Not his Netty! She promised to wait. What happened?

How many young men had he counseled who'd received a 'Dear John' letter? Too many to count...and now he had one. Comical. So ironic. Who would tell him things would be okay? What had he said to those devastated soldiers? For the life of him, he couldn't recall. Glancing at his wristwatch, confirmed time for chapel. William slipped on his shoes and coat, grabbed his Bible and headed to chapel.

The chapel was full. At least twenty or more sailors and soldiers filled almost every available chair. Several men in wheelchairs parked in the back.

William stood behind the lectern. The sermonette he had prepared was jumbled in his mind. He laid his Bible on the pulpit and flipped it open where his bookmark lay. Psalms 121...not the sermon passage reserved for today but one he had read the night before. He picked up his King James Bible and read:

"I will lift up mine eyes unto the hills, from whence cometh my help. My help cometh from the LORD, which made heaven and earth....The LORD is thy keeper; the LORD is thy shade upon thy right hand. The sun shall not smite thee by day, nor the moon by night. The LORD shall preserve thee from all evil; He shall preserve thy soul. The LORD shall preserve thy going out and thy coming in from this time forth and..."

Tears blurred William's eyes and heartbreak clamped his vocal chords. He could not see clearly to finish the remainder of the passage. The chapel attendees could readily see their chaplain's distress and his struggle to continue. One or two shifted in their chairs and looked around at their buddies.

One sailor sitting in the back of the room stood and began to sing. "My hope is built on nothing less than Jesus' blood and righteousness; I dare not trust the sweetest frame, but wholly lean on Jesus' name. On Christ, the solid Rock, I stand; All other ground is sinking sand, All other ground is sinking sand."

One by one the men who could stand rose to their feet and joined in singing the chorus and the next verse of "The Solid Rock." Those who couldn't stand raised their voices in worship. The song filled the men's hearts with hope.

William looked up. His earlier question had been answered...these twenty men were the ones who offered him counsel. God had ministered to him through these physically and emotionally hurting servicemen. The Holy Word and the hymn's simple lyrics brought solace to them all.

After chapel ended, William went back to his quarters. Withdrawing a sheet of paper from the drawer, he picked up his pen and words scrawled quickly across the page.

"Dear Caroline,

I have received a letter from Netty. Did you or Gwen know she was married? I do not ask to cast blame or place guilt by not telling me. I am in shock and that's an understatement. My heart lies in crumbled pieces. Hope that doesn't sound

too sappy. My men have been so supportive. I know God
has a plan for the rest of my life. I will continue to follow
His lead. Sincerely, William"

Two weeks later, William received two letters. The first letter read:
"My dearest, William,

My heart is breaking for you. I only wish there was something I could say to lessen your pain. No, neither Gwen nor I knew Netty was married. We were both equally shocked by the news.

God does have a plan for your life. You are answering His call right now encouraging those injured men aboard your ship. God will direct you to your soulmate as He will also direct me to mine. If I were there, I would offer a listening ear and a shoulder to cry on. Please know I am always here for you.

Your friend,

Caroline"

The second letter received that day read:

"Son,

When I read your letter about Netty, I knew you were in a dreadful state. I am so sorry. If I could take this pain from you, you know I would.

Sometimes the person we believe to be our soulmate is not God's perfect choice for us. God has a woman designed especially for you who will fill your life with joy and will truly be your other half. Be patient as God directs her to you.

We are all well. Your dad, as always, is extremely busy. It's flu season here. This may seem trivial to you…but meat rationing has ended. When you come home, I will cook your favorites. Everyone sends their best. Lean on God's Word.

Love you always, Momma"

Six weeks later, William hurried into the Mail Room. Seaman Gibson and one other sailor turned as William greeted them. "Morning, I have a letter to send out. Is it too late for the first batch of V-mail?"

"No, you're not too late," Seaman Gibson said as he took the letter.

"Ah, going to Belton. One or two letters a week now! Is this getting serious, Padre?"

"Maybe so," William grinned and hurried to chapel.

****

William stood on the top deck of the *USAHS Thistle* and watched as the tugboats on either side escorted the vessel under the Brooklyn bridge toward New York's Brooklyn Port. Skyscrapers with either flat roofs or tall pointed spirals aligned the coastline welcoming all travelers ashore. The hospital ship's brilliant white coating along with the broad green stripe and large red cross painted midship seemed out of place among the steel-gray vessels already berthed. From his elevation, William could see twenty rows of stretchers lined twenty rows deep on the dock's platform. Ambulances were parked nearby. The ship's Master Sergeant shouted orders to the crew as the disembarkation process would soon commence.

After six months at sea, the floating hospital had completed its assignment. The evacuation and transportation of critically and noncritically injured soldiers from Italy and from the coast of North Africa to Brooklyn had been successful.

William breathed out a deep sigh. He walked down the gangway and entered the covered walkway built to protect patients from extreme elements. As he passed the men waiting to be transferred to the ambulance stretchers, William shook their hands and bid them well.

With his duffle bag slung over his shoulder and knowing these men were in capable hands, William continued toward the Port Authority's main entrance. He was required to present his orders for shore leave. The *USAHS Thistle* would be sanitized stern to aft; medical supplies and food galleys inventoried and restocked. This turnaround process readied the ship to swiftly set sail on her next assignment.

William placed his sunglasses over his eyes before exiting the Port Authority, but the sun still blinded his view. A line of green Checker cabs with white roofs and white fenders lined the curb. Like ants searching for a stale piece of bread, weary travelers poured out of the building.

William was swept up within the mass and mingled among them—merchant sailors, seaman, naval officers, army doctors and nurses, cargo crewman—all searching for a ride.

"Need a cab, mister?" a woman's voice called. The woman—early twenties, slim figure, bright brown eyes and curly auburn hair, dressed in a light green two-piece linen suit and brown open-toed pumps—smiled cheerfully as she held open the passenger door of a Checker taxi.

Stunned, William stopped. "Caroline?"

Caroline with tears forming in her eyes, smiled. "When you wrote saying when your ship would be docking in Brooklyn, I took some vacation days to come meet you. You don't mind, do you?"

"No...no, of course not!" William stuttered. "You're a wonderful surprise!"

Caroline stepped from the curb. "May I give you a welcome-home hug?"

"Yes," he said, pulling her into an embrace. "May I kiss you?"

She raised her chin. He kissed her mouth; her lips as soft as he'd imagined.

"Our taxi driver is waiting." Caroline motioned. "Care to spend your leave with me in New York City, Lieutenant? Want to see Times Square? Central Park? Statue of Liberty? The Metropolitan Museum of Art? There's even an outdoor ice skating pond at Rockefeller Plaza. Maybe take in a Broadway show?"

"Yes, to all of that! Caroline, I'm so happy you're here!"

The two crawled into the back of the cab and William took Caroline's hand.

"Welcome home, William!" Caroline whispered as the taxi pulled away from the curb and veered into the congested traffic.

FAREWELLS AND TRAGEDIES OF WAR
1945

Stretched across her bed, Lucy lay on her stomach with her chin propped on her folded hands; her dress pulled up mid-thigh. Loraine sat on the bed's edge and held a Max Factor's pan-cake make-up compact in the palm of her hand. She dipped a flat sponge in a shallow bowl of water that sat on bedside table. Wiping the dampened sponge across the dry makeup surface, Loraine applied a medium beige color to Lucy's legs. Lucy lifted one hand and scratched her nose.

"Be still, Lucy! Mother will kill us if we get makeup on the bedspread!"

"Hurry up! You're taking forever!"

Arlo, who had been watching curiously, suddenly started pacing. He barked twice and trotted up to Loraine, nudging her knee with his wet nose.

"Stop, Arlo! I'm not hurting her! Just putting makeup on her legs. See?" Loraine held out the compact as if by seeing the object of concern, the dog would understand. Arlo sniffed the compact and then jumped in the middle of the bed landing in the middle of Lucy's back.

"Arlo!" the girls cried in unison.

Lucy rolled to her back and drew the black Labrador into a tight hug. She rocked him back and forth as he wiggled and bucked trying to break free. Loraine giggled at the two, placed the compact on the table, and joined in the play. Arlo's stiff tail pounded against Loraine's shoulders and arms as they wrestled.

"Girls?" Gran knocked softly and entered the room. "What's going on in here? Arlo, get off the bed! Girls, you know he shouldn't be up there."

The twins sat up quickly. Arlo jumped off the bed. He knew the rules as well as they. Gran smiled as the dog sat down obediently at her feet and stared back at the girls as if they were solely to blame for his bad behavior.

"We're practicing putting makeup on our legs since we won't have silk stockings for the Sadie Hawkins dance next week," Loraine volunteered.

"It's dreadful not being able to buy silk stockings," Lucy pouted. "Worse than that is drawing a line down the back of our legs with an eyebrow pencil!"

"I can only imagine! Dinner is ready." Gran turned and exited the girls' bedroom. Arlo followed; his tail swooshing side to side.

Valentine's Day had arrived. Maggie and Gran helped the girls dress for the Sadie Hawkins dance. Patrick and Franklin waited in the study. Franklin lit his pipe and leaned back in his chair.

"It's nice of you to take the girls and their dates to the dance, son."

"Yeah, I think I was tricked into it. I've never been able to deny my sisters anything! Being their chaperone means I can keep an eye on them. I already warned them! No funny business."

Franklin laughed and deeply inhaled his pipe. "I have little concern about either Tommy North or Arnold Blake. Something on your mind, son?"

"After hearing about President Roosevelt meeting with Winston Churchill and Joseph Stalin at Yalta on the Black Sea, it seems the war may be drawing quickly to an end. At least the U.S., England, and Russia have joined military powers to end it. General MacArthur and his troops have made an appearance in the Philippines to take over the three-year-stronghold Japan has claimed there."

"You're not considering joining up *now*, are you?" Franklin's voice was inquisitive and edged with concern.

"No, sir. But I am planning to go to Arizona and wait out the war."

"Why Arizona?" Franklin paused, "Oh, of course. Kim is there, isn't she?"

"Yes. The Japanese-Americans are being detained until the war is over. I want to be there when the camps dissolve. I must see if her feelings about us have truly changed. You understand why I must go, don't you?"

"Yes, son, I do. Have you told your mother?"

"No, I will tomorrow. She's so excited about the girls' dance, I didn't want to overshadow that."

"Patrick? Franklin?" Maggie called excitedly from the foyer. "Franklin, come see your beautiful daughters!"

Franklin set his pipe in the ash tray on his desk and placed his arm around Patrick's shoulders. "We're being summoned."

The two men entered the foyer. The girls were standing on the bottom step of the stairs. Lucy, wearing a dark rose-pink dress, smiled cheerfully. Loraine wore a royal blue dress with gold sequined flowers hand-stitched randomly around the skirt. Black sequined bows were clipped to the center of each of the girl's two-inch black pumps. Maggie and Gran beamed with pride as they stood behind them.

"Oh, my, you both look so beautiful! No longer two little girls! You are lovely young ladies!" Franklin kissed each of his daughters on the cheek.

"Let's see those legs," Patrick teased.

Loraine turned around and held her dress up to one side as she looked over her shoulder. "Lucy did a super job, didn't she?"

"What?" Frank looked quizzically at Maggie.

"I'll explain later. Patrick, take good care of our girls tonight," Maggie said, sidling next to Franklin.

"Have fun, you two," Franklin added and winked at his daughters.

Lucy and Loraine slipped an arm through Patrick's as he escorted them out the front door. Maggie, Franklin, and Gran peered through the sheer curtain panels in the parlor and watched until the car pulled out of the driveway.

****

On April 12, 1945, Franklin, Maggie, Gran, and the twins prepared to listen to one of their favorite radio programs.

"Come on, Loraine! The show's about to start!" Lucy burst into the kitchen.

Loraine shook a covered pan filled with Jolly Time popcorn kernels above the blue flames flickering from the gas range burner. The yellow kernels simmering in the hot oil hit the top of the lid with a ratta-tat-tat sound. After the last pop, Loraine removed the pan from the burner and slowly removed the lid. Steam and puffy white popcorn emerged from the pan. Loraine poured the hot popped corn into a large yellow ceramic bowl and grabbed a salt shaker.

"Not too much salt! You always get carried away!" Lucy scolded.

"Wouldn't Grant have loved this? That boy loved his popcorn!"

"Yeah, but it's all his fault….moving out of state to go to college. There're perfectly good law schools in Texas!"

Loraine laughed. "You sound like his dad!"

Lucy scooped the bowl off the pink granite cabinet top and the girls hurried down the hall to the study. They took their places on the floor in front of the radio cabinet with the bowl of popcorn staked between them.

The radio was tuned to *The Durante-Moore Show,* starring Jimmy Durante and Garry Moore. The weekly comedy variety show always began with their theme song, "Start Off Each Day With A Song," and was sung by Jimmy Durante.

The girls sang along, "You've gotta start each day with a song; now even when things go wrong. You'll feel better; you'll even look better. I'm here to tell you that you'll be a go-getter."

Then Jimmy Durante blurted, "Stop da music! Stop da music! You're supposed to follow da music not chase it all over da place!" The radio audience laughed wholeheartedly as the theme song continued softly in the background. Durante began his monologue, "My wife has a slight impediment in her speech. Every now and then, she stops to breathe!"

Franklin laughed and glanced at Maggie. Maggie swooshed her hand at him as if accepting the accusation of frequently talking too much. Durante continued, "My nose isn't big; I just happen to have a small head!"

As Garry Moore and Jimmy Durante began their next comic routine, a public announcement blared across the radio speakers. "We interrupt this NBC program with this important announcement! This afternoon at exactly 3:45pm, President Franklin Delano Roosevelt, age 63, died of a massive cerebral hemorrhage in his home in Warm Springs, Georgia. Our nation is in mourning. At 7:09pm this evening Vice President Harry S. Truman was sworn into office as the 33rd President of the United States. National Broadcasting Company will keep you apprised of upcoming events. We return now to the program in progess."[4]

The frivolity and laughter suddenly stilled as if it had been captured and stuffed into an invisible, impenetrable box. No one spoke. Gran began to cry. Abandoning the bowl of popcorn, Lucy scooted closer and laid her head on her grandmother's knee.

Gran patted Lucy's head, stroking her hair, and said between sniffles, "Oh, child, Roosevelt, our dear, dear President led this country four terms...twelve of our most trying years...even while coping with his own health problems. Tried his best to conceal the fact he had polio. His focus was our country not himself. In 1932 during the stock market crash when there were so many unemployed and the big banks began to close, the American people were losing hope. A blanket of doom covered our nation. During his first presidential inauguration speech, he said 'the only thing we have to fear is fear itself.' He brought hope to so many broken spirits. What will our nation do now?"

The telephone sitting on the edge of Franklin's desk began to ring.

"I'll get that. It's probably Ernie," Franklin said.

Early Saturday morning before breakfast had been served, Franklin left for town and returned with copies of three prominent newspapers...

The Austin American-Statesman, *The Dallas Morning News* and *The Houston Chronicle*. The top headline typed in a large bold font on one paper…**President Roosevelt Dies at Home in Warm Springs**… centered the front page. Two subheadlines in smaller fonts introduced articles from the United Press. The first one read: **Truman Sworn in at White House as 33rd President** and the next article: **Wife Arrives to Escort Body Back to Capitol**.

After breakfast, the Baileys spread the newspapers among them. Maggie and Franklin shared one; the twins the second; and Gran the third. The occasional slurping as Franklin drank his morning coffee or a random comment by one of the twins briefly disturbed the intensive concentration of the readers.

"This is so sad," Lucy sighed. "Have you read the article about First Lady Roosevelt not being with the President in Georgia when he died?"

"Read it to us." Gran removed her spectacles and placed them on the table.

"The article is written by a reporter named Merriman Smith. He writes, 'Death today removed Franklin Delano Roosevelt from a war-torn world and left peace-expectant millions shocked and stunned. Death gave the 63-year-old President of the United States short notice.'5 The article describes Mrs. Roosevelt receiving the phone call in D.C., and how she arrived in Warm Springs by a military plane. Reporters were expecting her arrival by train."

Loraine added, "President Roosevelt founded a rehab in Warm Springs for children stricken with polio and visited there often to swim in the springs for therapy for his paralyzed legs. Before President Roosevelt's casket was loaded on the train that would transfer him to Washington, Mrs. Roosevelt insisted the funeral procession drive by the rehab so that the staff and residents could pay their last respects. One thirteen-year-old boy, who had polio and had previously befriended President Roosevelt, was sitting on the front porch. It was reported the boy was sobbing as the hearse and the procession pulled into the circular driveway."

"The military personnel who arrived Friday night," Lucy continued, "were at least 3,000 strong all outfitted in ceremonial dress uniforms complete with swords and white gloves. For safety, soldiers barricaded the crowds from the train platform and the tracks at the Warm Springs station while the casket was loaded onto the funeral train. The First Lady insisted the train travel slowly. Crowds of people waited at each station along the route. One reporter said no one waved; they wept."

"CBS is broadcasting the funeral procession tomorrow and Arthur Godfrey was chosen as the announcer," Maggie added. "We'll have to listen in."

Gran nodded. "This article says the President will be lying in state in the White House East Room for only five hours before being transported to his hometown in Hyde Park, New York, for burial."

"I can't read anymore!" Loraine said. "I'm going out to ride Honey."

Lucy folded the newspaper and followed her sister to the barn.

****

As each of the thirty days in April arrived, a tick was placed on the family's calendar marking the day's conclusion. The month of May began with a new string of events to be recorded, remembered, and celebrated. On May 2, the Soviet Union announced the fall of Berlin while the Allies announced the surrender of Nazi troops in Italy. Three days later Germany signed an unconditional surrender with the Allies ending the European conflict. War still raged on with Japan. All the while plans were being made for Lucy's and Loraine's high school graduation party.

One night as the twins lay in bed and shared their comings and goings of the day as they did every night, Loraine noticed Lucy seemed quiet and terribly distracted. Something was wrong.

"Lucy? Are you okay?" Lorained rolled to one side to face her sister. The moon's glimmering light floated through their bedroom window emitting enough light to see without turning on the lamp.

"Arnie's moving to Boston in two weeks. He was accepted to Harvard. He plans to live with his sister Judy and her family."

"Oh, so that's what's making you so blue! I knew there was something! You're going to U.T. and that's just as exciting. You will be a famous concert pianist one day! You have no time to mope around about Arnold Blake!"

"But, he's my best friend! I'm going to miss him."

"I know," Loraine said sympathetically. "You still have me!"

Lucy smiled. "I told Mama today we didn't want a graduation party. Wouldn't be the same without our brothers and cousins. There's too much tragedy and uncertainty to find anything to celebrate!"

"I agree. Lucy? Can you keep a secret?"

Lucy sat straight up in bed. "Loraine Rae! What have you done?"

Loraine laughed and sat up. Wrapping her arms around her pulled-up legs, she said, "I took a job at the Austin telephone office. My friend, Bonnie Evans, and I start training next Saturday. You won't tell Mama or Papa, will you?"

Lucy flopped back on her pillow. "No, siree! Not a peep from me. But I do want to be there when you tell them!"

A few seconds later, Lucy giggled.

"What? What's so funny?"

"I thought you were going to tell me you were eloping with Tommy North!"

Loraine tossed her bed pillow across the space separating their beds and with skilled precision smacked her sister in the face. Lucy grabbed the pillow that had fallen into her lap. With full intentions to retaliate, Lucy stood in the middle of her bed and held the pillow high over her head. As she aimed the feather-filled weapon at her sister, she lost her balance and toppled over. The girls laughed hysterically.

THERAPY FOR THE SOUL
1945

L ucy tucked the *Life* magazine into her over-sized black purse together with her sheet music and opened the car door. She greeted her cousin and scooted in. "Thanks, Anne, for picking me up at the drugstore. Doc left for Temple earlier this morning...too early for me."

"Not a problem. I enjoy your company."

"Your house will be finished soon. You must be more than excited!"

"Indeed, I am! When Grayson took the full-time chaplaincy position at McCloskey, we didn't think much about the two hour drive. But with Grant away at school, there's no need for us to stay in Oak Hill. Did your family listen to President Truman's radio announcement? The war is over! Even after two weeks, seems surreal just saying the words! But, isn't it amazing?" Anne asked.

"Yes, after three years, eight months and seven days...that's what President Truman said. Finally an end! Such a relief after the depressing news reported a couple of weeks ago. You know the one I mean? The explanation Emperor Hirohito gave the Japanese people about why they must surrender? Did you hear it?"

"I'm not sure. What was said?"

"The Emperor said the Americans used a 'cruel bomb' over Hiroshima and Nagasaki and more cities would be bombed until the Japanese people surrendered. Can he honestly claim innocence in the part he played?" Lucy's voice quavered.

"I know. War is horrendous. But it's over now!" Anne remarked excitedly.

"Yes! Tommy North drove Loraine and I along with a couple of our friends to Austin to join the celebration there. We were lucky to find parking on West Ave and walked toward the deafening sounds. A throng of people marched down Congress Ave toward the Capitol. Couldn't really call it marching...more like being swept along in the current's flow. Traffic was stopped on all the sidestreets. Horns blared not because of stalled traffic but because of the celebration! I saw several children standing on hoods of cars to better see over the crowd. Church bells rang and people yelled and cried and screamed. It was thrilling!"

"Was that a magazine I saw there in your purse? Any good articles?"

"Yes, *Life's* August 27th issue. Look at this!" Lucy pulled out the 11x9 inch magazine from her bag and turned the front cover toward Anne. "Isn't it grand? The photo was taken in Manhattan thirteen days ago, on the 14th, when thousands of New Yorkers flooded Times Square to celebrate V-J Day...Victory in Japan Day. Not a breadth of a feather could be squeezed between them as they paraded toward Broadway celebrating the war's end! Bells rang! From the windows of the high-rise buildings, confetti flew everywhere. Posterboards with 'Victory over Japan' written in bright red lettering were held high. This photo is simply called 'the kiss.'" Lucy turned the magazine back around. "The article says a cameraman saw this unnamed sailor grab this unsuspecting nurse from the crowd....perfect strangers...wouldn't know by the kiss he planted on her! Look at them! What a great kiss!"

"What do you know about a great kiss? Oh, never mind...I don't want to know." Anne grinned and kept her eyes on the road; her hands on the steering wheel.

"Did Aunt Elizabeth tell you Clayton called us from the *USS Missouri?* The official signing of Japan's unconditional surrender will be held on his ship the 2nd of September. General Douglas MacArthur will sign and accept the document on behalf of the Allied Powers. Clayton was so excited! He hopes to have the opportunity to meet General MacArthur. Said he'd share all the details when he comes home... probably in a couple of months or so."

"Yes, Mama did tell us. How exciting! The signing will probably be broadcasted over the radio as well. Where's his ship docked?"

"Yes! I'm sure it will! Clayton's battleship is anchored in Tokyo Bay. Have you heard when Carter and Owen are coming home?"

"Owen maybe in a couple of months. Carter…I'm not sure. Dottie is back in Colorado and promises to visit as soon as the boys are home. Harold may come, too. Praise God! All my brothers will be home soon! When do your classes start?"

"In three weeks! I'm so excited!" Lucy looked out the passenger window as Anne turned into the hospital complex. "Are we here already?"

"Yes, we are. I'm volunteering on the East Wing. I'll be back around four."

"That's fine." Lucy opened the car door and got out. "Thanks again, Anne."

Opening the door to the hospital's main entrance and familiar with the surroundings, Lucy walked past the information desk and headed directly to the elevator. When the elevator stopped on the sixth floor, she exited.

Doc Lawrence, having previously made the arrangements, told her to introduce herself to the head floor nurse. Lucy pushed through the doors labeled 'Sixth Floor Amputee Ward' and proceeded to the first nurses station. No one was there. As she turned to leave, a young nurse dressed in a stiffly starched white uniform briskly approached; the crisp cotton dress rustled with her every step.

"I'm so sorry. We are very busy just now. Are you Lucy Bailey?"

"Yes, I am. I'm supposed to meet the head floor nurse…a Marjorie Adams…I believe. Doc Lawrence spoke to her yesterday."

"Marjorie's office is this way. Follow me. I'm Samantha Howard."

Lucy smiled and followed Samantha past three nurses stations, identical to the first, to an office at the end of the long hallway. After knocking softly three times, Samantha opened the door.

"Lucy Bailey is here," Samantha announced, holding the door open.

Lucy entered. A woman who easily looked to be in her mid-forties rose from behind a white metal desk. She smiled warmly as she came around and extended her hand to shake Lucy's.

"Lucy, I'm Marjorie Adams, charge nurse for the sixth floor. Doctor Lawrence spoke with me yesterday. Oh, where are my manners? Please take a seat."

Lucy sat in a chair in front of the desk as Marjorie returned to her seat.

"So," Marjorie continued, "Doctor Lawrence tells me your classes at UT start soon. A music degree. How nice. He speaks highly of you. Told me how your playing for those patients downstairs proved to be remarkable therapy. I've requested a piano be placed between stations three and four. The piano's nothing fancy....an upright. I'll show you."

Lucy followed Marjorie back down the hall. As they neared the piano, Lucy could hardly believe she'd walked right past it only minutes before. Pianos, to her, were like old friends; constant and true. This Steinway was at least fifteen years old; its beautiful wood cabinet in need of polish; its white keys slightly yellowed. But still a beautiful piece of furniture.

Marjorie noticed Lucy appraising the instrument. "It's been tuned. Should have a good sound. But then, I'm not a pianist. Care to try it out?"

Lucy pulled out the bench and sat down. She ran her fingers over the yellowed ivories, dusted the tops of the black keys and formed a chord. After playing through the G major scale followed by the E minor scale, she smiled.

"Yes, the sound is perfect. When do you want me to play?"

"Oh, definitely during the lunch hour. Otherwise, it's up to you. Our patients are military personnel transferred from hospitals across the country. This will be exactly the morale boost they need! Come to my office if you need anything."

Lucy's hands hovered above the keys. Playing the piano was not anything new nor unfamiliar. But the idea of just playing to the white wall in front of her seemed a bit ridiculous. Would the patients even hear her playing? Where had they served? Army Air Force? Navy? Coast Guard? On the land, in the sea, in the air...wasn't that how Bob Hope addressed them in an USO show where he thanked them for defending the rights of freedom everywhere? She thought of her brothers...Clayton and William in the Navy...John in the Army...Art the Coast Guard. What if one of these patients were one of them?

With tears slipping down her face, she started playing "Whispering Hope." Caught up in the melody and feeling somewhat isolated, she softly sang, "Wait till the darkness is over; wait till life's tempest is done. Hope for the sunshine tomorrow after the shower is gone. Whispering hope. Oh, how welcome thy voice, making my heart in its sorrow rejoice." After playing through the hymn a second time, she bowed her head and silently prayed for all the men assigned to the 6th floor.

FLEE FROM SELF-PITY
1945

The following Saturday, Lucy rode with Doc Lawrence to Temple. It was early....eight o'clock...but with classes starting soon, Lucy was unsure how her class schedule and the homework involved to make top grades would allow any spare time to volunteer at the hospital. Doc parked in the doctor's designated parking area near the hospital's front doors. Lucy bade him farewell.

Taking the elevator to the 6th floor, Lucy arrived a few minutes after eight-fifteen. She pushed through the double doors and entered a quiet hallway. Most of the patients were rousing awake or had showered and finished breakfast. Night shift ended an hour before; day-shift nurses were accessing their patients. Lucy saw Samantha at Nurses Station Two.

"Morning, Lucy," Samantha greeted, holding a clipboard in her hand. "Play something lively to get my blood flowing! I've not had a drop of coffee yet."

Lucy smiled. "Will do my best."

"Candy stripers are coming at eleven. They're high-school volunteers. The red-and-white pinafores they wear look like candy canes."

"Okay, I'll keep an eye out....of the back of my head!"

Samantha laughed. "Want to eat lunch together? Say twelve-thirty?"

"Yes, that sounds nice."

Lucy sat down at the piano and placed several pieces of sheet music on the music rack. Per Samantha's request, Lucy knew exactly which song would stir the morning. A smile broadened her face as she began playing "Oh, What a Beautiful Morning." Softly she sang the chorus, "Oh, what a beautiful mornin'; oh, what a beautiful day. I've got a beautiful feeling everything's going my way."

Lucy played three more pieces. Stretching her fingers, she got up to get a drink of water. As she drank water from a paper cup near Nurses Station One, four excited high-school volunteers pushed through the double doors. Dressed in a red-and-white pinafore worn over a short-sleeved white blouse, each girl seemed eager to start their assignments. Samantha greeted them with a friendly smile.

As Lucy walked away, she heard Samantha say, "Welcome to the 6th Floor. My name is Samantha. Simple things to do...serving lunch, reading to a patient or basically keeping them company. I'll introduce you to the nurses. Follow me."

Lucy returned to her piano bench and sat down. She looked to the right and to the left. No one even noticed she had left her position. She could play anything or nothing at all; no one would care. Glancing at her Bulova watch, she still had a little over an hour before lunch.

Bored with playing popular songs and knowing no one really cared what was played, Lucy softly played the song that gained her admittance into the University of Texas' music program—one of her favorite classical pieces by Johann Sebastian Bach—"Jesu, Joy of Men's Desiring." At the conclusion of the piece, Lucy closed her eyes and sighed.

"Get out! Leave me alone! Are you deaf? Get out!"

At the sound of a man's brusque shouting, Lucy abruptly opened her eyes. Looking over her shoulder, she witnessed one of the candy stripers running from the room located directly behind her.

"You're a monster!" the girl cried angrily and threw a book on the floor.

"Wait!" Lucy beckoned but the girl rushed past her.

Lucy stooped to pick up the hardback book. She took several steps toward the patient's door and stopped in the doorway. 'G. Lewis' was the name written on the plaque affixed on the outside wall.

"What do *you* want?"

Lucy stared. A young man wearing dark-lensed sunglasses lay

motionless in the bed; his right arm bandaged from shoulder to wrist; his left arm amputated above the elbow. The IV pole set to the right side of the hospital bed held two plastic bags; the line carrying antibiotics and pain killer was administered through a needle inserted into a prominent vein on the top of his right hand.

"Um...I don't want anything."

"Get out then!"

"Is this yours?" Lucy held up the book.

"No, that's not mine! That useless girl brought it in here. How did she think I could possibly read it?" Pointing the stump of his left arm at her, he jeered. "How am I supposed to hold a book?"

Lucy, clutching the book against her chest, took a step into the room. "That girl is not useless! If you'd given her a chance to explain, she would have told you she was here to read to you. She's a volunteer."

"I don't need anyone to read to me! I'm not a child!"

Lucy raised her eyebrows. "That's debatable."

Clearly angry and frustrated, the patient yelled, "Get out!"

"Gladly!" Lucy huffed out the room, closing the door behind her.

Thirty minutes later, Lucy followed Samantha through the cafeteria's buffet line. She wasn't that hungry but knew she needed to eat something. She placed her selections—a tuna salad sandwich, a small tossed green salad, and a coke—on the lunch tray and proceeded to the cashier.

The cafeteria was crowded; a few empty seats were available by the windows at the back of the room. Lucy took a seat across from Samantha. After removing her lunch items from the tray, she slowly nibbled at her sandwich.

"You're quiet. Anything wrong?" Samantha asked as she opened a carton of milk and poured its contents into a glass.

"What do you know about the patient in Room 34?" Lucy asked.

Samantha blew across a spoonful of tomato soup. "Why? Why do you ask?"

"Oh, just curious. He made one of the candy stripers cry."

"Oh, yeah. I heard. The girl's name is Georgia. Only fifteen. Poor thing. I'm sorry she encountered one of our surliest patients. Some patients are angels…easy going…pleasant…cooperative. And then there are the others…like Room 34."

Lucy placed her half-eaten sandwich on the plate. "What do you know about him? What's his story?"

Samantha studied her new friend's face. "I'm really not supposed to talk about our patients."

"I know, but even though he says terribly rude things, he seems lost."

"Do you want to save him?" Samantha laughed.

"I'm sure he could use a friend. I can't imagine what he's gone through."

"He's not a lost kitten you can take home." Samantha smiled. "Well, I guess just this one time. His name is Glen Lewis. Lieutenant Glen Lewis, a flight officer in the Army Air Corp. His plane was struck by German artillery flak during his last mission. He was able to land the plane in England, but the back of the plane exploded within minutes after landing. From what I've heard he pulled two of his crewmen from the plane before the plane was totally engulfed in flames. His injuries are due to the explosion. All the crew escaped. That's all I know."

"Thank you, Samantha, for telling me. He's a hero then."

"Yeah, I guess so. Are you going to eat that pickle?" Samantha pointed to the sweet pickle resting on Lucy's plate.

"No, you may have it," Lucy grinned.

The next morning, Lucy played through three pieces she'd selected for the day plus one that was personally requested by one of the patients…a Private Robert Baker. She was astounded the piano's sound carried to his room at the end of the hall; but was even more surprised he had requested a song.

She rose from the piano bench and walked the short distance across the hall to Room 34. Breakfast had been served; the food tray removed from the room and left outside on the floor to be picked up. The door was ajar. Lucy peered inside.

The room….a typical hospital room…small and stuffy; one bed; one single chair; uninspiring; lacking decoration or any semblance of home. The window shades covering the two windows on the west wall were tightly closed blocking any sunlight to alleviate the gloom. Odors of rubbing alcohol mixed gingerly with body sweat seemed trapped like adhesive to the walls and ceiling; the floor was swept but smelled of diluted disinfectant.

Lt. Lewis' head was propped against two pillows. The top of his dark mousy-brown hair was tousled and stood up slighty in the back. Was he awake or sleeping or just pretending to sleep? It was hard to tell. The sunglasses, protection for his retinas damaged by extreme flashes of light during the accident, sat perfectly perched on his nose. A growth of reddish-brown whiskers took up residence on his chin and jawline.

"Lieutenant? Excuse me. Are you awake?" Lucy stood in the doorway, wary of advancing any further into the room.

"Get out!" he grumbled and then shouted loudly. "Get out!"

"Wanted to know if there was a special song you'd like to hear this morning."

"Get out!"

"You are really beginning to sound like a parrot!"

"Get…." Lucy thought she briefly glimpsed a small curve at the corner of his lips. "Go away!"

"Nice to know you have such an extensive vocabulary. I'm just across the hall if you think of a song you'd like to hear. Or if you prefer, I could read to you."

"Who are you anyway? Missy Do-gooder? Oh, I know! You're the glad girl. Finding good in every situation. Pollyanna…are you Pollyanna?"

"No, I'm simply Lucy…Lucy Bailey. May I call you Glen?"

"No! Close the door on your way out!"

Lucy closed the door and returned to the piano bench. She sat down and sighed deeply. Her fingers, as if on their own volition, danced across the keys. Caught up in her own little world of cresendos, key changes, volume and tempos, was startled to see Samantha leaning against the piano.

"That was beautiful. Ready for lunch?" Samantha asked.

Lucy pulled the keyboard cover over the keys and nodded. Walking back to Room 34 and standing near the closed door, Lucy raised her voice. "I'll be back this afternoon, Lieutenant."

After lunch, Lucy picked up the light-weight piano bench and placed it near Lt. Lewis' closed door. She opened the book she'd rescued from the floor the week before and recalled the look on Georgia's frightened face as she ran out of the room to escape the lieutenant's wrath. Not knowing if the lieutenant could hear her and really not caring one way or the other, Lucy opened the book and read:

'The dawn came, but no day. In the gray sky a red sun appeared, a dim red circle that gave a little light, like dusk; and as that day advanced, the dusk slipped back toward darkness, and the wind cried and whimpered over the fallen corn.

Men and woman huddled in their houses, and they tied handkerchiefs over their noses when they went out, and wore goggles to protect their eyes.

When the night came again it was black night, for the stars could not pierce the dust to get down, and the window lights could not even spread beyond their own yards. Now the dust was evenly mixed with the air, an emulsion of dust and air. Houses were shut tight, and cloth wedged around doors and windows, but the dust came in so thinly that it could not be seen in the air, and it settled like pollen on the chairs and tables, on the dishes. The people brushed it from their shoulders. Little lines of dust lay at the door sills.'[6]

After reading chapters one through three, Lucy closed the book and carried the book as well as the piano bench back to the piano. She eased the bench in its place; set the book on top of the piano and grabbed her purse. After waving goodbye to Samantha, she left the 6th Floor for the day.

Lucy's hospital routine Sunday afternoon through Wednesday morning that week remained unchanged. A piano recital of sorts playing her favorite songs in the morning, a lunch break, then reading outside Lt. Lewis' closed door in the afternoons. Some afternoons she'd lean against the wall and just start talking as if dialoguing with the lieutenant....as if he were sitting across from her as they enjoyed a meal together. And possibly during the meal, he'd occasionally ask questions to get better acquainted. She would tell him blue her favorite color and cherry pie her favorite dessert; share stories about her family; tell him about Miss Daisy, her first kitten, and how the gray cat would ride upon her shoulders; express pride in her brothers and cousins who served in the war. Tell him how much she adored her nieces and nephews and expound upon her plans for the future…talk about anything to pass the time. She'd not seen him since Sunday afternoon when he had screeched at her and called her Pollyanna. Being compared to Pollyanna wasn't what was upsetting, but the belittling way he'd sneered at her as he said it. That was upsetting…demeaning.

Thursday afternoon as she lugged the piano bench across the hall, Lucy noticed the door to Room 34 wide open. Daring not to disturb the lieutenant and encounter more unbridled hostility, she sat down on the bench and opened the book to chapter fifteen.

After reading through three paragraphs, she heard her name.

"Lucy? Simply Lucy Bailey?"

Lucy rose with the book secured in one hand and stood motionless in the doorway. The lieutenant's face was freshly shaven, hair nicely combed and sunglasses removed.

"Lieutenant, your sunglasses! Does that mean your eyes have healed?"

"Please come in. I won't bite…I promise."

Lucy eased from the doorway and took two steps closer to the bed.

"My name is Glen. Please, call me Glen. And yes, the doctors think my eyes are 'healing nicely'—their words. Still need to avoid bright lights. There's one more skin graft scheduled early Friday morning for my lower right arm…obviously." He lifted the bandaged stump of his left arm as if appreciating his own humor.

"That's wonderful news!"

"Please, have a seat."

Lucy moved toward the chair beside the bed and sat down. This was the first time she'd seen him in a clean hospital gown; clean-shaven and without the glasses to obscure his eyes. His eyes…his eyes were a brilliant shade of crystal blue…the bluest of blues. A handsome face. Lucy's face reddened when she realized she was staring. He seemed to be staring back and smiled at her.

Struggling with what to say next, Lucy folded her hands on top of the book. "So, what's with this sudden change of heart? I must admit I'm a bit shocked!"

"I have been a brute, haven't I? Sorry, about that! My head's a mess!"

"I have no idea the horrors you've seen or what you've suffered, but I do know you have a future and a lot to offer others."

"Who says so?"

"Well...God for one. Me for the other."

"What does God know about it?"

Lucy, fearful Glen's sourer-than-grapes attitude had returned, bristled as she straightened. "Shall I bring my Bible tomorrow and read of His many promises?"

"If you'd like," he grinned. "Curious about one thing. Why did you choose to read from the *The Grapes of Wrath*?"

"You recognized it? Really? How?"

"I had just received a degree in English Literature at A&M College before fulfilling my obligation with the Cadet Corps and Uncle Sam. With my degree choice, I must admit I've read a few books." He laughed merrily. "That one, though, is one of my favorites of John Steinbeck's works. My dream was to teach secondary level literature and one day become a college professor. Anyway, it's impossible now! My dream was blasted to pieces along with my plane..."

"Oh, please don't say that! Teaching is still possible! You can do anything you set your mind to!"

"Lucy?"

"Yes?"

"Would you mind reading the letters in that top drawer? They're from home."

Lucy opened the drawer of the side table and withdrew six unopened envelopes. Her eyes filled with tears. "You've not read these? Have you not written to your family? Have your parents been here to see you?"

"No." He held up the stump of his left arm and shrugged his shoulders. "Hard to write...I told them not to come when they were first notified about the accident. I would refuse to see them even if they did!"

"Why? Do they live far away?"

"No, Abilene. You know it?"

"Yes, of course. But, Glen, your parents…of all people…would want to be here with you. They should be here!"

"No!"

"How sad…"

"Don't feel sorry for me. I don't want your pity."

"Oh, I don't! I feel sorry for your family. Knowing you're so close and they're unable to see you. You must see how upsetting that is for them. I could write to them for you."

"No….not yet." As he spoke, fear overshadowed his eyes. "I don't want them to see me like this. Just read, okay?"

She looked at him as he averted his eyes, not wanting to continue the conversation about his parents. "Okay, I'll read these then."

Lucy removed the first letter from its envelope. Was from his mom; the next from Gary, his brother. As she began reading the third letter, two male physical therapy techs barged boisterously into the room. Neither showing any regard for their patient who might be resting. The techs' physiques visible opposites…one short and muscular; the other tall and thin. The tall tech pushed in a wheelchair.

"Sorry," the short tech said. "It's time for therapy, Lieutenant."

Once Glen was safely transferred from the bed and seated in the wheelchair, the short, muscular tech replied, "Okay, Lieutenant, tell your pretty girlfriend not to leave. You'll be back in an hour."

"I'm not his girlfriend!" Lucy blurted too hastily.

"Too bad, Lieutenant," the tall tech joked. "Maybe you should reconsider….looks like the kind of girl you'd want to take home to meet the folks."

Glen smiled at Lucy as he and his wheelchair were pushed from the room.

Lucy, embarrassed by the tech's last remark, stood motionless until she realized she still held Glen's letters. She opened the top drawer to replace them. There in the back of the drawer she spotted another envelope and withdrew it to place with the others. This one was open; the envelope slightly crumpled. A corner of the letter jutted out at the top. In an effort to straighten the letter and return it to its proper position inside the envelope, she noticed a woman's handwritting penned on the paper's folded edge. *'My darling, just say when and where. My love for you and our plans together remain unchanged.'*

Lucy reread the sentence. She clearly wasn't the lieutenant's girlfriend. She tucked the letter inside the envelope, placed it where she found it, and closed the drawer. Feeling uncomfortable waiting for Glen in his room, she went down to the cafeteria for a coke. Sitting at a table near a window that overlooked the hospital grounds, her thoughts were solely centered around a certain Lieutenant Glen Lewis.

Before leaving for the day, Lucy wished Glen good luck on his upcoming surgery scheduled early the next morning. Knowing he would not want nor need visitors, promised to come see him after church Sunday.

True to her word, Lucy knocked softly on Glen's closed door Sunday afternoon and waited for his invitation to enter. She pushed the door open and stood beside his bed. He was lying back against his pillows. Two additional pillows were positioned under his right arm to prevent post-surgical swelling. He tried his best to muster a smile, but Lucy could tell he was hurting.

"How ya doing?" Lucy sat down on the chair. "Was the grafting successful?"

"Yes, the surgeon said I did great. Don't know what that means since I didn't do anything. My poor thigh is running out of skin!" Glen laughed. "At least I'm grateful they didn't graft skin from my backside!"

Lucy's face reddened. "Want me to read to you?"

"No, just sit with me. Will you do that?"

"Of course."

"I see you're wearing your favorite color. Blue is a good color on you."

Lucy self-consciously rubbed her fingers across the collar of her light blue dress. "How did you know blue was my favorite color?"

Glen cracked a smile. "I've learned a lot about you, Simply Lucy Bailey, as you persistently jabbered outside my door for hours on end."

Lucy's face darkened in embarrassment. "I didn't think you were listening."

A knock on the door caused the two to look around. A young man and a young woman, both immaculately dressed, entered the room. The young man—all smiles and an easy-going countenance—blonde hair slicked back with gel wore a blue shirt, yellow tie and dark blue trousers. The young woman, tall and reserved, showed no signs of emotion. She was stunning…long, dark perfectly coiffed brunette hair; tanned skin; shapely figure. She wore a dark green dress with a black clutch bag tucked loosely under her left arm.

Glen sat up. The pillows behind his head toppled to one side. Lucy stood instinctively to reposition them and helped Glen ease into a better sitting position.

"Glen, ole boy!" The young man, all spunk and charm, approached the bed. "Man! It's good to see you!"

The young woman remained by the door.

"Lucy, meet my best friend Steven Bradley. When did you get home?"

"Oh, about three weeks ago. So glad the war's over! It's good to be home!"

"Lucy, Steven and I grew up together and played football for the Abilene High School Eagles! Steven, this is Lucy Bailey, a volunteer here. She's done a lot to kick me into gear!"

"Hello," Lucy said warmly, pleased Glen finally had guests.

"Hello, Lucy." Steven brazenly winked then turned his attention back to Glen. "Boy, those were the days, weren't they? All-American. You should have seen this guy run down the field and snatch the ball out of the air! Clearly had great hands and sticky fingers. He was the best…." his voice trailed off leaving the sentence unfinished.

Glen wasn't listening to his buddy; his eyes were focused on the girl standing near the door. She kept avoiding eye contact by glancing at the floor, the walls, or her shoes; looking anywhere other than the man she came to visit.

"Holly?" Glen's voice trembled.

"Come on over, Holly." Standing at the end of the hospital bed, Steven motioned for her to join them.

Holly stepped reluctantly forward, but stood next to Steven instead of standing closer to where Glen lay.

"Lucy, this is Holly Larner…my fiancée," Glen said, keeping his eyes steadied upon Holly's face.

Lucy raised her eyebrows in surprise and looked down at Glen and then at Holly. Why hadn't he told her about Holly? He was engaged? Lucy noticed an uneasiness suddenly covered the room like a heavy goose-down feather blanket.

"Oh, I'm so sorry. You'll want to visit. I need to go anyway…to go…to get back," she stuttered. "Glen, I'm so glad your surgery went well. I'll check in before I leave. It was nice meeting you both."

Lucy left the room and closed the door behind her. She blindly walked down the hallway and waited by the nurse's break room for Glen's guests to leave. After getting a drink from the water fountain, Lucy turned the corner and saw Steven and Holly huddled beside the floor's exit doors. Lucy stepped back and waited for them to leave. They were speaking softly but not softly enough; she could hear them.

"I messed up! I'm so sorry, Steven!" Holly sniffled.

"Shhh, it's okay, sweetheart. We had to tell him sometime."

"But not that way! I should have paid more attention."

"Holly, are you sorry you married me?"

"No! Steven, you know I'll never regret marrying you! My feelings for you changed months before Glen's accident. Please, trust me about that."

"He's my childhood friend and all but I can't imagine your life with him! What would that have been like? How would he have supported you? You deserve more than being a cripple's care-giver! I've always loved you…even in high school when you and Glen were dating."

"I know."

"Let's go home," Steven whispered. Lucy peeked around the corner.

With his arms wrapped reassuringly around Holly's waist, Steven pushed through the doors. They are married? Unbelievable! Lucy briskly walked back down the hall to Glen's room. He must be in a state of confusion and anger, feeling betrayed on all sides. What a calloused trick to play. Glen's door was open. Lucy stood on the threshhold and waited for an invitation.

"Come in, Lucy."

"I overheard Steven and Holly as they were leaving. I'm so sorry!"

Glen looked at her but didn't say anything; his blue eyes were slightly red and moistened with tears. On his chest lay the letter Lucy had accidentally seen earlier. Lucy sat down on the edge of the chair. She reached out to pat Glen's right arm but quickly pulled her hand back. Touching him after his recent skin graft surgery was not a good idea.

"You can read it." He nodded at the letter. "The first few sentences will explain everything."

"Are you sure? Reading your letter feels like prying. I don't want to…"

"It's okay. Reading it is easier than trying to explain."

Lucy stood and carefully removed the letter from Glen's chest. She sat back down and unfolded it. Silently she read:

My dearest Steven,

I received your last letter and shed countless tears over it. Yes, I will marry you when you come home! I'll not mention 'us' to anyone. Don't want word getting back to Glen before we've had a chance to somehow tell him ourselves. I've not heard from him in months but know from his mother his plane crashed and he's terribly injured. He's currently in a hopital in Virginia but will soon be transferred to a hospital somewhere in Texas. I'm sorry he's injured, truly, but that doesn't change my feelings for you. Hurry home, my darling,……

Lucy had read enough. She refolded the letter and placed it in her lap.

Glen glanced at her. "Holly accidentally switched our letters. I got Steven's; he got mine. I've known about Steven and Holly for three months or maybe even longer. It was hard seeing them today and pretending I didn't know."

"I'm so sorry, Glen. That must have been so difficult! I can't begin to imagine. Is there anything I can do for you?"

"Play a song before you go home?"

"What would you like to hear?"

"Anything. I just want to sleep and forget this day ever happened."

Lucy stood and placed the letter back in the drawer of the side table. Impulsively and without much forethought, she leaned over and gently kissed Glen's forehead.

****

With class exams due in Music Theory and Music Appreciation plus a composition to be written and performed in her Music Composition class, Lucy had so little time of her own these days. And even less time to volunteer at the hospital. She felt guilty about not fulfilling her obligation to the hospital and more so about not seeing Glen.

Following Doc Lawrence's advice, she notified McCloskey General. When she spoke to Marjorie Adams to explain volunteering this semester was too difficult to manage, she felt relieved. Disappointment followed when Marjorie couldn't provide Samantha's home phone number...a strict violation of hospital policy.

Sunday afternoon Labor Day weekend Lucy somehow managed some free time and was able to convince Tommy and Loraine to take her to the hospital. She promised each a banana split before returning home. Lucy was convinced they would have agreed without being bribed, but she didn't want to risk it. She had to explain her situation to her friends and tell them goodbye.

"He's here!" Loraine called over her shoulder.

Lucy followed Loraine out the front door and watched Tommy pull off the road onto the gravel driveway. He drove his 1942 Dodge flatbed pickup slowly around the circular drive and stopped. The top of the black pickup's hood and cab as well as the fenders were rounded in shape. The truck's only windshield wiper blade hung askew over the driver's side; the headlamps sat securely centered on top of each front fender. Lucy smiled. Tommy's vehicle always reminded her of a giant praying mantis with big, bulging eyes that stared straight ahead. Was missing one antenna and the other drooped precariously over the left side of its head.

Tommy held the door open for Loraine. Lucy scrambled into the passenger side. She glanced at Loraine who had scooted closer to Tommy. It seemed her sister had finally acknowledged Tommy's affection for her and willingly returned it.

The ride to Temple passed quickly as the three recollected the skits from Bud Abbott's and Lou Costello's newest movie *The Naughty Nineties*. The movie's plot follows the antics of the two comedians who play entertainers aboard a showboat. Before setting sail, the boat's owner loses the vessel to a couple of card sharks. Abbott and Costello rig the onboard card games and recoup the owner's money. The owner reclaims his vessel and ousts the swindlers overboard.

"I think that's my number one comedy of all time!" Tommy declared.

"Abbott and Costello always make me laugh!" Loraine added.

"Who's on first?" Lucy asked.

"Yes!" Tommy and Loraine responded in unison.

"What about the part where Costello is auditioning for a singing role? At the same time, Abbott is shouting instructions to the stage crew to correctly align the height of the backdrop curtain," Lucy laughs.

"And Costello thinks Abbott is directing him?" Tommy pounds the steering wheel as he laughs.

"Costello lowers or raises his voice whenever Abbott calls out 'lower' or 'higher' to the stage hands!" Loraine laughs. "And then Costello stands on one foot when Abbott shouts 'raise the right!'"

The three were still laughing as Tommy pulled into the hospital's parking lot. He drove around two rows of parked cars before finding an empty spot. Sundays were always busy visitation days. Tommy parked and they got out.

Loraine and Tommy followed Lucy into the hospital and into the first floor elevator. At the sixth floor, the elevator door opened. Lucy disembarked first and pushed through the double doors with Loraine and Tommy close behind. As Lucy proceeded down the hall toward Glen's room, she heard footsteps advancing quickly behind her. When she heard her name called, Lucy stopped and turned.

"Lucy!" Samantha advanced briskly toward the three visitors.

"Samantha! I was hoping you'd be working today!" Lucy hugged her friend. "This is my sister Loraine and her boyfriend Tommy."

Samantha smiled brightly. "Hello! It's so nice to finally meet you. It's time for my morning break if you'd like to join me for a cup of joe in the cafeteria."

"I could use some coffee about now. That sounds great," Tommy replied.

"Sure, but I want to see Glen first." Lucy turned toward Glen's room.

Samantha grabbed Lucy's elbow. "He's not there."

Startled, Lucy raised her voice. "What? Where is he?"

Loraine saw the hurt painted across her sister's face and took her hand.

Samantha patted her friend's arm as she explained. "Glen... Lieutenant Lewis was discharged two weeks ago. His brother and parents came to take him home."

"His family came?" Lucy softly repeated.

"Yes, Lt. Lewis asked me to write and invite them to visit." Samantha reached into her uniform's pocket. "This is for you."

Samantha extended a white envelope toward Lucy. Lucy just stared at it as if it were poisonous to touch. Loraine gently took the envelope from Samantha and slid it into Lucy's skirt pocket.

"Thank you, Samantha. Lucy will read it later. How about that coffee?"

The three followed Samantha to the cafeteria and ordered four cups of coffee. Tommy kept the conversation lively. Lucy tried her best to participate in the conversation but her mind was directed elsewhere. The unopened envelope weighed heavily in her pocket.

After fifteen minutes, Lucy and Samantha hugged each other goodbye and exchanged telephone numbers and addresses promising to keep in touch. Lucy, Loraine and Tommy loaded into the truck. Once home, Lucy hurriedly opened her door and got out. Instead of going inside, she turned to her left bound for the gazebo.

"Will she be okay?" Tommy asked Loraine.

"I think so. I think she felt more for this lieutenant than she realized.

I just hope it wasn't too serious. Thanks for taking her…us…to Temple. It was nice meeting Samantha. Lucy talks about her all the time."

"Still on for dinner tomorrow tonight at Hoffbrau Steaks?"

"Of course! Reservations at seven?"

"Yes, we'll need to leave at six-thirty." Tommy got out of the truck and held the door open until Loraine slid out. Loraine leaned against the truck as Tommy kissed her goodbye once, twice, three times. She laughed as she ducked under his arms and ran to the porch. She waved and stood on the top porch step until Tommy's truck disappeared from sight.

Loraine stepped off the porch, rounded the corner of the house and headed to the gazebo to find Lucy. She stopped when she saw Lucy lying across one of the benches inside. The envelope's content was strewn across the bench inches from her fingertips. Presuming her sister might need more time on her own, Loraine turned back toward the house.

Thinking she'd heard something, Lucy sat up on the bench and looked around. No one was there. Perhaps she'd only heard dried tree leaves shuffled about by the wind. She picked up the letter and reread it.

My dearest Lucy,

I have so much to say to you. I've never been at a loss for words until it comes to expressing my feelings. I had hoped to say this to you in person; not in a letter. Samantha was kind enough to transcribe for me which makes what I want to say harder and much more embarrassing.

First of all, thank you for treating me gently when I needed a kind word and then again harshly when I needed correction. For I needed both. You treated me as if I were not a cripple. You made me see how foolishly I'd been behaving to those who were only trying to help me. I know God sent you to me to show me there is still hope for my life.

Because of you, I asked Samantha to write my parents. I explained to them my fear and reluctance for them to see me this way. You were right! They responded just as you said they would. When the doctor discharged me, they and my brother Gary came to get me. I am checking into a rehabilitation hospital in Abilene.

I have a long road ahead of me, but I am determined to carry on. I want to be a whole man, body and soul. All because of you. Thank you, for taking an interest in me for you alone are the reason I'm conquering my fears and moving forward. Don't be surprised, Lucy Bailey, if I don't show up on your porch steps one day.

Until then you may write to me in care of my parents: Bob and Ethel Lewis, 122 Hickory Street, Abilene

Sincerely,
Lieutenant Glen Lewis, United States Army Air Force
Or just simply, Glen

Late Monday evening with the lights off, Lucy leaned against three pillows propped against her bed's headboard. Feeling sorry for herself and having missed talking to Loraine the night before, Lucy pulled the pink chenille bedspread up under her chin. She wasn't chilled as it was still early fall…warm still…only sought comfort and reassurance Glen truly meant what he had written in his letter.

Lucy glanced at the clock on the bedside table as she heard steps approaching the bedroom door. It was after midnight. Papa was much more lenient with curfew hours now that the girls had graduated from high school. The door knob turned slowly and Loraine tiptoed into the room.

"I'm still awake."

"Oh! Lucy!" Loraine rushed to Lucy's bed. Plopping down, she missed sitting on her sister by inches. "I have so much to tell you! May I turn on the light?"

"Sure."

Loraine pulled down the chain on the lamp. Dim light illuminated through the white lampshade. Lucy looked at her sister whose face was beaming brightly…more so than the lamp.

Lucy sat up as Loraine scooted closer and held out her left hand. A gold band with a round solitaire diamond encircled her ring finger.

"Loraine? Is this what I think it is?"

"Yes! Tommy and I are engaged!"

"What?"

"I know! I was surprised, but then not really. Ya know? Tommy is such a wonderful guy. It just took me a long time...too long...to see that. He proposed after our steak dinner at Hoffbraus."

"Tell me all about it!" Lucy scooted over, brought her knees up and wrapped the blanket around them.

"Well," Loraine leaned back against the pillows. "After dinner Tommy asked to take me somewhere special. I thought Hoffbraus was special enough, but he drove us out to Lake Travis. We stopped overlooking the water. The sun had already set but we rolled down the windows and listened to the night sounds...crickets singing and frogs croaking. Romantic, huh?"

Lucy smiled as Loraine continued. "He told me he couldn't remember a time he hadn't loved me. Ever since we were just kids. But I seemed not to care if he were around or not. His older brother Mark told him to just be patient...persistent...but patient. I'd soon come around. Then he told me he couldn't imagine his life without me and was hoping I felt the same. He wanted to grow old with me and share every minute of our lives together."

"Well, I assume since you're wearing his engagement ring, your answer was yes? Has Tommy spoken to Papa? Does Mama know?"

"Papa knows. Tommy went to the drugstore to talk to him over a week ago! Papa suggested Tommy and I tell Mama. More special that way. Oh, Lucy! I am so excited. Who would have ever thought I'd be marrying the man who annoyed me so when we were kids!" Loraine laughed.

Lucy nodded her head and looked away.

"Are those tears? Aren't you happy for me?"

Lucy grabbed Loraine around the neck. "Yes, you goof! I'm happy for you! I'm sad for me! You'll move away and we'll never share nights like this again!"

"Oh, Lucy, of course, we will! Tommy works for his dad in the family's auto shop. We'll live here in Oak Hill. We may not live in the same house but you are my sister. You and I are two peas in a pod. We're like Abbott and Costello; Laurel and Hardy; Porky Pig and Daffy Duck. You'll always share in my life."

Lucy grinned and wiped tears away with the back of her hand. "One question. Which one of us is Porky?"

HOMECOMING
1946

"**M**aggie? Patrick's on the phone!" Franklin bellowed from the study. Maggie, hearing her name called, removed her apron and hurried down the hall.

"Repeat to your mother what you told me. She's here now." Franklin held the receiver to one side so they both could hear.

"Patrick? How are you, son? Are you okay?"

"Yes, Mama. I'm okay. I've told Papa I was able to find Kim and her mother and sisters in Salinas. The War Relocation Authority provided trailer houses and twenty-five dollars for the returning internees. It's a zoo here. The returning Japanese-Americans have no property to speak of. No place to go nor anyone to turn to. I have an appointment in the morning with the Relocation Authority."

"I'm so thankful you found them. What about Kim's father?"

"No word. All we know he will be returned to his point of origin which of course is Salinas. We just don't know when. On a happier note…. Mama, I called to let you and Papa be the first to know Kim and I were married yesterday."

"What?" Maggie searched Franklin's eyes and together they smiled.

"After much persuasion my proposal was not for convenience sake, she finally consented. John's friend, Ralph Morris, arranged with his pastor a simple wedding ceremony at his church. Kim and I along with her family are staying with the Morris's until I meet with the Relocation Authority. I'm hopeful all four will be released into my care. Mr. Morris and I agree Kim may have a better chance, under her circumstances now, being married to an American…although she is an American. This whole thing is so upside down. But so goes the world right now."

"What are your plans if your appointment goes as planned?" Maggie asked.

"I'm bringing Kim and her sisters to Texas. The girls are twelve and sixteen. Mrs. Yoshida refuses to leave without her husband. Mrs. Morris suggested Kim's mother remain with them. The prospect for a job seems doubtful as the racial bias the Salinas residents have against the Japanese people is as volatile now as they were during the war or even more so. Papa, I need to borrow some money. I hate to ask but most of my savings is depleted."

"Of course, son. How much do you need?"

"I'm not sure. Enough to get us back to Texas."

"I'll send the money through Western Union. We'll help however we can, son. You know that," Franklin encouraged.

"Oh, and honey?" Maggie asked, changing the subject.

"Ma'am?"

"Congratulations! We are delighted to welcome Kim into our family."

****

January slipped by almost unnoticed. By the middle of February Oak Hill received a sprinkling of unexpected snow. Any amount of snow was a novelty. A dusting barely covering the ground or a two-foot snowdrift banked against the house lifted the spirits of the Oak Hill residents. The Bailey family was no exception.

"Gramma? Papa?" a small voice called from the doorway.

Franklin rushed from the study. Polly, Sam's and Trina's youngest, decked in a light pink coat and matching pink mittens with a multi-colored knit scarf wrapped snuggly about her head stood in the vestibule. She laughed as she clapped her hands together; her knitted mittens produced a thump-thumping sound.

"Sweetheart! Come in! It's cold out there!"

"Papa, can we build a snowman?"

"Yes! Of course we can!"

Franklin heard his grandsons pounding up the porch steps. As usual, an argument was underway. Simon, now eleven, relished picking at his younger eight-year-old brother about anything and everything. David, willful enough and eager for any challenge, stood his ground.

"Papa!" David exclaimed excitedly as he removed his blue toboggan. A crackling of static electricity bouncing off David's hair caused Simon to point and laugh. Franklin hugged his grandsons and laughed along with them.

Maggie bustled down the hall just as Trina entered the house. Trina kissed her father-in-law's cheek and cautioned her sons to behave.

"Are they here?" Sam asked, stamping his snow-covered boots on the rug.

"Gramma, know what?" Polly asked, standing on tip-toe as her mother removed her scarf and coat. "I'm going to be a big sister!"

"What?" Maggie turned to Trina.

"We were going to tell everyone later when we're all together," Sam said, taking his wife's hand. "Was a surprise to us, too!"

Franklin grabbed Trina in a big bear-hug. "That's wonderful! Congratulations! Your baby makes our seventh grandchild!"

"I thought our family was complete," Trina whispered to Maggie.

Maggie patted Trina's arm. "Seems God has other plans."

"Let's go see our guests of honor!" Franklin beamed.

Sam's family...Polly skipping merrily; the boys scuffling about... followed Franklin and Maggie down the hall to the music room. As Sam and Trina entered, a tall, muscular young man who had been sitting next to a lovely young woman on the sofa stood.

"William!" Sam cried. Sam gathered his brother in a tight hug and clapped his back. "You look great, little brother! This then must be the infamous Caroline Hawkins I've heard so much about."

Caroline rose and joined William's side.

"Yes," William said proudly. "Caroline, this is my brother, Sam, and his family...Trina, Simon, and David.

"Yes, actually we met at Emily's before William shipped out. It's so nice to see you again."

"Of course! My apologies!" Sam shook her hand.

William hugged Trina and his nephews. "Where is my little princess?"

Polly, who'd been standing behind her mother, ran to her uncle. William picked her up and swirled her around. "Remember me? You were almost three when I saw you last!"

"Of course, Uncle William! I'm big now! I'm six!" Polly exclaimed; her brown eyes gleaming. "Mommy showed us your photo every night when we prayed for you. Is she your wife?" Polly, balanced on William's hip, pointed over her shoulder at Caroline.

William set the child down. Grinning like a kid lost in a toy store, he answered. "Close enough. We are engaged to be married Christmas Eve."

"Ah, William! That's wonderful! Congratulations!" Sam clapped William's back once more but with extra exuberance this time.

"Welcome to the Bailey family," Trina said, hugging Caroline. "They're a great family to be part of."

Lucy and Loraine entered. Lucy carried a blue floral ceramic bowl piled high with pink popcorn balls and Loraine a carafe of hot chocolate. The children flocked around the twins like three baby birds waiting for a wriggly worm to fight over.

"How come they're pink?" David picked up a popcorn ball for inspection.

"The corn ears got frostbite in the snow and the kernels turned pink," Simon, grinning mischievously, explained.

"Really?" Polly asked. "They got frostbite in the snow?"

"Simon, you goose. Red food coloring dropped in the sugar syrup while it cooks makes the pink color," Lucy laughed. "Help yourselves."

"Take turns. They're all the same size," Trina instructed her brood.

Loraine joined Caroline on the sofa. Soon their conversation turned to upcomming nuptials and wedding dresses. Lucy uninterested in talking about or listening to wedding plans, concentrated on her mug of hot choclate.

"The front door was opened…anyone could have walked in!"

"John!" William exclaimed and rose from the sofa.

The two brothers hugged each other firmly as if through that embrace their shared war experiences transferred silently one to the other. Eddie joined the other grandchildren at the popcorn bowl.

"Have you met Caroline, John?" Sam asked eagerly wanting to introduce his future sister-in-law.

"Yes, last week William brought her to the house. Caroline and her sister Gwen were Emily's constant companions while I was away."

"And she's a top-notch checkers player like Gran!" Eddie added; his mouth filled with big gooey bites of pink popcorn.

"Where is Emily?" Franklin asked.

"Here!" Emily entered carrying a plate of chocolate cake frosted with dark chocolate icing. "John asked that I bring a cake. Took it to the kitchen to slice it."

"Emily baked it herself," Gran said, bringing in dessert plates and forks.

"Gran, you make it sound like I can't bake. I did a lot of things on my own while John was away."

"Are you saying then that John baked all the cakes before the war?" William asked jokingly.

John winked at his wife as Emily answered. "Yes, William, that is exactly what I'm saying! Now, get over here and give me a hug!"

"Oh, what time is it?" Maggie asked anxiously. "Need to check the roast. Ernie and Elizabeth will be here any time now for lunch."

"I can help you, Maggie." Gran and Maggie headed to the kitchen.

"Me, too." Trina followed.

"Can we build a snowman now?" Polly asked; her lips smeared with chocolate icing; her fingers pink and sticky from clasping her popcorn ball.

Sam grinned at her. "Yes, let's wash up first. Then we'll put on your coat and mittens. Boys, want to help build a snowman?"

"Hey! I want to build a snowman!" William exclaimed. "Caroline?"

"Too cold out there for me. I'll check to see how I may help in the kitchen."

"Same for me!" Lucy agreed.

"I'm up for a little snow!" John exclaimed. "Come on, Em."

Emily shook her head. "I agree with Caroline and Lucy. It's too cold!"

"Count me in! You boys up for a little snowball fight?" Loraine challenged.

"You're on!" Eddie accepted eagerly.

Loraine hooked her arm within William's as they went to the entry hall where the coats were hung. The snowman crew followed. As the adventurers buttoned on coats and pulled gloves over their hands, the doorbell rang.

Loraine answered the door. "Tommy!"

"Hope I'm not too early." Tommy stepped side-to-side like a sheaf of wheat blown in the wind as the kids plowed through the opened door. Arlo vaulted off the front porch and ran toward a grouping of oak trees as if he knew the best snow drifts and perfect places to start the construction of a snowman.

"Not at all!" Loraine kissed Tommy as he stepped across the threshold. "We were on our way out to build a snowman and have a little snowball fight!"

"Who's this then?" William asked, pulling on a dark green knitted cap.

"Oh, William!" Loraine looked at her brother in disbelief. "Don't tease! You know Tommy North...we're to be married in four months."

"Not the same skinny kid who hung around here all the time with Grant?" John asked, stepping up behind William.

"The same," Tommy grinned. He shook William's hand and then John's. "Welcome home, William. John."

"Good at making snowmen, Tommy?" William asked.

"Not much practice around here. But yeah, I'm in!"

The four turned to join the others in the yard as a dark blue 1942 Ford pickup pulled into the drive. "Bond Construction" was stenciled in white lettering across the door panels.

Loraine hurried toward the truck before it stopped. "Uncle Ernie!"

Ernie got out of the truck and hugged his niece. Elizabeth held her door open for their guest passenger. A tall, dark-headed man emerged but remained by the truck and grinned.

"Owen!" William shouted as he gathered his cousin in a tight embrace.

John rounded the truck and grasped both men in an embrace. Loraine wrapped her arms around her two brothers and her cousin. The foursome clutched each other as Loraine cried.

Franklin hurried down the porch steps. "I thought I heard your truck, Ernie. Owen? We weren't expecting you for two weeks. Welcome home, son!"

Franklin hugged Owen tightly. "The kids are making a snowman and Loraine challenged them into a snowball fight."

"Sounds fun," Owen beamed and took Loraine's hand.

"Go see your aunt first, Owen, before you start playing with the kids," Elizabeth laughed.

"Yes, of course. Maggie will be thrilled to see you! Ernie, care for a cigar in the study?" Franklin asked. "Let's go in."

Ernie slipped his arm around Elizabeth's waist. "I'll take a cigar and a hot cup of coffee over a snowball fight any day of the week!"

"Chicken?" Loraine teased.

"Even chickens know when to roost!" Ernie winked at his niece.

Franklin led Owen, Ernie and Elizabeth to the kitchen. When they neared the door, Franklin whispered, "Owen, go in first. Better surprise that way! We'll wait here by the door."

Owen smiled and pushed through the swinging doors leading to the kitchen.

"Can a pilot get a decent cup of coffee around here?"

Maggie looked up from the platter of deviled eggs she'd placed on the granite counter. Tears puddled her eyes.

"Owen!" Maggie and Lucy exclaimed simultaneously.

Maggie reached Owen seconds before Lucy and hugged him tightly. "Looks like the Army Air Force fed you well."

Owen laughed. "That's exactly what mother said. What's up with whether I ate well or not your number one concern?"

Lucy patted Owen's abdomen. "A little too well, I'd say."

"Welcome home! It's so good to have you safely home!" Gran exclaimed as she hugged Owen.

Emily waited her turn to welcome Owen home. "Did you see John and William outside?"

"Yes, Loraine, too."

"Owen, this is Caroline Hawkins, William's fiancée," Maggie nodded toward Caroline. "Caroline, this is my nephew. Ernie's boy."

"Nice to meet you. Welcome home, Owen," Caroline greeted.

"Thank you. It's a pleasure to finally meet you. William wrote numerous letters about you. Congratulations to you both." Owen looked toward the door and raised his voice, "Okay, you guys can come in now."

Maggie, clearly puzzled, watched as Franklin, Ernie, and Elizabeth, appearing mysteriously devious, stepped into the kitchen to join the homecoming.

REUNITED
1946

Maggie sat up suddenly as if she'd been poked by a broken bed spring. She strained to listen for the sound that had stirred her from a deep sleep. Had she been dreaming? There...she heard it again. A pounding noise from downstairs. She leaned toward Franklin and gently shook his shoulder.

"Franklin? Do you hear that?"

Franklin opened his eyes and rubbed them awake. "What? What time is it?"

"It's 3:00. I'm sorry to wake you. But I heard something. There. Hear it?"

Franklin pulled back his covers, sat on the edge of the bed and turned on the lamp. He placed his spectacles on the bridge of his nose, slipped on his housecoat, and slid his feet into brown slippers kept under the bed. Maggie slipped on her houseshoes, wrapped on her housecoat and followed Franklin down the stairs.

The pounding became more insistent as they neared the front door. Franklin turned on the hall light. Through the stained-glass door panel, Maggie saw a blurred image on the other side. Standing to one side, she placed her hand against Franklin's back as he opened the door.

"Patrick! We weren't expecting you until Wednesday."

"We drove all night. I'm sorry, Papa, to wake you so early. Of all things, I didn't remember to take a house key."

Franklin pulled his youngest son into an embrace.

"Mama," Patrick greeted, peering over Franklin's shoulder. He stepped around his father and hugged his mother.

"Are Kim and her sisters in the car?" Franklin asked, straining his eyes into the darkness.

"Kim and Akira, her youngest sister, are."

"Well, bring them in!" Franklin encouraged. "Her mother and older sister?"

"I'll explain it all later. We are very tired and need to sleep."

"Of course!" Maggie said, "I'll get your beds ready and Franklin can help unload the car later. Akira may have John's room. Oh, Patrick, it's so good to have you home!" Maggie hugged her son again and turned toward the stairs.

Franklin stood in the doorway and watched as Patrick assisted Kim from the front seat of the car and Akira from the back. Exhaustion visibly apparent, Kim held her sister about the shoulders and directed her up the porch steps.

"Mr. Bailey," Kim bowed her head slightly as Akira slid behind her.

Franklin hugged her. "Please call me Franklin or Papa. You're family now, Kim. And we are so delighted you are."

Kim smiled. "Thank you."

Akira peeked around her sister to better see this tall, bespectacled man clothed in a blue plaid flannel robe. He reached out his hand but she ducked back seeking refuge behind her sister.

Patrick, carrying two small suitcases, marched quickly up the porch steps. Kim led Akira into the house and Patrick followed.

Franklin closed the front door behind them. "You know your way around. We'll see you in the morning. Sleep as long as you'd like."

Maggie was waiting in the upstairs hallway as the three weary travelers mounted the stairs. Upon seeing Kim, she rushed forward and hugged her tightly. "Kim, I'm so glad to see you! Welcome to our family, sweetheart! I've made John's bed down for Akira. Please, make yourself at home. I'll see you in the morning."

"Thank you, Mama," Patrick said. "I hope you're able to go back to sleep."

"I'll try. I'm so excited you are home! Sleep well."

Kim took a suitcase, held Akira's hand and led her to John's bedroom. Akira walked to the bed and sat on its edge. She looked around. The room seemed so large compared to where she had lived the past four years. Suddenly the absence of her mother and Asami consumed her with longing and grief. She began to whimper.

Kim sat beside her and wrapped her sister up in her arms. "Shhh... shhh," she cooed. The more Kim rocked, the more Akira cried.

"Haha! I want Haha!" Akira cried out as if she were five rather than twelve.

"Akira, shhh. I know you miss Mother and Asami. They'll come as soon as they can. Put on your nightgown. You'll feel better after some sleep."

Kim opened the small, badly scuffed brown case. Removing a light blue nightgown, Kim placed it on the bed beside her sister. Akira stood, undressed and slipped the nightgown over her head. Kim held up the corner of the sheet while Akira slid underneath. The sheets felt cool against her skin; the pillow firm; the bedding warm and comfortable. Was perfect.

"Stay with me, Kim! I don't want to be in this big room by myself!"

"Akira, I'll be just down the hall. Just close your eyes and sleep."

"No! Kim! Don't leave me!"

"I'm not leaving you!" Kim sat on the bed beside Akira. "You are safe here. This is Patrick's home; his family. My family now. Patrick will take care of us."

Akira gripped Kim's arm tightly. "Nooooo. Please, Kimika!"

Kim looked at her baby sister. Akira's big, brown eyes were rimmed in red from crying. She had cried herself to sleep every night since they'd left California. She looked so small and helpless lying in this big bed. Akira's chin quivered; her eyes pleaded with tears.

"One night. I'll stay with you one night. Okay?"

Akira nodded.

"Let me tell Patrick and change." Akira grasped Kim's hand tightly. "I'll be right back, Akira. I promise." Akira finally released Kim's hand.

Kim slipped down the hall, changed into her nightgown and kissed Patrick goodnight. She came back to Akira's room and eased the door open. Akira was sitting on the floor by the door, rocking back and forth; her forehead rested on her pulled-up knees.

Startled, Kim squealed. "Akira! What on earth are you doing on the floor? I said I'd be right back! Come, let's go to bed."

Kim pulled her sister from the floor and watched as Akira climbed into bed. As Kim eased under the top sheet, Akira rolled against her. Kim reached down and pulled the blanket over them. Akira nestled her head against her sister's shoulder. Finally as her breathing became less erratic, Akira closed her eyes and fell asleep.

The next morning at 8:30, Patrick trotted down the backstairs to find Franklin and Maggie sitting at the kitchen table. He kissed his mother's cheek and sat down next to his father. Franklin pushed his newspaper to one side.

"Ready for breakfast?" Maggie asked as she stood.

"Yes! I'm ravished. The smell of frying bacon pried my eyes open! Reminded me of Clayton when we were kids. On the mornings we smelled bacon cooking, we'd race down the backstairs to be the first in the kitchen. Remember?"

"I remember." Maggie laughed. "There're biscuits, butter and jam there on the table. I'll get your eggs."

"So why did Asami not come? Akira seems so shy and insecure. How's she coping with all this?" Franklin asked.

Between bites of a buttered biscuit, Patrick explained. "Asami would not leave her mother alone in Salinas even though Mrs. Yoshida is in good hands with Mr. and Mrs. Morris. We are hopeful Kim's father will be returned to Salinas soon and that Mrs. Yoshida will be able to persuade him to come to Texas. Akira is still adjusting. The last four years of her life have been miserable ones...almost as if she's a returning prisoner of war. Honestly, they're all prisoners of war."

"We will pray for a good outcome for the Yoshidas. I must get to work. Maggie will you come with me to the door?" Franklin and Maggie left the kitchen.

As Patrick poured coffee into his mug, Kim and Akira strolled into the kitchen. Akira, clinging to Kim's arm, was unwilling to release her hold. Kim looked anxiously at Patrick for help.

"Good morning, Akira," Patrick greeted cheerfully. "Here, have a seat."

Kim was finally able to coax her sister to sit down beside her. Once seated, Akria immediately grabbed Kim's hand.

"After you've eaten breakfast," Patrick continued. "I thought maybe you'd like to go with me to the barn. There are three horses out there waiting to meet you. Would you like that?"

"Can Kim come?"

"Yes, of course, she can! Now how would you ladies like your eggs? Scrambled or fried?"

"Patrick, let me do that." Kim stood.

Akira grabbed Kim's arm, pulling at her. "No! Don't leave!"

"Akira, honey, I'll be right over there by the stove. You can see me."

Akira remained seated, but eyed Kim constantly as Patrick placed a glass of freshly-squeezed orange juice in front of her. She stared at the glass briefly as if pondering whether it safe to drink. She took a small sip. A smile tugged the corners of her mouth.

Patrick sat in the chair across from her. "Pretty good, huh?"

Akira nodded, studied him closely, then asked, "What are the horses names?"

Patrick looked over his shoulder at Kim and smiled. "Oh, well, let's see….Honey is Loraine's race horse. Lucy's horse is Bluebonnet, but we call her Blue. And then there's Crockett."

"Named after Davy Crockett?"

Patrick grinned. "Yes, that's right. How did you…"

"Kim taught us Texas history at my school at Poston."

Kim served Akira's breakfast plate and sat down to eat her own.

"I'd love to hear about Poston one day. Would you tell me about it?"

Akira nodded as she spooned two tablespoons of strawberry jam into a biscuit and pressed the bread until jam oozed over the sides. She took a big bite and licked off the jam that slowly crept down her fingers. The strawberry jam smeared over her upper lip formed a sticky mustache.

Maggie returned to the kitchen. "Sorry, Patrick. Your father always thinks of a thousand things he needs to tell me before he leaves for work.

I think he forgets how effective the telephone service is these days. Oh, Kim! Good morning! Good morning, Akira. Did you sleep well?"

"Yes, ma'am," Akira replied softly.

"Akira wants to meet the horses this morning, Mama," Patrick said.

"That's a wonderful idea! Akira, I hope you'll enjoy staying with us."

Akira wiped her mouth and placed the crumpled napkin beside her plate.

"Ready?" Patrick stood and extended a hand.

Akira, panic-stricken, looked at Kim. "Kim? Aren't you coming?"

"Kim, go on. I'll take care of the kitchen. Santos has looked forward to seeing you for some time." Maggie patted Kim's arm.

Kim's face lit up. "Yes! I want him to meet another budding gardener."

"Who's Santos?' Maggie heard Akira ask as the three left the kitchen.

Patrick held the screen door open as Kim and Akira stepped out into the brisk April morning. The sun was shining but seemed to be in a sort of stupor for no heat radiated from the giant orb. Flower bulbs that had been resting in the frozen ground through the winter pushed up through the mulched soil. Yellow and white daffodils had opened fully. The bearded iris buds were still tightly wrapped on their stems with just a hint of color at the tips. It was not yet time to reveal their lovely purple and gold standards and falls.

Arlo ran from the side of the laundry house where he had been exploring and ran straight toward the newcomer. With his tail wagging furiously, the dog jumped up hitting Akira chest-high. Losing her balance, Akira took a step backwards.

"Down! Arlo!" Patrick commanded. Arlo sat. "I'm so sorry, Akira!"

"Ooohhh. Hello! Who are you?" Akira knelt and let the dog cover her face in kisses. "Is your name Arlo?" Arlo, as though he understood her question, extended his right paw. Akira laughed. "He's beautiful! Is he yours?"

Patrick nodded. "Yes...well, mine and the family's."

Akira placed her head against Arlo's and rubbed the dog's head and stroked his ears. She cooed at him and kissed his wet nose. Arlo's long tail wagged ferociously in response. She hugged his neck tightly. "You're such a good boy! Aren't you? Come on, Arlo. Let's go to the barn!"

Arlo popped up on all fours. With his tongue hanging to one side and his ears flying behind him, he ran full speed down the worn path toward the barn. Kim entwined her fingers within Patrick's and exhaled a sigh of relief as she watched her sister chase after the dog.

****

The lobby area with its shiny blue and white freshly waxed tiled flooring was small but well-lit. Finding space for a family of three to sit together on the wood benches proved impossible. Akira stood on tiptoes and looked out through the window onto the covered tarmac where Greyhound buses arrived and departed. Three buses parked in lanes A, B, and C were unloading passengers, trunks, suitcases, and U.S. Postal packages. Two lanes were empty. A bus from Salinas, California; the other from Little Rock, Arkansas, were due soon.

Akira glanced over her shoulder searching for Kim and Patrick in the crowded room. When she spotted Kim and Patrick leaning against the back wall, she mouthed at her sister, "How much longer?"

Kim looked up at the large clock that hung over the ticket counter and held up eight fingers. Eight more minutes of agonizing torture. Akira's French braid that ended with a small blue bow lay perfectly aligned against her back. She turned back around to resume her position as look-out.

"She's so excited!" Kim observed.

"And you're not?" Patrick teased.

"Oh, Patrick! I am as excited as a kid on Christmas morning. Honestly, I feel more like I do before a piano recital. Excited and scared. I can never thank you enough for all you and your family have done to bring my mother and sister here. And Akira!" Kim continued, "Look how she's changed! She's so happy! If she'd continued having those panic attacks, I don't know how I would have managed. Thanks to Maggie for letting Arlo move into her room!"

"Akira is waving at us. The bus must be here." Patrick took Kim's hand, and they made their way toward the door leading out to the tarmac.

"It's here! It's here!" Akira bounded toward the terminal's door.

"Wait! Akira! Only passengers are allowed out there."

Akira smoothed the front of her pastel blue skirt and readjusted the collar on her pink floral blouse. She looked up at Kim. "Do I look alright?"

Kim put arm around her sister. "You look wonderful."

"Haha and Asami are finally here!" Akira excitedly grasped Kim's hand.

Patrick, Kim and Akira stood near the window and watched as the passengers from the Salinas bus entered the terminal. Kim fiddled nervously with her hands. The bus driver, clad in a blue Greyhound uniform and a blue hat trimmed with a black brim, accompanied a group of six passengers inside.

Kim hurried up to the man. "Excuse me, sir. Are these the only passengers from Salinas?"

"Oh, no ma'am. There's three more."

"Three?"

Kim and Akira turned as the three stragglers entered the terminal. A man with slightly hunched shoulders wearing a dark gray suit a size too large for his small frame carried a round planter in his hands. A two-foot plant rested against his chest. Two women, each carrying a small suitcase, trailed behind.

"Papa?" Kim screeched. "Papa!"

"Haha! Papa!" Akira cried out. "Asami!"

Akira burst forward like a wad of paper shot from a peashooter. Kim followed. Upon seeing them, the man placed the planter gently on the floor and opened his arms widely. He crushed his two daughters to his chest and sobbed. Asami joined the huddle. Mrs. Yoshida smiled at Patrick.

"Thank you," she mouthed, tipping her head.

Patrick watched the scene, overcome with emotion. Reunited after four grueling years. These five would empathize over countless stories. Kim released her father's hold and walked briskly toward her husband.

The look on her face filled Patrick's heart with joy. With tears filling their eyes, she hugged his neck.

"Did you know? Did you know Papa was with them?"

"Yes, I did. Nice Surprise?"

"Oh, Patrick! I couldn't love you more than I do right now!" She kissed him, not at all concerned who saw them.

After several more minutes watching the Yoshida's family reunion—a mixture of tight embraces, tears, sobs, nonstop babble and laughter—Patrick stepped closer and asked, "Would you like to go home now?"

Thirty minutes later, Patrick steered the car he'd borrowed from Uncle Ernie onto Tenth Street and stopped. He crooked his arm over the front seat and grinned at the backseat passengers. The Yoshida women, all four, were jammed together with very little squirming room. But they didn't seem to care.

"We're here!" Kim exclaimed. "Welcome to your house!"

Mrs. Yoshida grasped Kim's hand. "What did you say?"

"Your house! Come on!" Akira exclaimed and climbed over her mother.

As the women exited the car, Patrick took the planter from Mr. Yoshida making his exit easier to maneuver.

"What kind of plant am I holding here?" Patrick asked.

"An orange tree," Mr. Yoshida answered confidently. "I found the pitiful thing behind our greenhouse among shards of glass. All the glass on the greenhouse had been shattered by rocks. This is all that's left.... all I have left."

Kim placed her arm around her father's shoulders to console him. The Yoshida family stood on the sidewalk and together observed the house at the end of the walkway. The house, simple in structure, was small...two bedrooms; one bathroom. The long, cedar clapboards had been painted white; the shutters either side of the front windows dark blue. The lawn was sparse in many places with visible skinny brown roots running haphazardly across the hard dried-out soil. The singular tree in the center of the yard, an oak, reached ten feet tall. The flower beds abutting the front porch deprived viewers of any green vegetation or floral beauty.

"The house belongs to my cousin Anne and her husband Grayson. They've recently moved to Temple," Patrick explained as he put the planter down carefully. "They have offered the house to you rent-free for a year to enable you time to find employment. After that, they'll negotiate a fair rental fee. If you're agreeable to those terms, the house is yours."

Patrick reached into his pants pocket, withdrew a set of keys and held them out to Mr. Yoshida. Kim's father stood rigidly, his mouth set; perplexed, as if he'd not understood the generous proposal.

"What a charitable offer. We are humbled by all you've done for us, Patrick. Thank your cousins for us." Mrs. Yoshida took her husband's hand. "Hiroto?"

Kim held her breath for she knew her father was a proud man and disliked charity or handouts of any kind. He had taught her to work hard toward a goal and never be satisfied until the goal was accomplished. But since the war's onset, all his dreams and aspirations...his goals... had been destroyed in the blink of an eye.

"The yard needs much attention. But is not hopeless. Shall we look inside?" Mr. Yoshida took the keys from Patrick and walked purposefully to the front door. His wife and two younger daughters followed excitedly.

Patrick took Kim's elbow. "Wait. I have something for you." Puzzled, Kim remained on the sidewalk and watched her husband retrieve a small black suitcase from the trunk of the car. "Thought you'd like to stay the night with your family."

"Oh, Patrick! It's been so long since I've seen my father! How did...."

Before Kim could continue, Patrick kissed her. "I'll be back tomorrow. Have errands to run for Loraine. I love you, Kim, and would do anything for you!"

"Oh, and I love you." Kim returned his kiss.

"Kimika?" he whispered. "Tell me you love me in Japanese."

"Aishimasu!"

Kim kissed him goodbye and hurriedly went inside to join her family.

VOWS AND PROMISES
1946

Loraine knocked softly on the glass-paneled door at North Body Shop. Tommy's dad, head bent over a ledger, sat behind his desk in his office. He looked up, smiled broadly and motioned for her to enter.

"Come in, my dear! Come in!"

Loraine lifted up three brown paper bags she held in her hand. "Brought you a ham and cheese on rye from the deli...extra mustard, chips, and a dill pickle."

Mr. North stood and walked around the old oak wood desk; it's surface marred and deeply scratched by years of not using a protective covering. He graciously took a sack and patted her arm.

"Thank you. This is very thoughtful. Tommy is working in bay two."

"Great! I also brought one for him." Loraine turned to leave.

"You know Tommy's mother would have loved seeing him get married." Mr. North glanced at the small framed family portrait on the edge of the desk. "And she would have adored you immensely. We always wanted a daughter."

"Now you have one!" Loraine smiled. She never knew how to respond when Mr. North spoke about his late wife. Although her death happened unexpectedly when Mark was twelve and Tommy only nine, her loss would always remain.

"Sorry, I seem to blubber and reminisce more often these days with the wedding coming up. Ellen would have loved all of this. Ah, but don't pay any attention to an old geezer like me! You two kids enjoy your lunch."

Loraine nodded. "Thank you. See you later, Mr. North."

"Tommy calls me dad. Was hoping you would too!"

Loraine kissed his cheek. "Nothing I'd like more, Dad. See ya later."

She closed the office door and spotted Tommy working under the hood of a 1945 Cadillac Fleetwood four-door sedan. The car's chassis was sleek; eighteen feet in length from its front grill to its rear fender wings. The baby blue body sported a solid white top and white-wall tires. The chrome was shiny and impressive.

A small radio sitting on a shelf at the back of the garage blared out the top-twenty weekly hits to anyone within a half-block's listening distance. Tommy's back was turned. Loraine tip-toed up and shook his lunch sack over his head. He jumped around and sliced the air with the wrench he tightly clutched in his hand.

"You missed me by a mile!" She grinned.

"Loraine! What are you doing here?" He wiped his hand on his navy one-piece coverall that bore 'North Auto Shop' stitched over the left pocket.

"It's lunchtime. I don't have to be at work until 2:30. Have the late shift. Oh, you've got a little something there." She pointed at his cheek.

"Here?"

"No, over a bit."

"Here?"

"Want me to get it?"

"Yeah, here." He removed a rag from his back pocket and held it out.

"How much good will that do, Tommy North? It's covered in grease and oil. Hold still." Loraine licked her forefinger and moved in closer. When within a breath's distance away, she kissed him. "There! Got it!"

"Have I just been bamboozled? You didn't get it all....there's still some here." Tommy pointed to his bottom lip.

"Come on." Loraine laughed and took his hand. "You're good for now. Let's eat on the picnic table out back."

Loraine and Tommy crossed through the garage...its floors splotched with oil stains and the four bays smelled of grease and rubber tires. They exited through the back door. The pecan tree which stood in the middle of the grassless yard provided welcomed shade from June's scorching sun. Five vehicles were parked near the back fence. Three cars....two completely repaired and one waiting in queue for repair... and, of course, the two pickups belonging to Tommy and Mr. North.

Tommy held Loraine's hand as she stepped in the space between the table and bench and eased down on the paint-stripped wooden bench. She smoothed her skirt over her knees as Tommy hustled around the table and plopped down across from her. He eagerly opened his paper bag and withdrew the ham and cheese sandwhich. He took a big bite. Loraine watched as he took another bite before swallowing the first. The way the food protruded from the side of his cheek reminded her of one of the brown squirrels that scavenged the yard; tucking away small bits of pecans into its cheek pouches until they ballooned as if filled with air.

"You've got something there," Loraine pointed.

"Oh, no you don't! I'm not falling for that again."

Loraine did her best to carry on a serious conversation without commenting again about the blob of mustard camped in the corner of his mouth.

"Patrick and Sam parked the camper behind your dad's house yesterday. Lucy will help me clean it tomorrow. Sam's coming back tomorrow afternoon to hook up electricity and add a butane tank. The camper will soon be livable. Anyway, it's not our forever home. Forever...doesn't that sound odd?"

"What? Living in a camper or getting married? Having second thoughts?"

"No, of course not!" Loraine squeezed his hand. "What was I saying? Oh, about the camper...it will be fine for now. Besides we'd be such a burden to your dad if we lived with him in his small house."

"He wouldn't mind; has said so numerous times."

"Yeah, but your dad's also said he doesn't expect us to live in his backyard more than a year. Less even. Has big plans for you it seems."

"Yeah, wants to expand and open another shop across town."

"We've never really talked about that. Is that what you want to do?"

Tommy stared at the back of the building as if his future was painted on a mural stretched across the wall. "Not really. Let's not talk about that now. So, Mrs. North, did you decide where we're spending our honeymoon?"

Loraine blushed and looked down at her half-uneaten sandwich.

"You're blushing!"

"Am I?" Loraine touched her cheek, surprised to feel heat, and laughed. "That's so unlike me."

"I know! You're adorable."

"Umm, not sure about that." Loraine smiled. "But to answer your question, Mr. North, I'd like to go to Carlsbad. Fish on the Pecos River and tour Carlsbad Caverns. I've read they're spectacular. I've seen pictures of the stalagmite and stalactite formations in a magazine. There are daily tours where we can actually hike down into the caves. A large population of bats emerge every evening at sunset. I want to see that, too."

"So, New Mexico it is!"

****

Lucy closed the camper's small refrigerator door, wiped the surface down and dropped her cleaning rag into a bucket of water-and-vinegar. She swept her hair out of her face with her hand. She turned as Loraine was coming from the bedroom; two white shirts and a blue dress draped over one arm.

"Well, that's done. Now what?" Lucy asked.

"Let me hang these up. Then how about a break? Mr. North sent out a pitcher of sweet iced tea. Said we could come to the house anytime for whatever we needed. The back door is unlocked. In fact, he's letting us use his spare bedroom for anything that doesn't fit in here."

"You'll certainly need that! With just your shoes and dresses and riding boots, Tommy can have one pair of pants and two shirts...no more!"

"Funny girl!" Loraine turned toward the bedroom. "I'll be right back!"

The camper's only door was propped open and the back bedroom windows were fully opened coaxing air to circulate through the cramped space. Placing her elbows on the horseshoe-shaped dinette table, Lucy leaned toward the oscillating fan that rhythmically moved side to side distributing cooler air. Or maybe Lucy only imagined cooler air. Being this close to the fan added a welcomed escape from the heat if only briefly.

"It's already a scorcher." Loraine handed Lucy a glass of tea and scooted into the opposite corner of the booth. "That fan feels good!" She shifted on the seat and propped her feet up on the faded blue vinyl seat cusion.

"Thanks." Lucy took a big swallow. "So what's the plan for this afternoon?"

"Kim wants to practice the arrangements for the ceremony on the church piano. Wants to hear how they sound in the sanctuary."

"It's so sweet of her to play for you. I would have ya know."

"But you're my maid of honor! Can't be two places at one time!"

"Guess not! Would be fun, though, running back and forth between the piano and the altar! Or I could just play an accordion and remain at the altar. Sure you don't want me to try?" Lucy laughed.

"Very funny! No, thank you. Any more letters from Glen?"

Lucy draped her arm over the back of the booth and fanned her face with her hand. "No, not in six weeks. He's been going to rehab weekly and several weeks ago added his name to a waiting list for a prosthesis. I think he's doing okay…"

Loraine reached out for her sister's hand to console her. As their fingertips touched, a loud banging noise erupted from the back of the camper. Someone or something was striking the camper's aluminum siding. Startled, the girls looked at each other. The pounding intensified.

"What is that?" Lucy asked.

Loraine hustled from her seat and marched bravely through the open door. She scrambled down the three make-shift porch steps with Lucy in close pursuit.

"Grant? I know that's you!" Loraine shouted. "Come out! Show yourself!"

Loraine, amid long strides, halted abruptly as she rounded the corner. Lucy plowed into her and stepped on the back of her sister's heels.

"Ladies…"

"Clayton! Oh, Clayton!" Lucy slipped around her sister and ran toward her brother. She jumped. He caught her mid-air and twirled her around.

"Loraine?" Clayton held out his arms and smiled broadly. Loraine didn't budge; tears streamed down her cheeks.

"Don't cry, baby sister. Please, don't cry." Clayton approached quickly and wrapped Loraine in a hug. Lucy still held a tight vise-like-grip on his right arm.

"You're here!" Loraine continued to weep. "But you reenlisted! I didn't think you could come!"

"Yeah," Clayton grinned. "I heard there's a wedding going on in four days and I wouldn't miss it for anything! Uncle Sam and the navy can do without me for a few weeks. So, what are you girls up to? How may I help?"

With their arms wrapped around either side of Clayton's waist, the girls led him back into the camper. There were four years of their lives to catch up on…cleaning and organizing, now the lowest priority, could wait one more day.

****

After adjusting Loraine's lace veil for the third time, Maggie placed her hand against her daughter's cheek. "You are so lovely!"

"Mama, don't start crying! I'm almost on the verge myself."

"I'll try. No promises! Your father wants to see you before we go out."

"Okay." Loraine waited for her mother to open the door.

Franklin sheepishly entered. He looked smart in his new dark blue suit and matching tie. A white rose was pinned to his lapel. He stepped toward Loraine and took her hands. Tears lined his eyes as he spoke.

"Loraine, you look beautiful!" He kissed her cheek. "I have known one day this moment when you marry would come and thought I was well prepared. But, seeing you now…I admit I'm helplessly unprepared.

I also knew one day I would step aside and allow another man to be the most important man in your life...."

"Papa, you will always be important to me!" Loraine choked.

"I know, sweetheart, but now it's Tommy who will care for you. He is a good man and I know he will oversee your every happiness. He promised he would." Franklin winked. "Or I'll sic all your brothers on him."

Loraine laughed nervously. Maggie, who remained by the door, suppressed tears as she laughed.

"I have something for you." Franklin reached into the inner breast pocket of his suit jacket and withdrew a necklace. "This is a blue pearl. I chose a solitaire rather than a string of pearls to remind you how rare and precious you are. May I?"

Loraine nodded as Franklin fastened the pearl necklace in the front and then slid the clasp to the back of her neck. Loraine reached up to feel the pearl.

"This is your something blue...your mother said you were lacking a blue object. Already had your something old, something new, something borrowed..."

Loraine, disregarding the time her mother had spent perfecting the position of her veil, grabbed Franklin's neck and hugged tightly. "I love you so much, Papa!"

A tap sounded on the door. "Mama? It's time."

Maggie opened the door. Lucy stepped in and addressed Loraine. "Ready?"

Loraine nervously pressed her palms together. "Is everyone here?"

"Yes," Lucy replied.

"And my brothers and cousins all wearing their service uniforms?"

"Just as you commanded, general! Eddie is waiting to be your escort, Mama."

Franklin extended his arm. "Shall we go get you married?"

Within the church sanctuary, Kim softly played the piano. An underlying current of excitement and anticipation mingled amid the piano key's sharps and flats and floated up toward the vaulted ceiling.

William, dressed in his blue naval officer's uniform, stood with Tommy on the top step of the altar.

As Kim continued playing, the doors at the back of the sanctuary opened. All guests turned to watch the wedding processional. Entering first, Loraine's best friend, Bonnie Evans, smiled brightly. She wore a lavender tea-length satin dress and carried a boquet of light green Peruvian lilies tied with long lavender ribbons. Arnold, wearing a blue suit and lavender striped tie, escorted her down the aisle. As they reached the altar they parted in opposite directions. Bonnie stood on the bottom step to the left; Arnold on the right.

Next to enter were Lucy and Grant. Lucy's lime green satin dress, similar to Bonnie's except for the color, rustled as she walked. She nervously gripped her bouquet of lavender roses wound tightly with dark green ribbons. Grant, donning a blue suit and matching blue striped tie, squeezed Lucy's elbow.

"We've got this, cuz," Grant whispered.

Lucy smiled as they parted at the altar and took their places on the second step. Polly, Sam's youngest, and Victoria, Art's youngest, held hands as they entered next. Each dressed in matching white chiffon dresses with light green sashes carried a white basket of white rose petals between them. As they stepped slowly up the aisle, Polly eagerly demonstrated for Victoria how to cast the petals onto the red carpet. William winked at them as they drew closer. The little girls joined Lucy on the second step.

"All rise," William instructed as he raised his arms.

Kim began playing "The Wedding March" by Felix Mendelssohn, one of her favorite German composers. The guests stood and turned to welcome the bride. A lump formed in Tommy's throat as he watched his future wife being escorted into the sanctuary by her father. Tears wedged in his eyes the closer she neared.

Loraine prided herself in being a no-frills-kind-of girl, but today was truly an exception. Her long form-fitting dress, constructed of white satin overlayed with white beaded lace, skimmed the top of her white shoes. Her blonde hair was perfectly coiffed. The lace veil, which she refused to use as a face covering, aligned at her elbows. The bodice's scooped neckline beautifully displayed her blue pearl necklace. She carried a mixed bouquet of white roses and white calla lillies.

As Loraine and Franklin eased slowly up the aisle, Loraine glanced to the left and then the right. All her family and close friends stood on either side of the aisle.

Before stepping up to to the altar, Franklin and Loraine paused at the first row of pews. She handed Mr. North a single white rose. She kissed his cheek then turned toward her mother. As she handed Maggie a white rose, she avoided eye contactat fearful they'd both start crying. She kissed her mother's cheek. Franklin then led Loraine forward toward William who motioned the audience to be seated.

"Who gives this woman in marriage?" William asked.

"Her mother and I." Franklin kissed Loraine's cheek then joined Maggie.

Reaching the top step, Loraine handed her bridal bouquet to Lucy who through tear-filled eyes smiled lovingly. Loraine then turned to face Tommy.

"You're beautiful!" he whispered, taking her hands.

Loraine gripped Tommy's hands tightly. She glanced at William whose sweet, warm smile settled her nervousness.

The ceremony began.

"Family and friends, today we are blessed to gather in God's Presence to witness the marriage of Tommy Eugene North and Loraine Rae Bailey. I am honored to officiate this ceremony for my baby sister. Marriage, instituted by God at the very beginning of time, is a sacred ceremony; a contract sealed between a man and a woman that carries a lifelong commitment to God and to each other." William opened his Bible and placed it flat across his hands. "In Genesis Chapter 2, we read these words, 'And the rib, which the LORD God had taken from man, made he a woman, and brought her unto the man. And Adam said, This is now bone of my bones and flesh of my flesh; she shall be called Woman, because she was taken out of Man. Therefore shall a man leave his father and his mother, and shall cleave unto his wife; and they shall be one flesh.' We know from Apostle Paul's letter to the Corinthians, that love is patient and kind. Love does not envy; love does not boast. Love is not arrogant nor easily provoked. Love bears all things; believes all things; hopes all things; and endures all things. Marriage is the melding of two persons into one unit. Today, Loraine and Tommy, you stand before God and these witnesses to profess your love to each other. Before exchanging rings and vows, Tommy asked to say something…Tommy?"

Tommy nodded and released Loraine's hands. Perplexed, Loraine glanced at William as this addition to the ceremony was clearly unrehearsed. Grant withdrew a folded piece of paper from his suit pocket and handed it to Tommy.

Tommy turned again to face Loraine and took a deep breath.

"Loraine, remember our senior year in high school when you sat behind me in 20th Century Literature class? You'd poke my back every time you caught me doodling and thought I wasn't paying attention to Mrs. Smith." The audience tittered; Loraine grinned. "Well, I was paying attention. William Butler Yeats could have easily written this poem years ago for me to share with you today." His hand began to shake. Loraine clasped both her hands around his to calm and steady him.

He read the words scribbled across the page; his voice strong and clear. "Had I the heaven's embroidered cloths enrought with the golden and silver light; the blue and the dim and the dark cloths of night and light and half-light, I would spread the cloths under your feet. But I, being poor, have only my dreams; I have spread my dreams beneath your feet; tread softly because you tread on my dreams."[7]

So overcome with emotion, Loraine no longer suppressed her tears. Droplets spilled untethered down her cheeks. She felt as if she were emerged under six-feet of water looking up at the surface; sounds mere vibrations; faces blurred; motions stiffled as if the water's current held some kind of power keeping her anchored underneath. The ceremony continued and she reacted as a marionette to its master….she the puppet; William the string-master. She spoke when questioned and moved when commanded. She finally became fully aware of her surroundings when she heard William boldly announce, "And now it is my extreme honor and utmost privilege to introduce to you Mr. and Mrs. Tommy North."

The audience stood, whooped, and applauded.

William added, "After photos of the wedding party are taken, please join our family at our home for some good ole Texas barbecue as we celebrate this newly wedded couple. Everyone is welcome."

SAILS INTO THE SUNSET
1946

T he festivities at the Baileys had been in full swing for almost two hours. The sun was slowly sliding down the vast blue western expanse and had at least one more hour before slipping entirely out of sight. Satin and lace had been substituted earlier for cotton and denim.

The French double-doors leading from the sunroom had been propped open allowing guests to mingle either inside the house or on the grounds by the grouping of chairs arranged by the gazebo. The younger grandchildren ran boisterously in and out or through the house enjoying the freedom the opened doors provided. Two tables near the gazebo held the last of the barbecue beef, roasted potatoes, corn-on-the-cob, baked beans, cookies and fruit tarts; each dish covered with a red-and-white cloth to keep the flies off. The two-tiered wedding cake securely harbored inside the sunroom away from the heat and flying insects remained uncut.

Elizabeth cornered Maggie who was talking with Matilda Lawrence, Dottie, Sakura Yoshida and Caroline Hawkins. "Maggie? Where are the bride and groom? I'd like to take family group photos by the creek before the sun sets."

"They're in the barn with Santos and Art and Rosa."

"Of course they are!" Elizabeth shaded her eyes as she gazed toward the barn.

"William and I can help round everyone up if you'd like," Caroline offered.

"Yes, thank you!" Elizabeth added, "If you two will gather everyone from the house, I'll send Ernie to the barn."

Caroline politely excused herself from the ladies' circle and scanned the yard for William. She spotted him leaning against an oak tree talking with Carter, Owen and Owen's fiancée, Julie Chapman. Owen and Julie had met at the Tech library during his pilot training. Caroline slipped next to William.

"Elizabeth asked if we'd gather everyone from the house. She wants to take family photos by the creek before the sun sets."

"Watch out! My mom has a new camera," Owen teased. "She's been dying to try it out. Julie and I….Mom's first victims…have been sufficiently tortured!"

Julie playfully poked his ribs as he tightened his hold around her shoulders.

Caroline laughed. "We've been forewarned! Thanks, Owen."

William took Caroline's hand as they walked toward the house. Caroline stopped after six steps. "With all that's been going on, I've not had a chance to tell you how beautiful the ceremony was. You are a wonderful pastor, William! I pray daily the church in Belton calls you to be their pastor. Shouldn't you hear soon?"

"By the first of the year at the latest. They're still interviewing candidates."

"As Tommy read the poem to Loraine, you were looking straight at me. I could hardly concentrate on what was said."

William kissed her. "From Tommy's lips to your heart…I hope. That poem could be ours as well. Only six more months until we are married!"

Caroline smiled up at him. "Unless we up the date! Wouldn't it be easier for the church to cast a favorable vote on a married pastor?"

"What? Stop teasing me!"

Grant trotted up behind them. "Okay you love birds! Break it up!"

William grabbed his second-cousin around the neck. "Help us get everyone out of the house and to the creek. Your grandmother wants to take photos."

"On it!" Grant exclaimed and dashed into the sunroom. "I'll take downstairs; you scour upstairs!"

Emily and Trina, their feet elevated on a shared ottoman, relaxed on the sofa in the music room. The ceiling fan above them offered a refreshing respite from the hot summer evening.

"Thanks for coming inside with me, Emily."

"Of course, your feet were swollen. Better now that they're propped up?"

"Yes, much."

"How much longer?"

"A month or less Doc says. But I look like I could pop any day. I'm huge! Was never this big with my others. And so restless...it's hard to sleep. Sam teases that he'll have to borrow one of Uncle Ernie's cranes to roll me over."

"Sometimes I regret John and I didn't have more children. But one can't cry over spilt milk. Isn't that the saying?" Emily laughed. "We're so thankful for Eddie. He is indeed our pride and joy. I'll just wait six or seven more years for him to marry and fill our house with grandbabies."

"May I tell you something only Sam and I know? Can you keep a secret?"

Unsure how to respond, Emily's brows burrowed slightly. Trina was elated; her eyes sparkled....so what she was about to disclose couldn't be bad news.

"Sure," Emily answered hesitantly.

"During my last doctor's visit, Doc heard two heartbeats."

Emily swept her legs from the ottoman and quickly sat up. "Twins?"

Trina grinned and grabbed Emily's hands. "Wouldn't that be something?"

"Why haven't you told anyone? This is wonderful!"

"Sam and I agreed to wait. False hopes, you know?"

Emily squeezed Trina's hand. "Oh, Trina, I am so excited for you both! I'll not say anything. But two babies! I can't believe it!"

"I don't mind if you tell John."

"Tell John what?" Grant asked, entering the room.

Sneaking a slide glance at each other, the women started giggling.

"Okay you two. You're behaving like two cats locked in a barn full of mice! We've been summoned to the creek for photos." Grant offered his hand to Trina to help her up. Trina willingly allowed Emily to be her escort to the creek.

Grant continued his quest. He peeked into the library as well as the study…no one was hiding out in either room. Hearing footsteps behind him, he looked up at the staircase. Lucy was descending. Her brunette hair was still pulled up the way she wore it during the wedding. She wore a cotton sundress…tiny blue-and-yellow flowers scattered over a white background….and white sandals. Grant waited for her at the bottom of the stairs and smiled as she reached the bottom step.

"You looked beautiful today. Ya know if we weren't cousins, I wouldn't hesitate to ask you to marry me!" Grant teased.

"Stop! Don't be silly! What about your little girlfriend in Nashville?"

"Which one?"

"You're incorrigible!" Lucy pounded his arm and laughed.

As the two made their way down the hallway toward the kitchen, three steady knocks sounded at the front door. Lucy looked back over her shoulder.

"Who could that be?" Grant asked. "All the guests are already here or know just to come around to the back."

"I'll get it…you go ahead. I'll be right there."

Lucy turned back toward the front door. She turned the brass knob and opened the oak door. Her eyes widened in surprise.

"Glen?" Lucy stood transfixed; her heart pounding furiously. He looked so handsome. Had gained weight and muscle mass which made his shouders look broader. His long-sleeved blue shirt covered the scars on his right arm; the left-arm sleeve pinned to the outside of his shirt covered the stump. His cotton shirt was neatly tucked into a pair of tan khakis. His blue eyes still pierced her heart.

"What….what are you doing here?"

"If this is a bad time…I'll come back. I see a lot of cars parked in the yard. Something going on? I don't want to intrude....Lucy? You're just staring. Are you going to say anything?"

"You did say you'd show up at my door one day...I just really didn't..."

"Believe it?"

Lucy nodded.

Stuffing his right hand into his pants pocket, Glen waited for Lucy to speak. When she didn't respond, a look of bewilderment lined his eyes. "Sorry...I should have called first. Lesson learned." Glen turned to leave.

"Wait! Where are you going?" Lucy rushed after him. "I've been waiting for you. Hoping you'd come...praying you'd come! Please, don't leave now."

Glen stroked her cheek with the back of his hand. As tears brimmed her eyes, he kissed her. "Then it's okay that I'm here?"

Lucy returned his kiss. "Loraine and Tommy got married today. Come meet my family," she reached for his hand. "Everyone is here."

"Nah, I won't intrude. I do want to come back to meet your parents."

"Glen, you're more than welcome to stay. But I understand. The Baileys make up an entire tribe of boisterous people." Lucy laughed. "Tomorrow afternoon there will be fewer family members here. Say 3:00?"

"Tomorrow at 3:00 sounds good."

"Where are you staying?"

"My parents and I are staying with my aunt and uncle in San Antonio...Aunt Joycee and Uncle Pete."

"Your parents are here?"

"Well, in San Antonio." Glen's eyes twinkled mischievously.

"Oh, I'd love to meet them. Will I be able to do that before you go home?"

"Yes, you can count on it. I best be going. You have a party to return to." Glen hesitated and then asked, "Lucy? I need to ask something. I was going to wait until tomorrow, but..."

Lucy's heart skipped a beat. "Ask me what?"

"Would you accompany me and my parents to the Army Airforce

Base in Stuttgart, Arkansas? I trained there and am being awarded a couple of service medals. I'd like for you to be there with me for the ceremony."

"Glen!" Lucy grasped his hand. "That's wonderful! Yes, I'd love to go! I've never been to Arkansas. Or out of Texas for that matter!"

"Stuttgart is a little German community…known as the Rice and Duck Capital of the World."

"That's funny! Rice and ducks…what a combination!"

"I know! Rice farming and duck hunting. Not much duck hunting going on while we were training there! I'll come back tomorrow to meet your parents and gain their approval for you to come with me."

"I'm almost nineteen. I no longer need my parents' permission."

"I know…but they don't know me. And we'll be driving across the state, staying in hotels along the way and in Arkansas, and…"

Lucy cut him off. "Always the gentleman…hey, Lieutenant? Wait! Did you drive here?"

"No, my cousin Lowell did…he's out there in his car." Glen motioned toward the yard. "But once I get my prosthesis, I'll be able to drive. Want to meet him?"

"Yes!" Lucy took Glen's hand as they stepped off the porch.

Lucy didn't recognize the maroon 1940 Ford two-door coupe and assumed it to be Lowell's. The young man, who had been slouched behind the wheel, bolted upright when he heard them approach.

Glen tapped on the side mirror. "Hey, Lowell, wake up!"

Lowell balanced his elbow on top of the door frame and leaned slightly out of the opened window. "If I were asleep, I'm awake now!"

Glen laughed. "I'd like you to meet Lucy Bailey. Lucy, this is my cousin and chauffeur extraordinaire, Lowell Riley. Sad to say….Lowell was a swabbie."

"It's so nice to meet you, Lowell. Two of my brothers and a cousin were also in the Navy."

"So you know what a swabbie is, then?"

"Yes, of course! The Army Airforce, Navy, and Coast Guard were well represented by my family. So I can't really say the Navy is the best.

Glen and my brothers would disagree with us if I did. Thank *you* for your service."

Lowell tipped his head as if he were wearing a hat and studied Lucy closely. "Ya know, Glen, she's a lot prettier than you described."

Both Glen's and Lucy's faces reddened.

"Lucy, we really need to go," Glen said, releasing her hand.

"Well, give her a big smooch and let's get going!" Lowell exclaimed.

Turning from his cousin, Glen kissed Lucy goodbye.

"Tomorrow," he whispered.

Lucy smiled and stepped to one side. "Nice meeting you, Lowell."

"It was nice meeting you, too. Just wondering…ya got a sister?"

Lucy laughed. "Sorry, you're too late! She got married today."

Lowell shook his head as he measured his misfortune and started the car. With a wink and a grin, Lowell revved the engine before backing up. Lucy watched until the maroon vehicle had turned out of the driveway onto the county road. Tomorrow! Glen will be back tomorrow. She felt as if she were floating on air…as if there were silver wings strapped around each ankle preventing her feet from touching the ground. As she rounded the corner of the house, Rosa, Vicky, and Polly stood on the side porch.

"The girls wanted a photo so we came to find you," Rosa explained.

"Of course! You two were such pretty flower girls. I'd love a photo."

"Aunt Lucy, was that your boyfriend?" Polly asked, emphasizing *boyfriend* in a melodic sing-song voice.

Rosa smiled knowingly as the two little girls circled giddily around them.

"Yes, I guess he is. His name is Glen."

"Glen kissed you!" Five-year-old Vicky snickered and grabbed Polly's hand.

"Kissy! Kissy!" Polly called excitedly over her shoulder and smacked her lips together, mimicking a kissing sound. Giggles bounced off the oak trees as the girls dashed toward the creek.

"Glen's coming back tomorrow. I'd love for you and Art to meet him."

"I would truly love that, but we're leaving early in the morning. Art, the kids and I are following Clayton and Carter to Plainview."

"To visit Pops and Gram? That's wonderful! How long are you staying?"

"Just a few days. We haven't seen them since Victoria was a baby. Actually, Carter is staying on to help out with the farm. May be a permanent move for him. We're bringing Clayton back. He wants some one-on-one time with you and your folks before he heads back to San Diego. And, of course, Art wants to be on the road by the crack of dawn."

"Wasting good daylight any time after 6:00!" Lucy interjected cheerfully.

Rosa tucked her arm within Lucy's. "You know your brother so well. It's been so good seeing you, Lucy. You should bring your young man to South Texas."

Lucy smiled. "I'd like that."

Jubilant laughter spilled across the sunroom as Loraine and Tommy cut the first slice of their wedding cake. Loraine used Maggie's silver cake spatula to ease the white cake onto a white china dessert plate. Tommy pinched off a piece and eased it towards Loraine's mouth. Loraine opened her mouth and he gently placed the cake on her tongue. He licked the icing from his fingers as she ate the cake.

Grant and Arnie chanted, "Your turn, Loraine! Show no mercy!"

Loraine grinned back at them and took the remaining cake within her fingertips. Tommy shied away as Loraine lifted the cake towards his face. When she smiled sweetly, he opened his mouth. Instead of placing the cake in his mouth, Loraine rubbed the icing-coated cake across his cheek and lips. Cake crumbles along with the icing formed a faux beard across his chin. Tommy laughed and lowered his head as he wiped at the icing that clung to his face. Loraine, unable to stop laughing, held out a napkin. Tommy rejected the napkin and smeared his icing-covered fingers down Loraine's nose and across her cheek.

The room exploded in thunderous laughter. Aunt Elizabeth, Eastman camera in hand, took numerous pictures of the bride and groom with their faces bedecked in buttercream icing.

Kim and Emily stepped up to finish slicing and serving the cake while Loraine and Tommy wiped their faces with napkins that bore their names in a lavender scripted font.

"Where are they going?" Loraine asked Tommy when she noticed Grant and Arnold sneaking out of the room.

Tommy kissed her cheek. "Not to worry. Ready to go?"

Loraine glanced about the room. Their families and wedding guests mingled about in small groups talking; clearly enjoying each other's company and the day's festivities. Loraine hesitated not wanting to leave the fun but then nodded.

"Our suitcases are in the study." Tommy led her quietly from the room.

"Where's Aunt Loraine?" Polly asked a few minutes later as Vicky repeated the same question like a trained parakeet. "Where's Aunt Loraine?"

The room bustled with activity as the wedding guests realized the bride and groom had slipped away. Eddie led the way down the hallway as they all scurried to the front door. Loraine and Tommy, waiting for their ride, stood on the top step of the porch. Everyone crowded around them exchanging hugs and well-wishes. Collective gasps could be heard as a baby-blue 1945 Cadillac Fleetwood sedan pulled into the circular driveway. Loraine grabbed Tommy's arm as the car stopped. Grant and Arnold got out of the car. Grant held the driver's door opened; Arnold the passenger door. John and William placed the luggage in the trunk.

"What's this?" Loraine shrieked in excitement.

"Our ride to New Mexico! You know Dr. Wallace Lancaster, superintendent of Austin schools? This is his car. When he heard we were getting married, he offered it to us to use on our honeymoon. It's his wedding gift."

"Oh, Tommy! I can't believe it! This is wonderful!" Loraine stepped off the porch toward the car and then turned back. Tears trickled down her cheeks as Loraine rushed back up the steps and stopped in front of her parents.

Maggie grabbed her daughter and held her tightly. "My baby...all grown up. I wish you two every happiness. I love you, sweetheart, and am so proud of you."

Loraine kissed her mother's cheek and stepped toward Franklin. Tears streaked his face as he pulled Loraine into an embrace.

"My little Lorry! You are a beautiful young woman. Your mother and I will always be here for you. I love you so much."

Loraine nodded but couldn't reply. Emotions choked out every word. She kissed her father's cheek. Mr. North cornered his son by the car and hugged him tightly, clapping his back affectionately. Loraine joined her husband. Tommy's dad hugged Loraine and then held the door open for her as she slipped into the car.

The combined families and their long-time friends stood in the yard and cheered and applauded as Tommy and Loraine settled inside the car. Tommy backed the car around. Old shoes and cow bells tied to the back bumper bounced and wobbled across the driveway as the car entered the road.

"Ha! Who did that?" Uncle Ernie laughed. "How long do you think it will be before the kids notice?"

"Two guesses!" Art exclaimed as he held Vicky up on his shoulder. Alex, who was standing next to Rosa, pointed at the shoes and bells and chuckled.

"Grant and Arnold for sure!" Aunt Elizabeth answered. "Would be fun to follow them out of town, wouldn't it?"

Ernie kissed Elizabeth's forehead. "Now I see where Grant gets his mischievous nature! Let's go in and have some more cake and punch."

Before leaving the outskirts of Oak Hill, Tommy pulled the cadillac to the side of the road and turned off the engine. He and Loraine removed the strings of shoes and cow bells from the back bumper and placed them in the trunk.

Settling back in the car, Tommy announced, "Before we go any further. I have something to tell you. Not only did Dr. Lancaster let us use his car, he offered me a job teaching three auto mechanics classes at Austin High School starting after Labor Day. With that schedule, I can still work with Dad at the shop."

"Tommy! That's wonderful! See? Things always work out!"

Tommy kissed her lips softly. "Shall we get going, Mrs. North?"

"Yes," Loraine sighed. "Wait! Was getting a job all you forgot to tell me?"

"Huh?" Tommy frowned in confusion.

"You forgot to say how much you cherish, respect, adore, and idolize me!"

"That will keep until Carlsbad!" Tommy grinned and kissed her cheek.

****

"There you are." Franklin stepped through the opened French doors which led from his bedroom out onto the veranda.

Maggie, sitting in her rocking chair, was enjoying the summer evening. The sky dimmed a bluish-gray as the sun prepared to ease herself into bed. Birds fluttered in small groups toward their favorite trees to roost for the night.

Franklin held out a cup of coffee. Maggie smiled and grasped the handle.

"Thank you. This is just what I needed."

Franklin scooted his rocking chair closer to hers. Maggie blew across the top of the hot liquid as she looked down from the second story to observe the side yard below. The grass and flower beds desperately needed a shower of rain to perk them up from the summer's drying heat, but rain was not in the forecast.

"Penny for your thoughts," Franklin said after lighting his pipe.

"Oh," Maggie turned her head and smiled. "Not one thing in particular...just a whirlwind of many, many thoughts."

Franklin patted her hand. "Thinking about those twins...no doubt."

Maggie grinned. "Yes, I can't wait to get my hands on them. But Trina's mother is still there. Doris needs time with her daughter and grandchildren. I would only be in the way. I'll get my time."

"What a surprise! Robert James and Rebecca Jeanette...a boy and a girl. Polly's wish for a little sister came true."

"Yes, with a little added bonus!" Maggie laughed and sipped from her cup.

"Think the babies will be nicknamed Bobby and Becky?"

Maggie smiled at her husband. "Is that what you'll call them?"

Franklin exhaled smoke from his pipe. "Maybe. It's a big ole quiet house now with everyone gone. My mother doesn't make much noise." Franklin mused after a moment's reflection.

Maggie laughed. "No, she doesn't. She and Arlo have become quite the pair. Did Patrick and Kim finally get settled into their house?"

"Yes, Ernie's and Elizabeth's rental houses are truly a godsend. Patrick said Kim's already plotting a space in the backyard for a garden."

"Of course, she is. I pray Patrick goes back to UT to finish his degree."

"He will."

"He'll make a fine druggist."

Franklin smiled. "Yes, he will. Perhaps he'll take over the family business."

"Perhaps. Has Kim decided what she'll do?"

"For now. Kim wants to help her father get his nursery business started again. Ernie offered Mr. Yoshida a contract to landscape the houses and office buildings that Bond Construction builds. Mr. Yoshida is thinking it over."

"That would be a perfect arrangement. Oh, William called this afternoon. He and Caroline are getting married Saturday afternoon in Baylor's chapel. A small ceremony. Family and close friends. Seems a Christmas wedding was too far away."

Franklin beamed. "Wonderful! Only two of our young'uns remain unmarried now...Clayton and Lucy."

"I think those numbers will decrease by one in April next year."

"Lucy and Glen?" Franklin asked and Maggie nodded. "Whatever happened with Glen's inquiry to teach at Austin High?"

"Tommy put in a good word with Dr. Lancaster. So, we'll wait and see."

"Sounds promising! I'd like to keep both girls close by. Did Clayton call?"

"Yes, this morning. Doesn't know yet where he'll be stationed. Will call when he knows. Said he's anxious to get back to sea."

"That's fine...just fine." Franklin, lost in deep thought, finally asked, "Maggie, have you thought how truly blessed we are? Think about it! From just starting out...with each day's blessings or setbacks leading us to this very day...this very hour. Through the hard times as well as all the good. Through all the changing seasons of our lives, God has provided and led the way. Our children are all upstanding, God-fearing adults and have married well. Our eight grandchildren are beyond delightful. Our family has tripled in size! Whatever life has in store for us from this day forward, we will see it through together."

"To have and to hold, for better or worse, in sickness or health...isn't that what we pledged to each other thirty-eight years ago?"

Franklin kissed Maggie tenderly. With their elbows crooked on top of chair's armrest, they interlaced their fingers and rested their hands on the smooth pine. They rocked their chairs in sync and watched as the sun bade them farewell and slipped out of sight...declaring an end to another day...another season.

RESOURCES

1   Honolulu Radio Announcement Pearl Harbor Attack:
    http://historymatters.gmu.edu/d/5167/ - Access Date 3.29.2023

2   First Lady's Address to the Nation:
    https://erpapers.columbian.gwu.edu/radio-address-december-7-1941-attack-pearl-harbor - Access Date 3.29.2023

3   FDR's Infamy Speech:
    McCuthcheon, Marc. *Everday Life from Prohibition through World War II*. Writer's Digest Books, an imprint of F&W Publications, Inc., 1507 Dana Avenue, Cincinnati, Ohio, 45207, 1995. Pages 75–76

4   Franklin Delano Roosevelt's Death:
    http://www.eyewitnesstohistory.com/fdrdeath.htm
    https://www.loc.gov/static/programs/national-recording-preservation-board/documents/RadioCoverageOfFDRsFuneral.pdf
    Access Date 4.03.2023

5   United Press Merriman Smith:
    https://www.upi.com/Archives/1945/04/12/Roosevelt-dies-of-stroke-at-Little-White-House/6802441123641/
    Access Date 4.03.2023

6   *The Grapes of Wrath*: Steinbeck, John, Penguin Books Ltd., Registered Offices, 80 Strand, London WC2R ORL, England, 37th Printing, Copyright John Steinbeck, 1919, Renewed John

Steinbeck, 1967, Notes copyright @ Robert DeMott, 2006, Pages 2-3

7 William Butler Yeats:
Aedh Wishes for the Cloths of Heaven by W. B. Yeats - Poems | Academy of American Poets - Access Date 01/05/2024

FROM THE AUTHOR

Each of us endured sitting in an American History class. To make a passing grade, we memorized names of important people and dates of major events. Some of us can proudly recite the first few lines of President Lincoln's Gettysburg Address. We recollect WWII's storming of Normandy beaches after viewing "The Longest Day," a black-and-white film starring John Wayne, Richard Burton, and Peter Fonda.

Once exams are taken, movies seen, and popcorn eaten, then what? History….what is its purpose? Why is it important?

We, too, have a history that is not recorded nor studied in a textbook. A retelling of our lives that should be shared and passed down from one generation to the next. A simple statement about who we are, where we come from and why knowing and keeping our family's lineage is so important. How many times did you sit with your grandmother or grandfather and drill them with numerous questions about the "old days?" Very few times, I fear. Our own lineage sometimes seems lost when the eldest generation dies, and no one remains to answer our questions.

Our todays earmark tomorrow's lineage for future generations.

FAMILY PHOTOS

Aviation Cadet Waymon M. Barker
Author's Father

Aviation Cadet Waymon Barker and Friends

Aviation Cadet Waymon M. Barker

Alvin B. Barker, 449th Bombardment Group
Author's Uncle

Author's Maternal Grandparents, circa 1940s

Waymon Barker and Friend, Skating Rink Bouncers

Printed in the United States
by Baker & Taylor Publisher Services